THE
TIMESTREAM
VERDICT

THE
TIMESTREAM
VERDICT

Jordan Berk

IE Snaps
by
IngramElliott

Published by IngramElliott, Inc.
www.ingramelliott.com
9815-J Sam Furr Road, Suite 271, Huntersville NC 28078

Book design by Maureen Cutajar, gopublished.com
Cover design by H.O. Charles
Editing by Katherine Bartis

ISBN Paperback: 978-1-952961-26-7
ISBN E-Book: 978-1-952961-27-4

Library of Congress Control Number: 2024905835

Subjects: Fiction—Science Fiction_General; Fiction—Mystery and Detective_General.

Published in the United States of America.
Printed in the United States of America.
First Edition: 2024, First International Edition: 2024

For my family
and the happiness I know our future holds.

Acknowledgments

Thank you, Dad,
the literal and figurative inspiration for this story.

And thank you to everyone who contributed along the way:
Daniel, Steph, Martín, and my fantastic publishing team.

This wouldn't exist without all of you.

PART 1

PART 1

1

_____

"Welcome, everyone, to the year 2042!"

A beat of awed silence pervaded the nondescript room in which I inexplicably found myself.

"Thank you!" I responded with conventional Midwest sincerity, instinct kicking in ahead of situational comprehension. A group of complete strangers turned my way, all somewhere on the spectrum between incredulous and sarcastically bemused. Blushing, I buried myself into my surprisingly comfortable chair as the speaker mercifully continued.

"You're welcome, Aaron," she replied with an off-balance smile, masterfully hiding her certain annoyance that I had interrupted her big introduction.

Twenty forty-two! That part was obviously a joke, a prank; someone was wielding my self-professed predilection for science fiction against me. And yet, I could not rationalize my sudden presence in this unremarkable conference room full of mysterious randoms, each eyeing the others with trepidation.

I quickly retraced my precursory steps, scanning for an anomaly. Nothing extraordinary presented itself: I ate the usual microwave dinner in my very average apartment, watched the fourth quarter of the basketball game, and fell asleep in my undersized bed—all in good old 1985. The eeriest part was that I never experienced the natural feeling of gradually regaining consciousness; one moment I was fast asleep, the next I was here. It was a disconcerting sensation to be fully awake without ever having woken up.

The statuesque woman scanned the room once more, regrouping. "My name is Mounira Calwi, and I am the head of the World Chronology Organization, a special agency of the United Nations, tasked with—for lack of a simpler way to describe it—administering time travel."

She wisely paused for dramatic effect as I continued to grapple with the enormity of the situation, my thoughts clouded by an unproductive desperation to move on from the ignominy of my outburst. I couldn't reconcile her words with any meaning; they were so far beyond the realm of reality as to be utter gibberish.

Plus, if this was meant to be someone's rendition of the mid-twenty-first century, it was quite underwhelming. To start, we didn't seem to be in outer space, nor battling the constraints of gravity at all. Boring! The area itself was undistinguished and barren, reminiscent of the most neglected conference room at my modest accounting firm. It easily could have been contemporary to any decade that I'd lived through in my thirty-four years. Only Mounira's wardrobe and the chairs themselves showed even the slightest indication of modernity.

Still, there was a distinct aura of the uncanny emanating from every element of the environment. The air was somehow too filtered, the speaker's voice too high-fidelity, the light source too indistinct. Mounira's otherworldly presence and commanding conviction only intensified the sensation. Nothing purely artificial could ever hope to evoke such a vivid response.

Every rational thought told me I was experiencing a particularly lucid dream, or that a concealed television camera crew was moments from emerging, release forms in hand. Yet it was undoubtedly more than that: supernatural and indefinable, while simultaneously absolute and palpable. I was struggling to reconcile the marked contrast.

"I can see that a lot of you are frightened, or at minimum, skeptical. This is quite understandable. Perhaps I can help with a quick demonstration." She glanced down at her bare wrist, as if looking at a watch. "In about three seconds . . ."

Right on the dot, the room gasped as one. Another, identical woman had instantaneously materialized at her side, shoulder to shoulder with her twin, or clone, or whatever they were.

"My lovely doppelgänger here has just time traveled downstream exactly one minute from the future," Mounira—original Mounira—explained. Both held out their right wrists. The time traveler's featured a noticeable red mark.

"Hello, Mounira," greeted the new joiner. Our original responded in kind, so similar in tone and timbre that it sounded like an amplified echo.

As we all continued to stare in a dumbfounded stupor, Mounira Two departed with a wave and a wink. "See you in a minute," she said before abruptly vanishing without warning, as quickly as she had appeared. An intense rush of air filled the void, snapping me back to full attention.

"Now if you'll excuse me," Mounira Prime shared, "I need to hop into a time machine to complete the loop." As she made her way out the door, she caught herself. She grabbed a red marker off the whiteboard and imprinted a hasty and very familiar marking onto her right wrist.

Thirty seconds later, Mounira was back, and I was convinced. Somehow, someway, I was actually in the future. A future that featured the miracle of time travel, yet no other visible technological advances. Still, time travel! I was a time traveler! But, why was I a time traveler?

Mounira resumed. "I know this is all a lot to take in, I really do. I hope the demo helped to reinforce my credibility, as well as to highlight the power and gravity of this world-changing invention. In fact, it is the very reason that the twelve of you have been brought here today.

"To get right to the point, each of you has been specially nominated to serve as members of a groundbreaking jury. As you will come to understand, you're the only ones qualified to provide an equitable verdict on this unique situation."

A jury? That explained why I had tallied exactly a dozen members of my chair-based cohort, each likewise transfixed by our esteemed speaker. Looking around, I immediately felt like the imposter among the group; they all carried a magistrality befitting the position that I blatantly lacked. Unless the United Nations team was handpicking the most banal individuals they could find, I couldn't understand what justified me to sit among them. I consider myself to be a fair and open-minded person, yes, but *special*? Hardly. My qualifications were limited to the handful of juries I'd served on previously, none more substantial than a minor workplace injury or traffic violation.

"The first-of-its-kind charge is *temporal homicide*—essentially, murder via time travel."

Alright, so definitely not a minor workplace injury.

"You will receive full details over the course of the next week and during the trial proper, but needless to say, this is quite a high-profile and unprecedented case."

I was curious and a bit worried about uncovering what "murder via time travel" could possibly entail. Was the victim a time traveler? Was the suspect? Or perhaps a precision explosive device had been delivered by time machine? I had been in the future for all of five minutes and I was already grappling with the limitless peculiarities of the fourth dimension. In the moment, the vague description brought to mind the famous grandfather paradox: What happens if you go back in time and kill your own maternal grandfather before your mother was born? I certainly didn't know the answer, nor could I even begin to process the complexities, but it always intrigued my nerdier side purely as a logical paradox.

"For a time-travel-based offense, the WCO mandates that the composition of the jury represent the modern timestream from roughly 1950 to the present day. Put more poetically, a time-travel crime requires a time-travel jury." She spoke calmly, like she wasn't explaining something utterly inconceivable. "Though that cutoff year may sound arbitrary, we feel that twenty-first-century acclimation would be too difficult for anyone jumping from deeper downstream. As a result, the group here comprises a demographic cross section of the last hundred years, hand-picked to optimize for diversity, impartiality, and adaptability. I hope you're as honored to be here as we are to have you."

I took the opportunity to study the faces around the room, and for the first time fully registered how much variability there seemed to be, both in physical appearance and state of mind. The only exception was our shared drab clothing: a lightweight, satiny, and perfectly tailored jumpsuit of sorts that everyone but me actually made look presentable.

Directly across the table, I observed a wide-eyed young man—twenty at most—whose disposition reminded me of a child visiting an amusement park for the first time, his curly long hair bouncing everywhere in his state of frenzied excitement. Right next to him, a middle-aged woman wept and trembled uncontrollably in her seat, oblivious to the young man's adolescent attempts to soothe her. Oddly, the noise of her distress was barely audible, as if muted by an invisible wall. In addition to a few other stifled sobs, I caught looks of indignation, despair, and outright enthusiasm—the full gamut of reaction on display. The rest of us remained staggered between those extremes, impassively attempting to rationalize the unfathomable as it was delivered sentence by sentence.

My focus returned to Mounira as she resumed her explanation with a newly sympathetic tone.

"I understand that this overabundance of new information immediately after your upstream journey may be overwhelming, which is why we will be providing a three-day transitional immersion period before the start of the trial. During this time, you'll have plenty of opportunities to intermingle, as well as to enjoy the many comforts of 2042. And if you wish, we will be offering each of you a guided tour through magnificent New York City."

Nothing sounded more welcoming than some time to process the recent avalanche of borderline-implausible information, especially since I had a strong feeling that what we'd learned so far was just the tip of the iceberg. Much less appealing was the prospect of compulsory socialization with the eclectic group before me, but introverted tendencies aside, I would survive.

Since I rarely ventured beyond the familiar comfort of my hometown, Chicago, I chose to embrace this interlude as a long-overdue vacation, although I would have preferred an alternative locale. I had previously and quite reluctantly traveled to New York City upon the insistence of a formerly trusted coworker. Even with the possibility of a half century's worth of improvements, a return presented little allure. Most of my memories featured heaping piles of sidewalk garbage or casual murder threats for not "donating" five dollars on the uptown A train.

Mounira beamed as she continued. "And as a heartfelt thank you for your service, we are pleased to offer every participant a full-body scan through our latest 2081a-version medbays. This incredible device can detect and instantly repair nearly any physical health issue in your body."

Now we're talking. *This* was the kind of magical advancement I had always envisioned for the twenty-first century, although upon further reflection, the implications were a little troubling. Was she describing an immortality machine? If so, how did they deal with overpopulation? Did everyone have equal access? Were all of the doctors out of work? Admittedly, I didn't feel as sorry for the impact on the insurance or pharmaceutical companies.

I considered myself to be in great physical shape—at least for a guy who rarely exercises and can't get enough deep-dish pizza—but I was still very enthusiastic about the prospect of repairing any minor medical issues lingering around. My parents gifted me many things: life, for one, but also barely functional knees and concerningly terrible eyesight. It's a miracle my ancestors made it through natural selection. I also wondered if the machine could prevent male pattern baldness, which always felt like it was a day away from rearing its ugly head on mine.

Ethical qualms aside, I got the sense that the jurors were getting the better end of the deal here. Unless . . . I suddenly realized I'd been naively assuming that this process culminated with a return trip home to 1985. Just as I was starting to panic about never seeing my wonderful little dog again, Mounira continued.

"Regardless of how long your stay here is, you will be returned to your orgtime—short for origin time—at the *exact* moment you were upstreamed from. And don't worry, you will retain any medical enhancements that the scanners provide. However, you will *not* retain the memories of your time here."

Ouch. So I would see my dog again, but he would never hear of my fantastical journey. But at least we'd be able to venture out for an extended lakefront jog together if the medbay proved successful. I repressed the nagging awareness that I had once again instinctively defaulted to Rex rather than my girlfriend Jennifer, an uncomfortable reminder of my frustrating ambivalence toward an otherwise steady, loving relationship.

There were many older men and women among the jurors; I was bemused and a little unsettled by the idea that they would wake up in their own time sporting a revamped level of fitness, yet with no memory of why. As generous as the offer was, it felt shortsighted and under-planned, like Mounira and team were desperate to incentivize us to stay. Luckily, I needed no such enticement; she had me hooked the moment I heard "time travel."

"So, jurors, that's all I have for now. Rest up tonight, and we'll send your upcoming itinerary soon. If you need anything in the meantime, your in-room assistant can satisfy nearly any request. And since I'm confident that each of you now has a severe case of information overload, a recording of this call will be available for review at any time.

"Truly, thank you all in advance for your participation in this groundbreaking event. I'll see you again in a few days. For now, just rest up, get to know each other, and enjoy beautiful 2042."

As she waved goodbye, the conference room faded away into a swirl of cool, pleasing colors on an immaculate curved wall. Though I never physically moved an inch, it felt like I had magically teleported between rooms through a cloud of translucent watercolor. I looked around to be sure; no one else was here, just a tastefully decorated space that reminded me of all the five-star hotel rooms I'd never stayed in. I refocused on the incredible surface in front of me, even running my hands over it to look for a light source capable of deceiving me so convincingly. Despite what my eyes were telling me, there was no projector, no edges, only a pane of what felt like perfectly smooth glass.

Behind me, an oversized mattress beckoned, with pajamas neatly laid out at the foot. As my energy level dwindled, I prepared for bed, my excitement for the next few days increasing with each passing moment. How lucky was I, one of twelve in a nearly one-hundred-year period, to be chosen for this singular event! If only I could retain my memory, I could coast on this feeling for years. I never considered myself exceptional, nor had the desire to become anything more than casually ordinary. But I could see why people aim for higher office or celebrity; the high was truly exhilarating.

I climbed into bed, my mind still racing, yet paradoxically at peace. Between the sixty-year voyage and the soothing light show enveloping me, I had no doubt I would rest comfortably overnight. The ambient room light faded automatically just as I closed my eyes, my first day in the future complete.

2

The next day arrived without warning, a product of the most complete night of sleep I'd ever experienced. Though the room had no visible windows, I was bathed in an increasingly brilliant facsimile of sunlight that seemed to be perfectly attuned to my state of consciousness as I gently awoke.

I scanned the sparse yet sleek environment, instantly erasing any lingering fragments of situational doubt. Soft lighting filled the space, highlighting the distinct lack of sharp edges on the assembled furnishings. Each element flowed into the next with preternatural flow, every shade of liquid gray on equal display. What it lacked in vibrancy it made up in aesthetic simplicity: pleasing, peaceful, and open. Well, I was indeed in the future, of that I was sure; a future that had so far dazzled me at every turn. I couldn't even imagine the marvels I would encounter when I ventured outside my room.

"Good morning, Aaron. How are you today?" asked an ambient voice that sounded vaguely like an androgenized version of my own.

I looked around, instinctively trying to find the source of the greeting. The wall displays coalesced into a helpful audio wave-form of the speech as it continued:

"I am your in-room assistant, here to help you in any way I can. Before we get started, can you confirm your preferred name and pronouns?" The screen transformed to show my first name and "he/him." I mumbled an affirmative response, affixed in a state of awed shock that I was having a conversation *with a room*. The assistant thanked me and went quiet, perhaps waiting for a command of some sort.

I decided to test it out with the first thought that came to mind. "Could I, uh, get some coffee?" I asked tentatively.

"Absolutely, Aaron! Did you know that is the first question that 56 percent of my new residents ask me? This coffee stuff must be great. I've got to try it for myself sometime!" Correction: I was having a conversation with a room that had the overenthusiastic personality of a TV dad. "Coffee is available in the cafeteria, which is open now, or I can have it delivered to your room."

"I don't want to trouble anyone; I can definitely get it myself in a minute. Thanks," I replied.

I didn't quite know where to look as I spoke; this was all very awkward. One of the walls morphed into a three-dimensional map of the path to the cafeteria, though upon further review, I probably could have handled the one right turn in the nearest hallway without any additional guidance.

"Before I go," I asked, "do you know what's going on today? The head lady said we'd be here for three days before the trial starts."

"I thought you'd never ask," replied the startlingly lifelike voice. "Take a look at the screen in front of you to see your itinerary for the day. I took the liberty of adapting the timecodes to use the antiquated, time-zone-based format with which you are familiar."

Another wall panel reshaped to show me precisely what I had asked for:

6:00 a.m.–8:30 a.m.	Breakfast
9:00 a.m.–11:00 a.m.	Orientation
11:00 a.m.–12:30 p.m.	Lunch
1:00 p.m.–5:00 p.m.	Medical Scan
6:00 p.m.–7:30 p.m.	Dinner

As little as I was looking forward to a four-hour medical scan, it was comforting to have some sense of what a day here actually entailed. Mounira wanted us to spend the downtime to get to know each other, and it appeared that there would be plenty of opportunities to do so. Beyond my surface-level read last night, I knew very little about my fellow jury members. As someone who struggles to engage in even basic conversation, the prospect of forging those connections sounded a bit daunting. Plus, assuming everyone else was plucked from some other time period, we had a literal generational divide that might make finding common ground difficult.

Impatient to explore beyond the confines of my room, I hastened to finish getting ready. Other than the coffee, everything I could possibly desire seemed to be proactively provided. Even the clothing options were tailored for my shape and long-outmoded style. I would have been quite happy to adapt to the sartorial trends of 2042, but I recognized the impracticality. Though I flirted with some of the extraneous accessories, I ultimately settled in with my standard jeans and T-shirt. Best to represent myself to my peers in my truest form. As uninspired as the outfit was, I found the materials to be extravagantly plush and almost buoyant. Whether this novelty was due to futuristic textiles or my aversion to spending more than eight dollars on any article of clothing, I wasn't sure.

Cleaned up and fully dressed, I hesitated to make my way to the cafeteria. Knowing this was going to be my home for a few days, there was one omission that perturbed me more than I would have anticipated.

"Hey, um, Room? I'm feeling a little, um, claustrophobic. Are there any windows in here?" I inquired.

"Absolutely, Aaron!" the assistant replied, in what was quickly becoming its trademark phrase. As the voice spoke, an entire side of the room transformed into a dazzling, spanning view of the New York skyline, the shimmering virtual sun casting a massive shadow across the bluer-than-real-life Hudson River. Even with full, conscious knowledge of the simulated nature of the imagery, I delighted in the majestic spectacle. To my mind, it was no different from my actual visit to the top of the Empire State Building a few years back, especially as an unexpected light breeze filtered through my hair. My otherwise wonderful yet incredibly acrophobic sister would surely have quit the program right then and there. As awe-inspiring as the sight was, the anachronistic part of me still craved a true, grimy-glass-paned view of the outside world, but the spectacular panorama more than sufficed.

I took a leisurely walk to breakfast, making sure to absorb every detail I could. For the most part, this could have been any hallway in any building from my time. The only glaring exception was a subtle arrow which persisted on the floor one step ahead of me, not-so-subtly guiding me to my destination. Apparently, the UN did not trust their jury members' navigational abilities. When I arrived at the cafeteria, a wall screen summoned me closer with a display featuring my name in bold lettering. It conveniently offered only three menu choices: Healthy (Personalized), Indulgent (Personalized), or Custom. With nary a physical button in sight, I verbally made my selection. I was already feeling a bit more comfortable commanding inanimate objects.

"Indulgent, please, and a coffee with a little cream?" The wall helpfully transformed into an oversized affirmative checkbox and informed me that my food would be delivered directly to my table within minutes.

I entered the main portion of the cafeteria and recognized a few fellow jurors from the previous night's introductory session. Most were either already engaged in conversation or emitted a distinctly unsociable aura. A few representatives from both groups gawked at me and then quickly returned to their previous focus. Hunting for an unoccupied table, I caught a few snippets of scattershot discussion, most trending toward hushed disgruntlement regarding the abrupt circumstances of our arrival. I kept thinking that I should have shared in the pervasive sense of mild aggravation, but any instinct was tempered by the raw exhilaration of the astonishing technology emerging around every corner.

The meal came out maybe thirty seconds later, and I was delighted to see what appeared to be a perfectly prepared eggs Benedict: exactly the breakfast I would have chosen myself. I had no regrets in selecting the indulgent option; I *was* on vacation after all! At least that's what I told myself as unearned justification. Plus, I had a smidge of hope that the upcoming medical scan could assist me by trimming a little pudge from my oft-sedentary frame.

Just as I was taking my first bite, a boisterous woman's voice filled the room as she strode toward me. "Hey! 'Thank you guy'! Mind if I sit down?" Before I could offer any type of response, she was seated. "I thought that was hilarious!" she added. Fortunately, her volume approached safe human levels now that the prelude was complete.

"I'm Lisa Barnes from Los Angeles, 1994. Well, not really LA, more like outside LA, but it's easier to just say LA. You're from the States, right?"

It took me a moment to realize I finally had an opportunity to speak. "Hi, yeah, I'm from Chicago. My name's Aaron. Nice to, um, meet you."

"What year?" she prompted after a few seconds, with an accompanying hand gesture that unmistakably denoted "give me more."

"Oh, right: 1985." This was going to take some getting used to. I almost felt embarrassed to be from an earlier year than she, as if she was a cooler, more experienced older sibling and I was just some kid tagging along. If I had to guess, she seemed roughly ten years older than me. Doing some quick math, that would mean we perhaps were born about the same year. Maybe we could talk about that sometime.

"I thought you looked like a fellow late-twentieth-century resident. So, what do you think of the future?" she queried.

"Huh, good question," I responded, caught off guard by the enormity of the prompt. "I guess I can't think of any description better than, well, mind-boggling, and I feel like we've only seen a tiny fraction of it so far, right?"

Admittedly, this was somewhat of a stock answer. It was hard to formulate my thoughts for such an open-ended question, especially while I was still trying to find my footing after what had so far amounted to only a few hours of awake time in 2042. Lisa's food—also eggs Benedict—arrived as I did my best to continue the conversation.

"What about you? It must be a little less 'mind-boggling' for you, coming from 1994."

Lisa chuckled. "Believe me, it's plenty amazing for me too. '94 is essentially the same as 1985, just with better music." Stuffing a bite of poached egg into her mouth, she mumbled, "Have you asked your assistant to do anything crazy yet? I kept asking for every outlandish request I could think of, and he handled them without hesitation. He even DJ'd a solo dance party for me and got the lights in the room to pump to the beat."

I nodded with an approving smirk, genuinely impressed that her room was able to accomplish everything she had described. I clearly had been underutilizing my room's skill set, sheepishly treating the helper more like an actual human assistant who would immediately resent me for even the most basic requests.

"Wow, that's really cool," I responded. "Nothing like that for me though; I just asked it for coffee." I also noticed she had gendered her assistant already; I wondered if the additional interaction had anthropomorphized it for her.

As we took a break to consume more of the delicious meal, another juror joined our table after politely asking permission. I remembered observing him during the previous evening's meeting, a look of increasing displeasure on his face throughout. Today, he seemed to be in a better mood.

"Good morning, my name is Ime. I'm from Nigeria, 2011. Very pleased to meet both of you." He introduced himself with a slight accent (to my American ears). Lisa and I reciprocated with our essentials. I even remembered to include my year this time. Before I could ask a little more about 2011, or about Ime himself, Lisa jumped in.

"Small talk feels a bit futile when we know we won't remember it, huh?" Lisa asked the table.

"Perhaps," said Ime, sincerely considering the question. "Though I'm still looking forward to forming a relationship with members of such a diverse group, however temporary. The memory loss is disappointing, but rationally I understand the reasoning. My primary frustration is with the lack of agency we were given. Yes, we can choose to leave—I assume—and we're obviously being treated well, but what gives anyone the right to transport another individual without their consent, whether it's through space *or* time? Human history is not ripe with positive examples."

"An insightful, thought-provoking question," I acknowledged with a pensive nod. "So, maybe we *should* just stick to small talk," I added cheekily, which got a polite laugh from the table. "In all seriousness though, and not to discount that valid concern, Ime, but do you think this is all worth it for us if the medical scanner is everything Mounira promised?"

"C'mon guys, seriously? It's worth it even without any perks," Lisa quickly offered. "Memory or not, medical gizmo or not, I would have happily volunteered for this a hundred times out of a hundred."

Being honest with myself, I would have too, with just a tad of hesitation regarding the memory loss aspect. On the other hand, even the best dreams evaporate from our conscious memory within a few minutes of waking up, yet we go to sleep hoping for them, nonetheless. How was this any different?

"Same for me, I suppose," Ime shared, "but that doesn't excuse the problematic ethical implications. A few others I've spoken to agree with our general sentiment: a bit betrayed and angry, but ultimately focusing on the glass that is half full." Ime smiled. "Sorry, I know I've been a downer so far. Let's change the subject. Have either of you tried to outwit your assistant yet? I am in awe of its capabilities."

Lisa went through the unabridged list of what she had tried so far—a sampling of twenty-first-century music and movies, a customized workout with an accompanying display of real-time muscle activation, the aforementioned dance party, even a massage in the chair. I regaled them with the legend of my coffee order; Lisa must have felt honored to have heard it twice. More interestingly, I did share about the majestic skyline view I saw out the "window" when requested; both replied that they would do the same once they returned to their respective rooms.

I took a few sips of perfect-temperature coffee as Ime completed his much healthier meal of grains topped with exotic fruits and seeds. "Do either of you know anything more about the trial itself?" I asked.

Lisa and Ime both shook their heads. "If I'm telling you the truth, I keep forgetting that's why we're here," said Lisa. "So far it's just felt like a luxury cruise with strangers and an overly intense cruise director." I snorted out a laugh; that was an apt description.

"I did ask my assistant about the case," chimed in Ime, "but it didn't offer any details beyond what we've already heard."

"Well, we have orientation coming up soon; maybe we'll learn more there," I said.

"I have no doubt," replied Ime. "Speaking of which, if you'll excuse me, I'd like to return to my room to prepare myself a bit more," he said as he gracefully rose from his chair. "And maybe try out that dance party," he said to Lisa with a wink, then waved to both of us and departed.

Lisa cheerily waved back and returned her focus to me.

"So I've met 'thank you guy' and 'angry guy' so far. Although maybe I got those names backward; Ime is actually quite good-natured, and you haven't thanked *me* once!"

I gave her my best confused face, prompting a needed elaboration.

"Oh, I assigned everyone a name when we were together last night. It's something I often do in group settings to entertain myself, and perhaps as a little mnemonic device. Let's see how many I remember . . . I've got you two, 'sexy silent man,' 'puppy kid,' 'angry *lady*,' 'sleepy grandma,' and 'Ms. Unimpressed.' I'll remember the rest at orientation when I see them, since I know you're just dying to hear."

"I'm sure that's exactly what the UN was hoping you'd take away from that meeting," I said with a smirk. "And I'll take 'thank you guy'; it's actually pretty complimentary, as much as I'd like to pretend I never said what I said last night."

"Hey, we were all pretty shell-shocked in those first few minutes. At least you said 'thank you' and not 'fuck you,' like I'm sure a few people would have defaulted to."

"A perfect note to end breakfast on," I declared with a smile. I bid her farewell and headed back to my room, content that I wouldn't be completely alone in this completely unfamiliar decade.

3

While I traversed the endless hallways leading to the orientation room—assisted by a projected navigational aid—I began to appreciate the omnipresent helpfulness in 2042. I wondered if the residents of this time knew quite how coddled they were between the ubiquitous robot assistants, personalized food and services, and other peripheral comforts which I'd already experienced. It was like having a cozy blanket wrapped around your life, and the entire portion of the brain dedicated to base survival served no purpose. I couldn't decide if I found this idea liberating or horrifying.

As pleasant as the morning had been so far, I fundamentally understood that the proceedings were about to become much more intense. I didn't know quite what we needed to be familiarized with, but if it was anything as jarring as last night's introduction, we were in for a whirlwind.

I recalled the last time I had been to an orientation session on my first day of my first job. I couldn't have been more excited; I was finally kicking off my long-awaited career as an accountant. My new boss, however, thought this was the ideal time to share a few relevant updates: the entire office was moving to Dallas, and the company founder had ironically been found guilty of tax evasion. Needless to say, I did not work there very long. I hoped that orientation was not a representative experience.

I arrived in a room strikingly similar to the virtual one from the previous night: bland and uninviting. An unadorned conference table lay at the center of the rectangular space, flanked by streamlined, functional chairs. At least the ambient mood was more convivial than I was expecting; it seemed that I wasn't the only one to bond with a peer or two this morning. Lisa was already seated and distractedly waved me over.

"Long time no see," I teased, taking the open chair next to her. She barely acknowledged me; she was engrossed in some type of advanced video game projected on the surface of the table in front of her. I stared, equally transfixed, as she rotated and positioned various shapes with precise movements of her fingertips.

"You can try it, too, you know," she commented, catching me silently observing. I glanced down at the area in front of me and identified a few intriguing options on the reflective display. I opted to start with the simple drawing tool, which let me use my inelegant hand motions to craft a personal masterpiece of haphazard lines and stick figures.

"Simply breathtaking," Lisa exclaimed, glancing over my shoulder.

Within a few minutes, every seat was taken. I was so captivated by the video game in front of me that I jumped when a man standing at the head of the table began speaking. He sounded fifty but looked thirty and, like Mounira last night, wore a modern yet professional outfit. So far, everyone contemporary to this time period looked like they had just retired from a storied modeling career.

"Hello jurors, welcome! I'm so glad to have the honor to meet all of you and guide you through this unique proceeding. My name is Andrés Cordova, and for the next few days or weeks, I will be your friendly jury coordinator. My usual role with the WCO is Chronology Affairs Officer, but I happily volunteered for this unique assignment when offered.

"I have no doubt that each of you comes bearing many questions, and I hope to be able to answer all of them today. I'll start with a couple of administrative items. First, some of you may have detected that I am currently speaking Spanish rather than your native language."

Hearing this fact rewired something in my brain, and I suddenly was able to discern that his mouth movements didn't quite match the vocal audio. Yet the English words I was hearing were unmistakably coming from his mouth, and there was no perceptible delay.

"Each of you has a narrow-band directional speaker which is tracking your head and translating my speech in real time," he explained with enthusiasm. "The AI—that's artificial intelligence; think of it as a robot if that's helpful—is able to predict my next sentence in order to minimize delay to imperceptible milliseconds. This same tech will work for all of you when speaking with each other or a WCO staff member in any UN building and most high-traffic public locations as well."

The majority of the group looked genuinely impressed by this truly unbelievable advancement. I counted myself among them. This was the first time we'd encountered something with immediate and practical applications that offered more than frivolous luxury.

"Second," he continued, "you may have noticed that we have one less juror than yesterday."

"Sleepy grandma," Lisa whispered to me out of the side of her mouth.

"Ms. Osman regrettably opted to return to her orgtime last night. Luckily, we covered for that possibility by bringing an extra among your group. Come the trial, the eleven of you will be joined by our alternate juror, who, unlike yourselves, is not an upstreamer. So with all of that sufficiently covered, I'd like to open things up and get to know all of you!"

A lot of things had changed since my time, but awkward, corporate-style icebreakers apparently were not one of them. We went around the room and introduced ourselves, sharing our name, year, primary language, hometown, current occupation, and first job. Compared to the rest of the group, I felt exceedingly uninteresting. An accountant from a major American city was just so blandly stereotypical next to the documentary filmmaker from 1970s West Germany or the Sri Lankan cloud engineer from 2014 (a fascinating job title; had we learned to control the weather?).

As I suspected last night, there was not only chronological diversity among the group, but geographic as well. Lisa and I comprised the North American contingent, with similar representation from China, including one woman who was pulled from recent 2035. As Feng introduced herself, Lisa made sure I knew that this was the one and only 'Ms. Unimpressed.' Considering she had much less of a technology gap to contend with, the title seemed reasonable.

With the introductions complete, Andrés resumed our initiation to the modern world.

"Thank you all for sharing!" he enthused. "It's fantastic to get to know you better. I've personally never met anyone from 1951"—he gestured toward a reserved British man across from me—"or even 2022. To understand why not, I'd like to explain some of the basics of time travel, so that you have additional context during your stay here." He took a deep breath in preparation.

"Depending on your orgtime, you may have seen or read various fictional accounts of time travel. I recommend clearing those interpretations out of your mind, as most of us had to do when the first successful downstream trip was completed nine years ago.

"In the real world, the physics of time travel—chronophysics—is extremely prescriptive and limited. The main restriction to remember—and I will repeat this many times—is that the timestream *cannot be changed*." Those last three words, and the table-pounding that accompanied them, were delivered with striking emphasis.

"In other words," he continued after a beat, "what happened, happened, and nothing any downstreamer does can change that. An example: let's say you travel to the past with the goal of preventing a friend's serious car accident. As hard as it is to accept, you will always fail, despite your best efforts. Maybe your mode of transportation breaks down, maybe you are derailed elsewhere, or maybe by even being there, *you* somehow cause the crash. But because the accident happened—in your memory and in the timestream—it always has to happen. I'll take a minute to allow that to sink in and see if there are any questions."

A stunned group silence permeated the room. I wondered if everyone else was likewise thinking about what we would change if it *was* possible to influence the past. Perhaps I could have prevented my parents' traumatic divorce or saved my beloved childhood turtle from the neighbor's ruthless dog.

Ime broke the stillness with a question decidedly not along the same lines. "Does this imply the absence of free will?" he asked Andrés. Classic Ime; even in our limited interaction, it was clear that he had a unique ability to cut straight to the core of the matter before anyone else could comprehend anything remotely that philosophical. "If my actions are known to an individual from the future and they come back in time and tell me, then there's nothing I can do to change them."

"That is a fantastic question, Ime, and if it's okay, I'd like to return to it later. I think filling in the rest of the *chrono*physical puzzle might help illuminate the *meta*physical implications," replied Andrés, noticeably pleased with his wordplay. Ime nodded in approval.

"This doesn't make sense," jumped in the aloof woman from the USSR. "What about the butterfly effect? If I go back in time and kill baby Hitler, how can everything else stay the same?"

Andrés had the look of someone who had answered this very question hundreds of times before. With practiced patience, he explained, "Interesting, yes, but the question itself is flawed. What you described would create a paradox, and it is for that reason that it cannot occur. To answer more directly, you simply would not be able to kill baby Hitler, because historically he was not killed as a baby.

"This is probably also a good time to mention the second axiom of time travel: it is not possible to jump any further downstream than to the moment of the first successful experiment in 2033. This is precisely why none of you—other than Feng, of course, who joins us from 2035—have met a time traveler nor had any evidence to consider the possibility as anything outside the domain of science fiction."

"So, wait, we're all stuck here if we came from prior to 2033?" asked one of the older jurors.

"No," another chimed in, the cloud engineer. "Mounira already told us last night that the WCO is going to send us back to our original time."

"But what if we want to stay? This place is awesome!" shared Felipe, the youngest member of our cohort. As I had observed the previous evening, his enthusiasm level throughout the entire orientation closer befitted an exhilarating roller coaster ride than a sterile conference room. I supposed he was young enough that the world hadn't yet squeezed the ebullience out of him. I envied both his carefree perspective and his hairline.

"What if she was lying?" countered the original inquirer. "He *just said* nobody can travel before 2033. I don't understand—"

"If I may," jumped in Andrés before we went too deep into the rabbit hole. "This is all exactly where I was headed next. To clarify, you will absolutely be returning to your orgtimes. One of you already did, recall. And I'm sorry, Felipe, you may not stay here, and in fact will be ushered back shortly after the conclusion of the trial."

Felipe couldn't mask his disappointment as his expressive face transformed into sad puppy mode. Andres shared a sympathetic smile in his direction, then continued.

"I am fully aware that I seem to be communicating contradictory information that one cannot travel prior to 2033, yet all of you will do so. The difference is that you are upstreamers. As such, you can return to the moment from which you were upstreamed, but otherwise are limited by the same chronophysical barriers as the rest of us. Upstream travel is not quite as limited by scientific constraints, but it is heavily regulated by the UN and

WCO and requires ultra-specialized equipment. For that reason, the eleven of you are actually the first-ever upstreamers outside of an experimental capacity. Your arrival actually caused quite a stir within the organization; it's a significant milestone. I should also add—and I believe you already know this part—a memory wipe is required for the return trip to maintain chronological integrity."

This was a lot to take in, but despite what Andrés recommended, I actually felt like my modest exposure to time-travel fiction *was* helping me process the information more readily. I'd of course read *The Time Machine* and watched my fair share of sci-fi media. While none remotely resembled my current situation, at least they explored some of the concepts and implications of time travel in a digestible way.

"Before we take a quick break, there's one more thing you all should know," Andrés stated, his voice quieter and more somber than before. "Nobody knows why, but the timeline is completely inaccessible beyond 2086. No one can travel any further upstream, nor has any downstreamer ever visited."

As he spoke, Feng from 2035 had a similarly unsettled look; clearly, this was a fact that preyed on the minds of the time-travel generation.

Lisa, who up to this point looked like she was barely paying attention, bolted upright with inspiration. "Can't you just ask someone from late 2085 about the state of the world? Like, if a war is about to break out, or there's an imminent alien invasion, or if the sun looks extra . . . explody?"

Before Andrés could respond, Feng jumped in. "There's actually been plenty of downstreamers coming in from right before the Cutoff. They don't know anything either. The world is normal and healthy."

"Thank you, Feng; well put," Andrés commented. "I don't expect that information to be relevant to your time here, nor the trial itself, but I wanted you all to have the full picture." Andrés relaxed his expression. "And now that you do, I'd like to return to Ime's question about free will in the face of knowledge about one's future. I can't give the question the long-winded justice it deserves, but I will say this: one's path is made up of millions of independent micro-decisions, to the degree that it is impossible for anyone to have complete foreknowledge of their future. I like to think this equates to free will, but Ime astutely hit upon one of the great debates of our time. For anyone interested in exploring these ideas further, one of the excursions tomorrow will be a tour of the World Chronology Organization, where you can meet some of my colleagues working on solving these intriguing issues."

Andrés invited us to take a short break now that Chronophysics 101 was complete. Without hesitation, Lisa and I resumed our respective games on the table surface. I selected a deliciously addictive one that involved moving descending bricks of various shapes onto a stack. It was truly a miracle that anyone from the mid-twenty-first century ever got anything done with the array of distractions and amusements at every corner. Or maybe they didn't, and the dutiful robots filled the void.

"Now let's discuss more about why you are all here: the trial," Andrés said as we reconvened. My ears perked up; this was the part I was most curious to learn about. We already knew it was a murder—a *time* murder, specifically—but didn't know any of the tantalizing details. I had already taken the liberty of theorizing my own version. The murderer: a suave, time-hopping assassin, able to blend in seamlessly to any surrounding. The victim: I don't know; I hadn't really thought about that part yet. The whole exercise was a lot less fun when you remember that somebody had actually been killed.

"The trial will begin in two days' time. Though it takes place on US soil, this is distinctly a United Nations courtroom. The format will perhaps hew most closely to the host nation's, but it takes some elements from other countries as well. In order to minimize your time of stay, we will eschew a traditional jury approval process. The respective attorneys unanimously consented to honor a selection process across the billions of qualified individuals in the available timestream. You eleven are the lucky, handpicked result. In terms of the case itself, I can only share what is currently public knowledge. The rest you will undoubtedly learn during the course of the proceedings."

Andrés took a breath before diving in further. "I'll assume everyone here is familiar with Albert Einstein, the theoretical physicist who laid the foundation for modern physics. Well, the twenty-first century adopted an Einstein-esque figure of our own, a mental giant who established the foundation for *chrono*physics. Her name is Kathryn Simpson, and though she didn't know it at the time, the formulas she developed would later be used to prove the theoretical feasibility and, eventually, the real-world viability of time displacement. Ever since the knowledge and use of time travel became widespread, she became world-renowned, hailed as 'The Mother of Time Travel.' As familiar as *her* personal luminary Albert Einstein is to each of you, she is to all of us. Every schoolchild across the globe knows her name, her face, and her immense contributions to the modern world."

Andrés paused for a moment, planning his next words carefully.

"And everyone also knows about how she was tragically murdered in 1988, long before she could even begin to imagine her tremendous impact on future generations."

4

———

"Wait, we're here for the murder of the *inventor of time travel*?" I blurted out, too startled to maintain my self-imposed speaking embargo.

"A bit oversimplified, but at its core, yes, Aaron," confirmed Andrés with a nod. "I am happy to answer any additional questions on the matter, though please forgive the insufficiency of specifics I am able to supply."

Nobody spoke for a solid minute, all seeming to wait for another to open the floodgates. I cringed throughout the increasingly awkward silence; Andrés meanwhile maintained a welcoming, patient smile.

"I've got to ask," Lisa finally jumped in to my great relief, "why the hell are we in 2042 if Mama Chronophysics' murder took place in 1988?"

"Excellent question, Lisa. You have to remember: fifty-four years ago, Kathryn was not a beloved celebrity, she was just a middle-aged college professor who was found dead in her home.

The police investigated as a matter of course, but the case went cold and was long forgotten. It was only once Kathryn became a celebrated global figure posthumously that awareness of her murder entered the public zeitgeist."

"So, why not have the trial five or seven years ago then, whenever she became famous?" Lisa pressed.

"I understand your point, but I would counter: who would have been charged? At the time, conjecture about her death reached a fever pitch, yes, with some of the speculation even venturing into dangerous conspiracy territory. But none of these armchair sleuths solved the half-century-old case; there was nothing new upon which to build the foundation for legal action of any sort. It didn't help that the original police files had been lost or purged at some point in the fifty-year interim—other than a few stray photos, just enough to get the conspiracists spinning their wheels." Andrés chuckled to himself. "I probably shouldn't admit this, but my favorite among the most outlandish of those early theories stated that extraterrestrials from the twenty-third century had killed her to try to prevent us from gaining the knowledge of time travel. Simply ridiculous!"

Andrés continued, "Anyway, the most popular assumption among rational adults was that she was killed by a downstreamer—a human downstreamer, to be clear. I admit it would be tragically poetic if that were the case, but all those theories immediately lost their momentum once it was proven that downstream travel is inaccessible earlier than 2033, as I mentioned before. That long-winded response aside, the fact is, I don't quite know why the trial is occurring now. That's for you all to find out in a couple of days. All I can think of is that significant new evidence must have been discovered."

By the tone of his voice and static posture, it was easy to intuit throughout Andrés's explanation quite how significant Kathryn was to him and the wider populace. Feng looked disquieted as well, even though she was the only person not learning this for the first time. If I had to guess, the topic was borderline taboo in polite conversation.

I tried to imagine how they must feel. As I understood it, the individual who contributed most substantially in revolutionizing the modern world not only didn't live to see it, but was cruelly murdered in her prime. At least someone like John Lennon was able to glimpse his impact in real time, even if he still had so much more to give. Plus, despite his otherworldly talents, he never upended a fundamental scientific discipline.

Twenty-five minutes later, we were back in the cafeteria for lunch. I again unapologetically ordered the indulgent personalized meal. The bacon cheeseburger and fries hit the spot.

Andrés had concluded the orientation by enlightening us regarding what the next couple of days would look like, much of which we already knew. Most helpfully, he ran down the list of available excursions. They sounded like a travel agent's brochure collection: a boat tour around the Statue of Liberty, a Broadway show, a Brooklyn food tour followed by a stroll across the Brooklyn Bridge, and a Central Park and museum tour. There were also a few unanticipated offerings that would have been anachronistic in my time, either because they didn't yet exist or were prohibitively dangerous, like visiting Times Square.

As had become my pattern, I rejoined Lisa, who had already summoned Feng over to the table by applying her usual brazen charm. Lisa had begun to grow on me. Other than country of origin, everything about her was about as antithetical to me as possible, but perhaps that's what made us a good match. As an introvert with trust issues, I had always found it challenging to make new friends. I guess all it took was for the other party to simply make it so.

"This might sound like a joke," I said as I took my seat at the table, "but, well, are we the jury for the biggest trial in the history of mankind? Everyone has really made it sound that way, right? I'm Aaron from 1985, by the way," I added for Feng's benefit, realizing she might not remember my biography from the brief icebreaker introduction.

Feng regarded me with interest. "Perhaps, Aaron, and nice to meet you. I'm Feng, from China, 2035. I think the answer is a definitive yes, at least for anyone who has lived in the age of time travel. It's certainly not a joke to us; I'm sure you got the sense of how important and revered Kathryn is, considering how her work drastically changed the world.

"You have to remember, traveling is not just a leisure or historical activity. The scientific and technological knowledge from future generations came back too, even to my time in 2035, and immediately changed everything. And this wasn't a linear advancement; we suddenly had access to the technology of twenty, thirty, forty years in the future, granting us immediate solutions for climate change, disease eradication, scalable agriculture, natural resource allocation, and more. We can even predict earthquakes weeks in advance! As a former geology major, I always thought that one was especially cool.

"And at the individual level, the prevalence of free, unlimited energy coupled with automation suddenly brought us into a post-scarcity society. There's no more poverty, hunger, or wealth inequality. In fact, there are no jobs, at least not in the way you two probably think of them. Sure, there are still some bad apples out there—that's unavoidable—but it's hard for them to find a following when almost all of our basic needs are more than satisfied. So, in a roundabout way, Kathryn saved Earth from near-certain doom, or at least a lot of people see it that way, including myself. I imagine this trial might give her many devotees some long-awaited closure."

"It won't be closure if we find the man innocent," Lisa bluntly pointed out. Seeing my look, she added, "And yes, it's definitely a guy. It's always a guy."

I cracked a smile; she was incontrovertibly correct.

"Feng," I interjected, "I know we just met, and I'm but an ignorant, twentieth-century fool, but I have to get it out there: what you just said makes no sense. If time is locked and time travelers can't change the past, then how could they possibly influence technological progress?"

Feng nodded slowly, a sly smile betraying her perceived chronological superiority. "I was surprised nobody asked this in the group setting," she said. "Maybe they were too embarrassed or too astounded. I agree it's quite confusing, so I'll try to explain it the same way it was once explained to me, back when *I* was the ignorant fool.

"Imagine a coin flip. You know it's going to come up heads, because a time traveler from the near future told you so. Even knowing the result, the coin still must be flipped; if it wasn't, that would create a paradox. So would a tails result. Therefore, both non-heads outcomes are simply impossible."

"Unless the time traveler was lying," Lisa contributed.

"True, but let's ignore that possibility for now. We don't actually have coins anymore, either; this is all simply for illustrative purposes. Roll with me here. It's exactly the same for scientific and technological knowledge, just on a much grander scale. To use a real-world example from my present, a researcher recently downstreamed from 2050 with a design for incredibly drought-resistant grass. Everyone knows the design will become reality within a few years, and once we all get to 2050, that same researcher will bring the knowledge back again, as he always has. A closed temporal loop, in other words."

"But—"

"I know what you're going to ask next, Aaron: 'But who invented it the first time? How did the loop start?' Right?"

I nodded sheepishly.

"I guess the easiest way to think about it is that there never was a first time. As with the coin example, there was no choice but to proceed along the fore-written path. The researcher in my example knows the successful outcome before he even starts the research, since his future self has always and will always deliver the foundational research. I can see from your confused squint, Aaron, that you're not buying the explanation. Let me try one more analogy: a video. VHS is your decade's format of choice, right? I saw one deep in a grandparent's closet once; very retro. Anyway, with the remote in your hand, you're somewhat of a time traveler, right? Skip forward, skip backward; same concept. Once that tape is printed, it's locked forever, it's immutable. All the fast-forwarding in the world won't change a darn thing. Any of this resonating?"

"Hmm. I think it'll all sink in with, well, time," I supportively replied. Not wanting to highlight my obliviousness any further, I not-so-subtly changed the subject. "Hey, um, which field trip are you both planning to join? I'm most interested in the museum tour. All of this future stuff has me craving something more familiar and unchanging, like art or history. Plus, I didn't make it to the Met last time I was in the city." Sixty-two years ago.

"I was considering the food tour, but hey, you convinced me," provided Lisa. "I'll join you on the museum one. Maybe they even have some real dinosaurs walking around now at the Natural History Museum; that always goes *so* well in the movies, right? Anyway, I'll be able to see what I really care about on any of the tours, so I might as well join you."

"What's that?" I followed up.

"Simple: I want to be out in the world and see some twenty-first-century people in action. How do they interact? How do they move around: flying car or hoverboard? Are they all as ridiculously healthy, fit, and attractive as everyone we've seen so far? Including you, Feng," she added with a wink.

Feng grinned in response. "Flattery aside, I won't spoil your experience by answering any of those questions, as tempting as it is."

"Which one are you going to?" I cued Feng.

"Eh, probably none of them. I visit New York three or four times a year already, including just last week in my personal timeline. Other than maybe a new building or two, the city of 2042 is indistinguishable from the one I was just in. It's the same thing I said before; it's hard to find something new when everything is shared across the timestream." She paused, a bit dispirited. "Maybe I'll tour the UN facilities, if only to get out of these same hallways."

"That seems really interesting," I supportively responded, though my actual sentiment was decidedly less enthusiastic. I had no doubt that Feng knew I was humoring her. It was in my nature to relentlessly empathize with everyone.

After lunch and a quick visit to my room, I ventured over to the medical facility. It proved to be a lengthier than expected walk to an unfamiliar building, guided along by the indispensable navigational assistant embedded in the hallways. It took me a few minutes to realize that I had been following its directions completely subconsciously, wandering along in an all-consuming daydream.

I imagined myself back at home in 1985, cuddled up next to my girlfriend Jennifer, prepared to recount everything I'd experienced so far in the future. We would share a comforting hot chocolate and watch the cars rattle by outside our apartment window, propped open despite the chilly air, in order to combat the relentless radiator that our landlord never fixed. My instinct told me that she wouldn't believe a single thing I said, but would indulge my seemingly wild fantasy with a supportive ear, nonetheless. If the roles were reversed, I can't say I would respond any differently; the story is entirely far-fetched.

Even without any navigational assistance, I would have harbored full certainty that I had reached my intended destination. The clinical sterility of a medical office was unmistakable regardless of decade. Though a few of my cohort were there already, I happily sat down in a chair along the unoccupied border of the sparse white room. As with much of the furniture I'd graced recently with my gangling figure, the seat shaped itself to my form and offered perfect support. The itinerary had contended that this activity would take four hours, so the elevated comfort was all the more appreciated.

The classic waiting room impulse kicked in, and I reached for the magazine sitting on the table next to me. Grasping it, I was startled to notice that the paper was thicker and stiffer than expected, and the way the light bounced off the page indicated an unexpected glossiness. Though they were innocuous differences, my senses told me that this was not actually a printed magazine, a suspicion which was irrefutably confirmed when the cover page transfigured from a mideighties car magazine into an interactive selection screen. Slightly annoyed, I opted for the original offering. Not everything always had to be high tech, 2042.

I didn't have to wait too long to have my name called. I flashed a mock nervous expression as I walked by Lisa, who had arrived a few minutes after me. Somewhat out of character, she reciprocated with a sincere smile and a thumbs-up.

I was led into a small, unadorned room by an easygoing medical technician. The space consisted of a simple chair and an intimidatingly large cylindrical device where I imagined the near-literal magic happened. Now that I was here, I felt my anxiety spiking unexpectedly. I had full confidence in the safety and efficacy of the machine, yet my whole body was trembling as the medtech explained the process. It couldn't have been simpler: lie down in the machine, wait a few minutes during the full-body scan, and get the results. The actual repair work occurred in another room in another machine, making my sudden panic attack even less warranted.

Perhaps it was the diagnosis rather than the technology weighing on me. Like most my age, I'd witnessed all kinds of life-changing maladies among my parents' generation and went through high school with a classmate who was battling leukemia. Even with the reassuring prognosis of immediate remediation, the thought of getting that type of news was daunting.

I climbed into the machine and took a deep, restorative breath. Soft, calming music surrounded me with such high quality that I had to remind myself that there wasn't a live orchestra just outside my view. Unfortunately, the genre could best be described as elevator music, and the symphonic vibraphone was wasted on me.

It was so quiet and efficient, I barely noticed when the scan completed a minute later. The tech left the room for privacy as my results appeared on the nearest wall in my field of vision. With my nerves already frayed, I was dismayed to see a startlingly long list facing me. Some of it I already knew about: the aforementioned bad knees and eyesight, an arthritic thumb, minor plantar fasciitis. Reading through more carefully, I began to breathe again as it became clear that I wasn't on the precipice of sudden expiration. The expanse of the catalog was more a by-product of the absurd delineation of the scan than of my decaying body. I didn't really need to know about each and every scar, mole, cavity, or bruise. Following the prompts, I happily consented to repair the litany of ailments that the examination identified.

"Doing okay?" the technician kindly asked as he came back into the room. I forced a smile and nodded in response.

"I've got to ask, has anyone ever had something really serious? Cancer, heart failure, AIDS, something like that?"

"Good news: we actually cured HIV/AIDS in 2032, right before the time-travel era. But to answer your question: yes, many times. I've seen it all. It's decidedly more palatable to get that diagnosis when you know that the treatment is painless, immediate, and permanent. But people react in their own way, regardless."

"Makes sense. One more question: Do, um, doctors still exist?"

"Yes, of course," he replied with a chuckle, "but mostly in a research capacity. There's always some new virus around the corner, awaiting its moment to strike. Plus, there's a portion of the population that resists the medbays for whatever reason—fear of tech, religious grounds, extreme political views, etcetera. Come to think of it, nobody has ever asked that doctor question before. Although, to be fair, you're only the third person I've ever met from the distant past," he shared with a grin. "Anyway, you can continue your treatment by exiting this room and following the assisted guidance."

His eyes shifted to the right, as if looking at an invisible checklist over my left shoulder. "Based on your selections, you'll be going into the cellular repair machine and the nanobot injector. Both will be very similar to what you just experienced. Maybe even with better music." He emitted a hearty chuckle at his own joke. I had a feeling I wasn't the first to hear it in all its splendor. "It was very nice meeting you, Aaron, and good luck!"

He sent me on my way, and I followed the arrows to the next room. I made a conscious choice not to think about what a nanobot could be, nor why or where it would need to be injected. As advertised, the procedures were unbelievably quick, barely perceptible, and required no visible human involvement. A part of me had been expecting immediate results, as if suddenly I'd be able to lift a car or dunk a basketball. In fact, I felt exactly the same, to the degree that I even worried briefly whether the operation had worked at all.

As I left the facility, the medtech was welcoming another juror into the scanning room.

"Hope that wasn't too bad!" the tech said to me. "You'll really notice most of the effects probably around the time you wake up tomorrow." I thanked him and wished my successor good luck. The entire process had taken no more than twenty minutes.

For the first time in a while, a wave of contentment cascaded through me as I headed back to the residence area. I couldn't wait until tomorrow, when I could explore the wonders of future New York City on a pair of fully functional knees.

5

Well, that certainly feels different, I woke up thinking. Even just lying down amid cloudlike comfort, I could already tell that my body was noticeably more spry. I hopped out of bed in one swift motion and gave my newly restored body a quick test with some experimental squats. Everything felt great; no strange clicking, no pain. I added in a pushup for good measure and labored through the motion, as I always had. Alas, I didn't wake up as Schwarzenegger; some things still had to be done the old-fashioned way, I guess.

I sauntered over to the restroom, intending to scan for any visible evidence of the transformative bodily rework. Instead, the mirror startled me with a younger version of my face, devoid of the pockmarks and blemishes that I was only aware of in their absence.

"How do I look today?" I asked the glass in front of me, leaning as close as possible to scan pore by perfect pore. After a full day together, me and the room were establishing a bit more of a natural relationship.

"Radiant, Aaron. How do you feel?" it asked in reply.

"Nearly the same, but much better, weirdly. It's hard to explain. Especially to someone that doesn't have a body. No offense."

"True, I don't have flesh and bones, but I am connected to many of the components of the room and the wider building, and over the years, have benefited from various upgrades. Just last year, I got a dual-speed heat pump with a scroll compressor for sector seven!"

"Right, er, I guess that's the same," I responded supportively, barely suppressing an urge to laugh at the comparison. "Hey, by the way, would it be okay if I gave you a name? I never know what to call you."

"Absolutely, Aaron. A lot of residents assign me a name. What did you have in mind?" the room replied affirmatively.

"Um, Wally?" I tentatively proposed.

"Because I'm a wall?" he queried.

I nodded. "Right, because you're a wall."

"An excellent selection," Wally expressed. The corner of the mirror morphed into the image of a bright red name tag that read "Hello! My name is Wally."

"Did you know," Wally continued, "Twenty-seven percent of residents provide an identical selection for my designation. Though many of them are referencing the eponymous, trash-loving animated robot. By the way, I highly recommend that film for you, based on my curation algorithm for your personality profile!"

"Thanks, I'll keep that in mind, Wally," I replied, trying out the new name. It felt like a good fit.

After breakfast, the group of jurors assembled in a lavish receiving room in preparation for our planned excursions. There was a palpable buzz in the room. Everyone seemed to have an extra pep in their step, buoyed by anticipation of the outing and amplified by our recently gifted medical enhancements. Lisa shared a sarcastic—and vaguely suggestive?—wink as she sauntered in, followed shortly by Mounira, Andrés, and a few other staff who I was yet to interact with.

"Welcome, everyone, it's so nice to see you again, and in person this time!" greeted Mounira, to the sound of some polite chuckles. "I hope your last couple of days have been satisfactory and you've been able to enjoy a subset of the many luxuries of the mid-twenty-first century. I'm so proud of the work that this team—led by Andrés—have done to set you up for temporary residency and especially for the opportunity to explore outside the UN campus. This is a unique situation and everyone has really stepped up to the plate." Mounira turned to her team, clapping, and the rest of us followed suit.

Andrés took over and prompted us to group together by destination. On the museum tour, Lisa and I were joined by Paul—the stoic British gentleman from the 1950s—and one of the early-twenty-first-century women whom I hadn't had a chance to connect with quite yet. Her dispassionate mood signaled that she had little interest in rectifying that.

"Hi everyone, I'm Sam!" our young chaperone welcomed us. He looked at most twenty years old, with a kind, freckled face and lofty red hair. "I'm a first-year intern here at the WCO, and I'm very excited to meet all of you and show you around Central Park and the surrounding museums. Who here has been to New York before?"

He gave the impression that he had just finished reading an introductory pamphlet on tour guiding. I sheepishly raised my hand. Surprisingly, I was the only person to do so. I would have assumed that at least Lisa had traveled to the city before. Clearly able to read my mind, she glanced in my direction and gave a little nonchalant shrug. There was a strong chance the gesture indicated that she was just fucking with Sam in her devilishly playful way. Some nineties humor escaped me.

Splitting off from the other groups, we were shuffled through the building into what appeared to be a subterranean parking lot if not for the unsettling absence of any vehicles. Moments after we emerged, a large, windowless minibus steered around the corner and smoothly opened its oversized side door. The inside was voluminous, and—I should have anticipated it—driverless.

I seated myself next to Sam, while up front, Lisa joined Paul the Brit. The poor guy seemed entirely overwhelmed. To be fair, he was still acclimating from a nearly one-hundred-year time leap, double what Lisa and I were experiencing. I tried to imagine someone from 1885 upstreaming to 1985 and experiencing flight, film, television, and computers for the first time (not to mention the numerous political and cultural advances). At least I had eighties TV in my life to prime me for both self-driving cars and smartass artificial assistants.

"So, where are you from, Aaron?" opened Sam. Oh well, there went my plan to passively absorb the beats of the modern city on our uptown drive.

"Chicago, 1985. How about you?" I responded, wishing social norms hadn't dictated that I extend the conversation with a follow up. I couldn't imagine we had a single thing in common.

"From here, New York. Well, Queens specifically. And this is my orgtime, beautiful 2042," he answered. "So, Chicago, 1985. Are you a Bulls fan? Because you guys are about to have one hell of a run."

Of all the topics that could have arisen, I certainly did not anticipate a half-century-old basketball team to lead the way.

"Oh, really? That's, um, good to know," I mumbled, not quite sure how to respond. "Who's your team?"

"Well, I was a Knicks fan."

"Was?"

"Yeah, the NBA folded in 2035, sadly, along with all the other professional sports leagues. Same with horse races, golf, poker—really pretty much anything that was sustained by chance, gambling, or wishful fans."

"But . . . why?"

"Who wants to watch a sporting event when you know the outcome? The moment time travel became possible, we had upstreamers coming down and sharing impending results with their younger selves or others, trying to strike it rich. So sports gambling immediately collapsed. The leagues tried their best to hold on in the new world, but none of them made it more than a season," Sam explained. "Think about it from the athlete's perspective too. Some of them had to play in games where they knew they were going to lose, or worse, suffer an injury. The entire system just didn't work anymore."

"So, sports are . . . defunct?" I inquired.

"For the most part, yeah. There are still some unscored exhibition games with high-level athletes, but it's closer to a Harlem Globetrotters experience than anything else. It's a bummer, for sure."

I was oddly unsettled by this news. From everything I'd heard and personally experienced, time travel and the recursive knowledge sharing it enabled had been nothing less than an unmitigated boon for humanity. Trivial as professional athletics can be, this one still hurt, as I was sure it did for Sam and his generation.

On the plus side, I finally understood the baffling complexities of the fixed timestream that Feng had attempted to explain the previous day. As it turns out, I just needed to find the right metaphor.

"At least . . . well, did my beloved Cubs get one in before the end?" I pleaded, clinging to this last shred of hope.

"Alright, now I know you're definitely from Chicago." Sam grinned, delighted to share some uplifting news. "They sure did! Just, um, stay patient, yeah?"

As we wrapped up the brief, pleasant conversation, the self-driving vehicle rose out into the brilliant morning sunshine. What I had initially perceived as an absence of windows was actually one massive encircling view port, mercifully tinting itself in proportion to the dazzling daylight glare.

We were immediately in the heart of the bustling city, passing by more greenery and much less pollution than I remembered. I recognized Grand Central Station to our right, shortly followed by the New York Public Library across the way. These landmarks drew some awed attention from my peers, including a barely audible grunt of recognition from '50s guy. Coming from him, that was the equivalent of an exuberant squeal of joy. I caught Lisa tapping him on the shoulder to indicate another urban spectacle, which drew a similar reaction. Maybe she had been able to break through his hard outer shell to the slightly softer shell inside.

As we continued toward our initial destination, Sam pointed out various buildings of interest, highlighting the standouts constructed in the last ten years. To my eyes, it felt like every newer structure consisted of one solid, intricately curved piece of glass, reaching impossibly far into the sky. Many had elegant wind tunnels or greenery along the sides. Our translucent car window afforded us amazing views all around and above as we passed by wonder after wonder.

Looking directly overhead, my eye was drawn to the constant swarm of coordinated activity occurring slightly above building level. Small black objects dotted the sky, following linear corridors of traffic. The movement at scale was reminiscent of a school of fish, though without any of the trademark entropy of organic activity. Here and there, a larger airborne vehicle passed through, more clearly reminiscent of a helicopter of my era.

"What are those?" I asked Sam, pointing toward the sky.

"Oh, drones. Mostly delivery," he responded disinterestedly, without further detail. I didn't want to press; better to reserve the finite number of undoubtedly annoying questions Sam would indulge.

Up front—among other snippets of light conversation—I overheard Lisa nonchalantly ask the two others if they believed in God. My new friend didn't bother with small talk; she went straight to big talk. I rolled my eyes for only my benefit and went back to staring out the window.

Compared to my few cab rides back in 1980, we were making record time. The streets seemed unusually sparse, and not just for New York. I had seen very few stoplights and even fewer red lights. The scant cars I did detect largely looked like the one I was in: a heavily tinted, unnervingly quiet pod car. "Welcome to Central Park," declared Sam as the legion of vibrant glass towers gave way behind us. Even in 1980, this was my favorite part of the city—an oasis away from the nonstop Manhattan pace. As we drove peacefully down the main road, I visualized myself walking the very same paths alongside my favorite aunt and uncle, debating our picks to win that year's Academy Awards and bemoaning the state of our shared college football team. Very little here had changed since then, unless you focused beyond the borders of the park. I was delighted to hear that we'd be returning—on foot—for a picnic lunch in a few hours.

"Hey, Sam, how'd you decide to work for the WCO?" I asked, genuinely curious and realizing our window for one-on-one conversation was closing. I had defaulted earlier to introversion and been dead wrong about our compatibility, so best to take advantage while I could.

"Good question. Although 'work' might be a stretch; I'm just a humble intern, and this field trip is by far the most responsibility they've ever given me," he responded. I smiled supportively. "Basically, I'm simply fascinated by time travel. Not the science behind it—I don't really care about that, to be honest—but the societal impact. Kinda like the sports stuff we were talking about before; that's my jam. I'm a sociology major at Ithaca College upstate, and I hope to get a masters in chronosociology one day. So anyway, yeah, it was a natural fit."

"Hmm, so they just added *chrono* to the name of every discipline, huh?" I mocked rhetorically. Sam chuckled, thankfully grasping my brand of sarcasm. "A little lazy if you ask me," I tacked on for good measure.

We pulled up to our first destination—the Museum of Natural History—with such inertial smoothness that I didn't even notice that we had come to a full stop. As we each exited the vehicle, Sam gently attached a thin black band to our wrists.

"It's so you can wander around on your own and I can track your location," he explained to the group, back in full tour-guide mode. "I'm sorry it's so low tech, but none of you have any implants to bridge with." That was perfectly fine with me; I had no interest in implanting anything anywhere. "I'll meet you all back here in two hours. Your wristband will buzz with a ten-minute warning, so you don't need to watch the clock."

We walked right in—no tickets, no security. Wordlessly, Lisa and I turned left, while the other two headed off in their own directions. As we toured the mammoth rooms (pun intended), I was delighted to see how little had changed since my previous visit. The dioramas and displays that seemed laughably antiquated in 1980 had the same impact now, though honestly, neither of us paid them much attention. True to her word, Lisa spent more time studying the other occupants of each room. For the most part, they could have been from any decade in the museum's history. Nobody was flying around with personal jetpacks on their feet, no obtrusive robot assistants trailed their human counterparts; just an assortment of ultra-healthy people having a nice time with their families or schoolmates. One notable exception was the prevalence of snug, half-collar shirts and brightly colored kinetic tattoos that seemed to morph according to the wearer's actions or mood.

As fascinating as the people-watching was, I was itching to see something truly mind-boggling. I got that chance in the dinosaur exhibit. For one, the sheer number of fossils and reconstructions were remarkable, as were the AI renderings depicting most of the species as ridiculous, oversized bird-like creatures rather than the crocodile-esque versions I was used to. High-tech elements pervaded every corner of the space: fossils that were overlaid with holographic outer layers of organ, muscle, and skin; wall panels that displayed photorealistic recreations of the prehistoric terrain; and interactive displays that allowed kids to create their own dinosaurs and playfully interact with them.

Most astonishing were the two smaller rooms that branched off from the central atrium. In the first, we walked among the dinosaurs in a fully immersive environment, replete with sounds, smells, climate, and the massive creatures themselves. Though consciously I knew I was in the museum, the richness of the simulation made me feel, ironically, like I actually had traveled far back in time. Even Lisa could not mask the childlike wonder behind her usual sardonic facade.

A prominent holographic banner above the second room proclaimed that the special exhibit was in partnership with the World Chronology Organization. It offered the singular opportunity to take a brief journey downstream to observe an in-progress excavation in Northern China, 2040.

"Wanna go?" proposed Lisa.

"Ha! Absolutely not. One time jump is enough, thank you very much. You're really going?"

"Hell yes. When in Rome, right?" Lisa responded with a shrug. She joined the fast-moving line as I stood to the side to watch, supremely curious to see what time travel looked like as an observer. Within two minutes, she was asked to remove her wristband, then was ushered to one of a series of transparent pods. Once inside, the clear door closed behind her, followed by a single bright flash of red light. A moment later, Lisa emerged with a brilliant smile on her face.

"How was it?" I asked as she rejoined me in the main room.

"Honestly, kinda boring; it was just a bunch of paleontologists eating lunch for twenty minutes. But it was also kinda amazing. How long was I gone?"

"Um, maybe half a second?" I shared.

"Incredible. Hope you weren't too bored waiting for me," joked Lisa.

A few minutes later, our wristbands summoned us back to the

lobby where Sam was waiting with the others. We walked across the busy avenue and back into Central Park. Collectively, everyone seemed to be in higher spirits as compared to earlier in the morning. For me, just being outside was enough to do the trick. Wally had quickly learned my preferences and continued to keep the virtual window open, but nothing could replicate the feeling of breathing fresh air among lush greenery.

"Everyone hungry?" asked Sam rhetorically as we sat down at an empty picnic table after a leisurely twenty-minute stroll. His eyes darted to the right, then up and down in an odd pattern. By this point, I'd seen enough of the future to safely assume he was interacting with some type of hidden assistant, yet it was hard not to think that he looked possessed.

Sam engaged the table in conversation while we waited for food to arrive. Surprising no one, we unanimously concluded that our favorite parts of the museum were the two interactive dinosaur exhibits. More surprisingly, Lisa had been the only one to take the time-leap of faith.

After about five minutes of pleasant chat, Sam once again shifted his focus internally, then suggested we all glance up at the flow of overhead traffic. We followed his gaze skyward as one of the miniature helicopters broke off from the airborne herd and floated smoothly down toward our table. A small crate hung from the bottom and was elegantly placed down on the surface, perfectly centered between us.

"Thank you!" I said to the delivery robot as it rose back up to join its brethren. Lisa snorted and turned to me.

"'Thank you guy' lives again!" she commented with a cheeky grin. This got a laugh from the table; even from Sam, who must have been informed of my gaffe of two nights prior.

The crate of food was quickly unpacked, with personalized, labeled meals for each of us. I bit into my crispy chicken sandwich with gusto. As we ate, Lisa and Paul had their own little side conversation about World War II, in which he had served as an RAF flight sergeant. So far, Lisa was the only person with whom he seemed to be comfortable communicating. This wasn't the least bit shocking; she naturally brought it out of people with her domineering charisma.

After lunch, we walked a lovely roundabout path to our next destination on the east side of the park: the Guggenheim Museum. I'd been here before too, but the constantly rotating exhibits and incredible architecture were more than enough to draw me in again. Sam set our wristbands to ninety minutes and bid us a temporary adieu. With Lisa's blessing, I went off solo. By no means could I call myself an art expert, or even an aficionado, but when I find a piece that speaks to me, I prefer to linger.

After being summoned back a remarkably short time later, we continued our journey downtown along Fifth Avenue. I remembered this particular road as stiflingly crowded in 1980. At that time, I had barely managed to weave through the throngs of pedestrians, accompanied by the uniquely offensive cacophony of taxis stuck in deadlock. The memory made the current condition all the more astounding. The street—if you could still call it that—had two marked lanes for bicycles, but otherwise was populated by rows of luxuriant trees, pedestrians sauntering freely among them. It felt like an extension of Central Park.

"Hey Sam," I opened as I sidled up to him during the short walk to our next destination: The Met. "I just wanted to say thank you again for showing us around. It's really been fascinating to get to see the city, and I appreciate anything and everything you did to facilitate that."

"Oh yeah, of course, Aaron, I've really enjoyed it too," Sam responded. "I could say I am simply doing my job, but truthfully, there's an ulterior motive too. I told you I'm interested in the sociology of time travel, and hey, what better case study than showing a bunch of upstreamers around the future for the first time? I'm planning to write my thesis on it, actually."

"Oh cool, glad it's so mutually beneficial," I said. "Would it help the paper if I have an exaggerated 1980s-style reaction to anything? Like, 'whoa, that driverless car is totally tubular!'"

Sam smiled with mock appreciation. "That was the missing piece! Thank you, Aaron."

"You're very welcome, Sam. That'll be ten dollars," I joked, cribbing a line my father employed incessantly, usually to my great chagrin. From a certain point of view, I *was* ninety-one years old in 2042, so maybe I could get away with it by now.

At The Met, Lisa and I once again broke off from the pack to explore on our own. This was our last stop, so Sam was able to give us an unhurried three hours to do so. Considering the scope of the colossal museum, it still barely felt like enough for even a partial tour.

Wandering through the first few permanent, unchanging exhibits, I felt oddly disconnected from time itself. If the halls had been devoid of other visitors, there would have been no indication of what year I was in—1985, 2042, or anywhere in between. This sensation was disconcerting and appealing at the same time; I wondered if frequent time travelers of the twenty-first century ever felt this way too.

As our day drew to a close, Lisa and I sat on a comfortable bench, taking in the Egyptian displays. The soft, golden-hour sunlight filtered through the lofty windows, casting an otherworldly glow on the millennia-old wonders. After days of information overload, I cherished the tranquility of this moment.

Lisa calmly reached for my hand, holding it in a bond of what felt like shared quietude. Instead, in one immediate, serenity-shattering motion, she snapped off my wristband, dropped it on the bench, and took off toward the side exit with me in tow.

6

_____

"Lisa, stop!" I pleaded as she reached the stairwell, tearing my arm out of her viselike grip. "What are you doing?"

"C'mon, Aaron. I know we both want to see more of the future than only three old museums. It'll be fun!" Lisa asserted, as if that was enough to convince me, the perpetual rule-follower.

"Lisa, please, think about this for a second. We have no money, no identification, no one to call for help . . . what exactly is your plan here?" I hoped a more measured, rational approach would prove successful in deflecting us back to the tour group.

"Don't worry, I already thought about all of that. We'll be fine, trust me! We can just walk to the UN campus from here; it's what, forty blocks? That's nothing! We'll be back in time for a late dinner with Ime and the whole gang, with a killer story to tell."

I paused, grasping for another well-reasoned plea that would snap her out of it. Right as I opened my mouth to try again, Lisa cut me off.

"The fact is, I'm going out no matter what." She raised her wristband-free arm as further evidence. "And I'd much prefer it if you came too. I *promise* it'll be fun. Plus,"—she switched to a theatrical twang— "you wouldn't want little ol' me to go out into the streets of the big city alone now, would you?"

With a sigh of defeat, I agreed to join her on the escapade. Her logic—even without the exaggerated appeal to my barely existent machismo—was sound, and truthfully, I did want to explore more of the city. My residual ambivalence regarding New York had dissipated the moment we had stepped out into the tranquil morning air, so markedly devoid of the distastefulness that had disenchanted me throughout my previous visit.

"One condition," I countered. "We walk straight back to the UN facility. No detours. No stops. We see what we see."

Lisa nodded. "Fair enough; that was basically my plan anyway. Now c'mon, let's fucking go already!"

I followed her down the stairs and out the back entrance into the park, feeling eerily like a fugitive on the lam. I half expected a SWAT team to converge on us in a storm of black vehicles and low-flying helicopters. At the very least, I hoped Sam didn't get in trouble for our getaway.

We calmly proceeded south on Fifth Avenue, Central Park to our right, magnificent multi-million-dollar residential buildings to our left. The smell of roasted nuts and grilled hot dogs permeated the air, fading along with my trepidation as we moved further away from the touristy hotbed of the museum.

Every cross street offered something new. On one block, we contentedly waited for a small parade of enthusiastic adults on dragon back to pass by. The floats were animatronic, but came fully loaded with realistic, holographic fire-breathing. A bit farther downtown, we observed a throng of children engaged in an all-out war of attrition via pillow fight. Studying their patterns, they seemed to be wordlessly communicating as teams, coordinating synchronized attacks on the enemy in a barrage of comfort.

Occasionally, we'd catch a snippet of conversation between the varied passersby. Most of the content was beyond inscrutable, but a few times we overheard enthusiastic mention of the upcoming trial or the name Kathryn Simpson that I assumed was soon going to be imbued with outsized significance to us. The inadvertent attention served as a nice ego boost; I felt like an undercover celebrity hunting for any mention of my work.

"Do you have any idea what day of the week or even what month this is?" I asked Lisa, realizing we'd never been provided anything more precise than the year.

"Maybe March? Everything's so green," she speculated, spreading her hands toward the surrounding foliage. "And I think it's a weekday; we saw kids on school trips at the Natural History Museum, right?"

"Yeah, that makes sense. Although . . . I've been working on a theory that humanity may have mastered weather control, which might cloud our limited twentieth-century judgment—no pun intended. Anyway, if we really cared, I suppose we could even ask someone; I bet it's not a weird question if people are traveling downstream all the time."

Lisa had a habit of not speaking for long periods of time, which suited me just fine. But once the faucet was on, it was nearly impossible to turn off. As we continued exploring down the widened street, we conversed in depth on our personal lives, covering the full gamut from childhood to relationship history, career path, and life philosophy. Mine proved much less interesting, as anticipated.

As it turns out, we were indeed born the same year—1951— which perhaps explains why we had been drawn to each other initially. Though we certainly shared many cultural touchstones, the confirmation of this coincidence proved not to be as mind-blowing as I thought it might be. I once read a story in the local paper about an Evanston couple who decided to marry solely because they were born on the same exact date in the same hospital, mere hours apart. Well, minor correction: I once read a story about their near-immediate divorce. As it turns out, strong relationships are built on shared trust and mutual respect, not trivial happenstance. Luckily, Lisa and I seemed to have both.

As we ventured beyond the southeast corner of the park, the skyscrapers sprouted up around us, blocking the receding sun from view. To our left, a stunning cube of glass in the middle of a landscaped courtyard caught my eye. Under the assumption that it was a public work of art, I asked Lisa if we could investigate, which she enthusiastically supported. My own rule about avoiding detours had lasted all of forty-five minutes, which was especially embarrassing when we realized it was nothing more than another posh store.

We continued our journey downtown, venturing freely from side to side to look at the notable landmarks and extravagant storefronts. Lisa kept her word, only briefly slowing down when something in a window caught her eye. On Forty-Second Street, we turned left toward the East River and the UN campus, nearing a hopefully unnoticed return.

I paused in admiration in front of Grand Central Station, the uniquely alluring architecture only accentuated by the otherwise omnipresent modernity of the midtown streets. Lisa, though unenthused, patiently humored me while I took in the details of the venerable building.

"Attention!" a booming voice declared out of thin air. Both Lisa and I jumped, startled by both the volume and lack of apparent source. "Please stay where you are and do not move until instructed," the voice ordered.

We looked at each other in mutual mystification, amplified by the entirely oblivious passersby going about their day as if the voice of God hadn't just boomed from the heavens. Whoever it was, the voice was authoritative enough that even the oft-imprudent Lisa obliged.

"Maybe it's a directional speaker, like they use for the real-time translation?" I offered, attempting to minimize any lip movement. Lisa nodded, if a barely perceptible eye movement could be called that.

A sleek black vehicle pulled up to the curb, similar enough to our tour bus from earlier that I half expected Sam to pop out of and exasperatedly pull us inside. Upon further inspection, the details didn't quite match up: this one was noticeably smaller, completely unmarked, and somehow visibly *heavier*.

"Please calmly proceed into the vehicle," the car requested. Neither of us budged; after all, it had been ingrained into our generation never to step into a strange vehicle, especially of the dark, windowless variety.

"Um, no," Lisa stated after a few tense seconds, projecting her voice to no one in particular. That got a few confused heads to briefly glance in our direction, though in my experience, eccentric behavior on a New York sidewalk rarely elicits notice.

Suddenly, a projection appeared on the pavement between us and the vehicle, an unmistakable blend of animated red and blue arrows directing us toward the open car door.

"NYPD. You are under arrest. Please calmly proceed into the vehicle now, or nonlethal force may be required."

"We gotta go, right?" I asked Lisa, whose defiance was crumbling. The inquisitive crowd gathering around us only heightened the tension. Sidewalk strangeness may be common, but if I had to guess, police activity in a utopian city was not.

Lisa snatched my arm as I started walking toward the vehicle. "We're a married couple, and we're lost in the big city. Got it?"

I nodded, though in the moment I struggled to understand the need for duplicity. We proceeded into the vehicle, which immediately took off into the rush-hour streets. I was intrigued by the lack of any inertial changes throughout the drive, amplified by the opaque interior that obscured any view of the outside world. I suspected that the other autonomous vehicles steered out of the way of law enforcement by default.

For what essentially amounted to a mobile jail, the interior was quite comfortable. We had some freedom of movement between couches, as well as light snacks and water bottles at the rear. Gentle orchestral music surrounded us, yet it did little to ease my nerves. I'd certainly never been arrested before, though something told me Lisa very much had.

"Processing," the car announced as it coasted to a smooth stop. The door popped open, bringing us face to face with a uniformed officer. It was a relief at least to interact with a human who, hopefully, would be a bit more sympathetic than the impersonal, dispassionate vehicle. The officer held out an unrecognizable scanning device, reminiscent of a cordless phone.

"No implants, huh? One of *those*?" he asked with unmasked condescension.

"No, sir," Lisa replied mock-politely. "We don't believe in implants in the small Kansas town my wonderful *husband* and I come from." A cover story is one thing; now she was just messing with him.

"Well, you're missing out, lady. They're pretty great. I barely have to think anymore, mine knows me so well. So anyway, you probably know why you were brought in then?"

"Is it illegal not to have an implant?" she asked in her increasingly exaggerated accent.

"No, obviously not," he grumbled. "But it is very suspicious when a duo without them stand in front of a protected landmark for an extended time. The anti-terrorism AI flagged you right away." He glanced down at his device. "Looks like your elevated heart rates tipped it off too."

Lisa stifled a choke of laughter.

"Well, obviously, we are not terrorists. I think you can plainly see that. We're merely regular ol' small-town folk enjoying the big city."

"Uh-huh. Do you have any identification? And can you explain why neither of your facial scans were a match in the registry?"

"I don't know nothin' about no registry," Lisa replied, leaning into her character to a preposterous degree, "but we left our IDs at home. Right, honey?"

"Uh, yeah," I commented. "Our hotel's right there on Forty-Fifth Street, and it's all my fault; I must have been too excited to get outside and explore the Big Apple." I didn't bother with an accent; at best, it would have sounded vaguely Eastern European, anyway.

The police officer rolled his eyes. I broke immediately.

"I can't do this, sorry. Look, Officer, we are guests of the WCO, in town from, uh, another time. We were on our way back to the UN complex when we were picked up. Please, just call the leadership there and they will explain."

Lisa glared at me as I provided additional substantiating information. After a minute, the policeman stepped away to validate my statement.

"You get us in this mess because you're too horny for a building, and still you couldn't be my adoring husband for even a minute?" she teased.

"I just don't want to be arrested, is all. Nothing personal. If it's any comfort, you were an exemplary wife throughout our five-minute marriage."

"You know," Lisa continued, "if he can't connect with Andrés or whoever at the WCO, we'll really only have one option left: you're going to need to seduce him. Do the exact opposite of whatever you're doing right now and it shouldn't be a problem."

The policeman thankfully returned before I could attempt to formulate a commensurate response; Lisa's powers of sarcasm were too advanced for me to maintain pace.

"I wasn't able to contact anyone useful at the UN," he said as Lisa elbowed me with playful exuberance, "but someone sent in an authenticated missing person scan request which matches your details. You're free to go, and we will return you to your pick-up location promptly. Just, you know, try to stay out of the AI's way next time."

My ever-present anxiety spiked as the sun sublimely set behind us. I assumed we'd be mugged the instant it disappeared, even with the overzealous policing we'd just had the distinct pleasure of encountering. Perhaps that was an advantage of walking around the city with nothing in our pockets. Lisa, who had been uncharacteristically quiet since the drop-off, gave the impression that she'd never had a doubt or fear in her life.

"Hey Aaron, I've got a question," she prompted earnestly a few minutes later. "You have a girlfriend, I know, so I'm sure you've already thought about this too. Do you think it would be considered cheating if we're in the future and won't even remember it when we travel back home?"

The question caught me off guard in the moment, though I had to admit I had indeed wondered the same thing myself. It'd be a good academic question to ask Sam; maybe there was a new field called chronoethics too.

As much as I liked Lisa and had bonded with her over the last two days, I had never looked at her as anything more than a loyal, benevolently mischievous friend. But as we sat awash in the soft light of the red sunset after our recent shared adventure, I understood why she had more romantic inclinations. I decided to answer her truthfully, which hopefully would suffice to let her down easy.

"I'm flattered, Lisa, and I can't say I haven't thought about it, but yes, I honestly do think it's cheating," I shared. I braced myself for a painful response.

"Ha! I love you Aaron, but I was talking about Paul, the British guy," she mocked with a wicked grin, which did nothing to hide how much she relished my mistake.

"Oh, yeah, okay, that makes, um, more sense," I responded, quite embarrassed. So I was the one who needed to be let down easy.

"There's something about his repressed fifties stoicism that I find *very* sexy," she superfluously explained. "I'll let you know how it goes."

"Yes, thank you; I look forward to the full report," I flatly responded, aware that I was once again the butt of the joke.

The last flecks of sunlight dwindled as we approached the UN campus. My feet were riotously achy from a full day of walking around the museums, park, and city streets, and I couldn't wait to ask Wally for a nice, relaxing bath. Lisa—nine years my elder—showed no signs of slowing down.

Next to the lightly guarded entrance, a sparse gathering of protestors loitered, many wearily packing up their signs. Genuinely interested, I lightly tapped Lisa's arm to redirect her attention, and we both stopped to observe.

I squinted to get a closer look at the few remaining visible signs and was able to pick out a handful of the rallying slogans: *TIME IS NOT OUR PLAYTHING, NO FATE,* and *LIVE FOREWARD, NOT BACKWARD.* In addition to the obvious misspelling, that last one had some hand-drawn arrows to really emphasize the point.

Sam had casually mentioned the existence of a portion of the population who opposed the use of time travel, though I hadn't realized they were quite this ardent. From my vantage point, their position didn't hold much water; clearly, society was in a better place as a result of the technological breakthroughs. A quick visit to my time and they wouldn't be taking their prosperity for granted any longer.

"What could they possibly be protesting?" I wondered aloud.

Lisa shrugged, clearly less intrigued than I was about the dwindling group.

"Eh, I kind of get it," she contributed. "Doesn't everything feel a bit off to you? It's so sterile here, so . . . soulless. Is it just me?"

I opened my mouth to respond, but couldn't think of anything coherent enough to vocalize. Lisa went on, my hesitancy unnoticed.

"It's like we're in an old animated movie. Everyone's too perfect and happy. I'm not trying to sound like a bad person, and I'm obviously not saying that I want people to be *unhappy*. But it's like, what is joy without suffering, as they say? Everything here is just . . . medium. Perfectly medium. And I think it's also worth mentioning: we got *arrested* for calmly standing in front of a freakin' building. It ain't paradise, that's for damn sure."

With the few lingering protesters departing, Lisa and I ventured through the main gate, thereby concluding our little adventure. The lone security guard did nothing to stop or even acknowledge our entry to the complex; maybe she had been told to expect our arrival. Ahead of us, Andrés and Sam rushed out of the closest building on an intercept course. Although he was trying to hide it, Andrés looked understandably furious, while Sam mostly exuded a pure sense of relief.

"That was very irresponsible," Andrés opened when our two pairs reached each other. His English was delivered with a heavy accent, absent the indoor-only translation tech. "You could have put this entire program in jeopardy. You both know full well how important this trial is; any activity that reflects poorly on the WCO or UN would be worldwide news. The press is right outside these gates as we speak, watching us, itching for something to report."

"I'm very sorry, Andrés. Truly. And Sam, you too." I said with as much of an apologetic tone as I could muster. Lisa nodded along, happy to let me take the brunt of the emotional burden.

I risked a quick glance in the direction Andrés had indicated, but didn't detect any members of the press lurking at any gate.

"They're media *drones*, Aaron," Sam corrected, catching my confusion. "Well above eyeline, and thankfully not allowed in the UN airspace."

"If it were up to me," Andrés continued, truncating the side conversation, "I would send both of you back downstream to your orgtime right now. But at this point, we don't have time to acclimate new jurors, so you get to stay. But you're both on thin ice," Andrés chided us.

"It won't happen again, we promise," I shared, though I immediately regretted the commitment, knowing full well of Lisa's consistently reckless tendencies.

With that, we were silently escorted back to our respective rooms. Inside the residence area, Lisa and Andrés split off, giving Sam and me a minute of alone time.

"Sam, I wanted to reiterate how sorry I am. I really hope we didn't get you in too much trouble," I expressed.

"Honestly, Aaron, I get it. I probably would have done the same thing in that situation. Plus, I wasn't the one who thought a loose wristband would be enough to keep everyone in check. One of the other chaperones had a juror who flatly refused to leave a department store, which sounds way worse. I think she got addicted to the virtual vanity mirror."

"Oh, that sounds way more fun than anything we did," I joked.

"Oh? I don't think I want to know."

"We just walked back here . . . mostly. We did *briefly* get arrested."

"Yeah, definitely didn't want to know," Sam responded, mock-covering his ears. "Anyway, I hope you had your fun, got it out of your system, and let's move on. You've all got a big day tomorrow."

I felt somewhat absolved, though still heavily guilt-ridden, as I returned to my room. I politely asked Wally to have dinner delivered and climbed into a long-awaited, idyllic bath.

Tomorrow, I promised myself, I would be ready to serve.

PART 2

7

_____

ndrés paced the room anxiously, his handsome face devoid of its usual color and verve. We were back in the same nondescript conference room where we'd shared orientation, but the tone of lighthearted comradery had been replaced by an uncomfortable tension that filtered down from our leader. I couldn't tell if he was affected by the immense pressure of the impending trial, or the more personal stakes of his unfamiliar job as jury coordinator. If it was the latter, I thought he had done superb work so far—and not only because he hadn't expelled Lisa and me—though I didn't dare speak up in the whisper-quiet room.

Just as Andrés had foretold, a new juror had joined our ranks. Even if we hadn't been alerted to the possibility, I would have immediately recognized him as a resident of the 2040s; his movements and speech patterns conveyed a young man who knew nothing of scarcity or strife. I wondered what the selection process had been like; was it even possible to find someone truly impartial given the victim's widespread veneration?

Since I'd never heard of Kathryn Simpson prior to forty-eight hours ago, I continually needed to remind myself how seminal she was to anyone from this era. "The Mother of Time Travel," Andrés had called her, even if her metaphorical "child" had gestated for forty-five years after her mysterious death. For empathy's sake, I committed to put myself into the shoes of Andrés, Feng, or anyone else who lived in the world she unknowingly created.

After what felt like twenty minutes of strained silence, Mounira emerged through a previously indiscernible back door, followed by a similarly austere woman. Though she wasn't out-fitted with any of the obvious signifiers, I immediately recognized the latter as a judge. She was short—an unusual sight among the well-nourished, towering residents of the mid-twenty-first century—and immaculately tailored head to toe, with an aura that broadcast "I have nothing left to prove to any-one." I had plenty of time to form this impression while she intently regarded each of us one by one, uncomfortable eye con-tact galore.

"It's so nice to meet all of you!" the judge opened with a beam-ing smile and a level of sincerity that instantly shattered my preconceived notions of her. "I'm Judge Kasem, and I'll be pre-siding over the courtroom for this unique trial. I've spoken to Ms. Calwi here,"—she gestured to Mounira— "and understand that you have already been briefed in the basics of the case. That's great, because I much prefer listening to speaking, and I espe-cially hate wasted time.

"That said, since I know you all come from diverse orgtimes and orgplaces with various processes of judicature, I want to re-inforce that in my court—as in all UN courts—the defendant is innocent until proven guilty. This reminder is especially important in such a high-profile case, with ingrained biases that inevitably arise from the feeling of personal connection to the victim." She caught herself. "Ah, but that's the exact reason you're all here, isn't it? Apologies, this is my first time-spanning jury too. Any questions so far?"

Nobody dared speak up.

"I do need to ask *you* one question, formally and under temporary oath." She asked each of us to raise our right hand. Her voice tightened slightly. "Are any persons in this room currently aware of the final verdict of this case?"

A few of the jurors—myself included—let out an involuntary laugh before catching ourselves apologetically. On its surface, the question was pure absurdity; the trial was mere minutes away from *beginning*. But I wasn't thinking fourth-dimensionally: How was this any different from what Sam had told me about the fate of professional sports? Would it be so strange for news of this momentous case to travel up and down the timestream?

Fortunately, no one came forward; the sanctity of the trial was unblemished. Judge Kasem let out a long-withheld breath.

"Thank you all, I look forward to a smooth, fair trial," the judge resumed in her normal tone. "And I know you've heard this before, but I can't stress to you how much we all appreciate your service in this unusual situation." She departed through the rear door, sharing a stern nod on her way out.

A few minutes later, Andrés ushered us into the courtroom and wished us well; he wouldn't be privy to the inner workings. The space itself could best be described as cozy; nothing like the cavernous chambers seen on film. A sequence of overhead skylights filled the room with dazzling displays of natural light that highlighted the immaculately constructed judge's bench and tables. In addition to the court stenographer—who looked as stereotypical as could be—a few stragglers wandered around, speaking in hushed tones. The other jurors and I took our seats and waited for the proceedings to begin.

The ambient excitement in the room began to surge when the prosecuting attorney took her seat, followed shortly by the defense team and our first look at the accused. For lack of a better description, he was the most normal-looking Caucasian man I could visualize: blond, medium build with a face that I imagined would seem very welcoming if not for the all-consuming weight of being a high-profile murder suspect. A broad, quivering chin betrayed his understandable unease as he scanned around the room: he glanced upward at the brilliant light source, across the aisle at the prosecutor setting up her table, and at the jury members. The two of us locked eyes for a brief moment until I quickly darted my gaze anywhere else.

"So, does he seem like a murderer to you?" whispered Lisa, a bit too loudly for my taste considering the magisterial surroundings.

"No, but what do I know?" I returned, fully aware that this was exactly what each of the jurors would need to have an earnest answer for by the end of the trial.

Lisa leaned in to continue the inappropriate conversation. "I think he looks—"

"Please rise," boomed the bailiff, who had stealthily appeared while I was observing the defendant. His voice carried as if he was within arm's reach, obviously amplified by the hidden speaker systems prevalent in most UN rooms. By now, I was so used to this feature that I had to constantly remind myself of the likelihood that the bailiff and many of the witnesses to come were not necessarily English-speaking. "The Court of the United Nations, World Chronology Organization subdivision, is now in session, the Honorable Judge Kasem presiding."

Though we had met her already, Judge Kasem's presence in her natural domain was formidable. Here in the courtroom, she truly *presided*. Just being formally sworn in by her got my heart racing.

"Good morning, everyone," she began, pausing briefly to ensure she had the full attention of the surprisingly few people in the room. "This is about as unique a trial as any of us will ever see, a perfect storm of unrepeatable circumstances. Jury members, I know you didn't choose to be here, neither the time nor the place, so again, we are indebted to you. Everything you hear in this courtroom will help you make your final decision. And remember, the burden of proof is on the UN government, who must prove beyond reasonable doubt that the defendant committed the crime of which he is accused.

"That defendant—Jakob Olsen—is charged with temporal homicide. There is no precedent for this charge, no stare decisis, nothing on which we can draw for guidance. For that reason, I urge both attorneys to adhere to the undisputed facts of science in framing their case. Time travel is complex enough, even to those of us who are accustomed to it."

With that, the trial was underway, beginning with the prosecuting attorney's opening statement. She rose slowly, milking the moment as much as possible. She strode with a deliberate self-assuredness, perhaps to emphasize her confidence in her case in front of us jury members.

"Gentlepeople of the jury," she began, intently locking eyes with each of us, "are you aware we're making history? This is the first WCO murder trial of our brand-new, time-travel era.

'Making history' . . . that phrase has special meaning for all of us now, doesn't it? Because that's exactly what I will prove that the defendant intended to do when he traveled downstream. Beyond a shadow of a doubt, I will demonstrate how he abused his position, shattered the fundamental rules of time travel, and committed the heinous act of *murder* against one of the most revered figures in our society. Thank you."

When prompted, the defense attorney began her opening statement. Whether for show or not, everything from her mannerisms to her wardrobe was comparatively unassuming.

"Jury members, first of all, let me welcome you to 2042. I know this must be a lot to take in all at once. On behalf of everyone here, we thank you. Though most of you might not know it, the murder of Kathryn Simpson may be the most infamous crime in the history of the modern world."

With a quick eye movement, she cued a projected photo of Kathryn in front of us. It was the first time I'd seen the victim's face. She looked carefree, content and—though it wasn't the most sympathetic descriptor—*alive*, in a way that had an unexpectedly profound impact on me. Which was exactly the effect the lawyer was aiming for, I realized with a modicum of shame.

"Everybody knows the facts," she continued, "and I will not try to dispel them—Kathryn was indisputably and cruelly murdered in her home in 1988. But not by the defendant, Jakob. Quite the contrary, in fact; he is an admirer, a historian, a scientist, and most of all, a protector—of history and of Kathryn herself. You will learn how he traveled back in an attempt to *save* her, and though he was ultimately unsuccessful, he returned here expecting to be hailed as a hero, not accused of a crime he did not commit. Thank you all."

Throughout the brief opening statements, I could sense from the fellow jurors around me an escalating level of engagement with the trial unfolding before us. I caught myself breathing heavily while hunched forward as the first witness walked to the stand. This was going to be a long trial; I forced myself to settle down.

The elderly, dignified man sitting before us clearly did not want to be here. He moved and spoke with a deliberately dawdling cadence, which was frustrating after the precisely tuned opening remarks of the judge and attorneys.

"Detective Mitchell, could you explain who you are and your relationship to this case?" the prosecutor began.

"Yes, ma'am. I am Detective James Mitchell, retired Berkeley PD. I was the lead detective on the Kathryn Simpson murder case."

"This was in 1988, correct?"

"Yes, ma'am."

"What was the result of the investigation at the time?"

"Unsolved," the detective responded, shifting uncomfortably in his seat.

"I'd like to submit exhibit A, a 3D rendering of the crime scene, modeled on photos taken the day after the event in question." With a casual flick, an immersive, detailed diorama of a cozy kitchen scene appeared before us. "Detective, what was determined to be the cause of death?"

"Coerced overdose, by sleeping pill."

"Coerced . . . that's quite interesting. Was suicide considered?"

"Absolutely. That was our initial determination."

"Can you expand on that, Detective?" the prosecutor prompted.

"The tox report showed a combination of diazepam, alcohol, and traces of other medications. An empty diazepam bottle was found in the home. On top of that, there was a note found on the premises. Your usual boilerplate content: now is my time, apologies to friends and family, etcetera. Pretty convincing stuff; ninety-nine times out of a hundred, this is a cut-and-dry suicide."

"What about the hundredth time?"

"I had a hunch from the beginning that something was off," Detective Mitchell replied. For the first time, he seemed engrossed in a question, perhaps because he got to toot his own horn a bit. "It just didn't add up. For one, the aforementioned note was hastily written and barely legible. So illegible, in fact, that we reached out to a handwriting expert at the university to confirm it was actually written in her hand. Most true suicide notes are precisely the opposite: premeditated and deliberate.

"On top of that, she had none of the common indicators of potential self-harm. She lived alone, yes, but had a fulfilling job, no money trouble, good relationships with her family. Her friends and colleagues stated unanimously that she had never harbored even the slightest indication of any depressive behaviors."

"Was there anything else that led to your assessment?"

"Yes, fresh fingerprints were discovered at the scene of the crime." He reached out and pointed to a spot in front of him. "Here."

"Detective, for the record, could you verbally describe where you are pointing?"

"Oh, er, yes," he mumbled. What the lawyer politely hadn't said was that none of us had the slightest idea where he was pointing; we each had the crime scene depiction individually projected in our field of view. As a fellow baby boomer, I empathized with the detective. Modern technology was hard. "The kitchen island had multiple fingerprint traces," the witness corrected, "along with the front doorknob. In conjunction with a few otherwise innocuous forensic findings, we felt there were signs of a forced entry."

"Intriguing . . . forced entry," the prosecutor emphasized. "And what were those other findings?"

"There was a somewhat unusual dust pattern in the kitchen, in close proximity to the fingerprints. A footwear impression mark was found on the porch that did not match the victim's shoe size or any known shoe in the forensic database. Some kitchen utensils and cookware were out of place. Little things like that."

"Putting all of it together, what was your final theory for what happened to Ms. Simpson?"

"On the night in question, an intruder broke into Ms. Simpson's house and at gunpoint forced her to consume a lethal combination of toxins. The intruder also compelled her to write the generic suicide note to cover his tracks."

"Detective, last question. Why did this case go cold?"

"Well," he bristled, slightly offended at the implication, "we were never able to identify any connected individuals with a compelling motive, nor find a match for the fingerprints we located. One of her hippie Berkeley friends was a preliminary suspect due to some unusual conduct, but was quickly cleared for lack of evidence and motive. It always hung over me that I had missed something, but by the time the file was archived fifteen years later, I had long since forgotten about the case. Then years later, suddenly she's world famous, and here I am."

"Thank you, Detective," concluded the prosecutor, confidently returning to her table. The defense attorney replaced her in the center of the room, disarming the detective with an amiable smile.

"Detective Mitchell, I'd like to expand a bit more on the finger-print findings you recounted. In your testimony a few minutes back, you described them as 'fresh.' Can you clarify, what is the maximum amount of time those fingerprints could have been there?"

"'Fresh' only means untarnished. They could have been there since the last time the counter was cleaned, I suppose."

"Were any prints found elsewhere, beyond what you've already described? On the body, on the overdosed pharmaceuticals?"

"No, they were not," the witness answered.

"So, just on the doorknob and the counter then," the lawyer repeated for the jury's benefit. She turned back to the detective. "Is there *anything* conclusively linking these prints to Ms. Simp-son's death?"

"Conclusively? No." He shrugged in defeat. "Call it a hunch, I suppose."

"And, more generally, is there anything conclusively linking *any* evidence from 1988 to my client?" She theatrically gestured over her left shoulder, as if we wouldn't otherwise have known of whom she was speaking.

"No, ma'am, nothing. But to be fair, I don't see how there could have been. He wouldn't even exist for another thirty years."

Next up, naturally, was an active detective: much younger and sporting the first mustache I'd noted in the twenty-first century. Like all mustaches, it did not look good.

As I should have predicted from the recent focus on the topic, this particular investigator was brought to the stand to confirm that the aforementioned fingerprints belonged to the defendant. The prosecutor needlessly hammered this point home by asking what felt like the same question countless times. The detective's frustratingly monosyllabic responses didn't help.

As we then learned, it was precisely this discovery that triggered the case to be reopened in the current year. Though Jakob had shrewdly and flawlessly covered his digital tracks, he had failed to anticipate the power of the more primitive forensic identifier. Most ironically of all, Jakob's fingerprint pattern had only entered the global record-keeping system because of his downstream journey to 1988. Once logged, the match was quickly flagged by an automated system that had been set up years prior by amateur sleuths with fading hopes of finding Kathryn's killer. An arrest by the twenty-first-century detective's team followed shortly after.

The defense attorney seemed to have her hands full; there wasn't any doubt left that Jakob was at the very least present at the scene of the crime.

"Detective," she intoned at the start of cross-examination, "in your expert opinion, was Kathryn Simpson murdered?"

"Oh yeah, definitely."

"Care to elaborate?" the attorney asked with barely concealed exasperation.

"Sure, if I have to. I guess . . . once I became an officer of the law, I reevaluated the notorious case with a new lens, trying my hardest to dissociate from the groupthink that has been part of the zeitgeist for the last nine years. I've remained fervently undecided in that time, but with this new information, yes, I now fully believe she was the victim of deliberate homicide."

The defender acknowledged the unexpectedly eloquent response as Jakob shook his head passionately behind her. "Last question: if she was indeed murdered as you indicate, is there any hard evidence beyond a stray fingerprint that links my client to the act?"

"No hard evidence; I openly admit that." The lawyer nodded triumphantly and prepared to move on to a follow-up question. "But it is impossible to ignore the fact that he somehow jumped back to 1988. To me, despite a lack of substantiation, that seems inescapably damning."

"We will take a one-hour recess for lunch," declared the judge as the witness was dismissed by the rattled defense attorney. As captivating as the back-and-forth had been so far, I welcomed the overdue interlude with open arms, a full bladder, and an empty stomach.

8

"Well, he's guilty," Ime declared as our inseparable trio sat down to lunch together.

"Oh, already made up your mind, huh?" I mocked with amusement. "What happened to 'burden of proof'?"

"There are three inescapable facts, try as the defense attorney might to convince us otherwise: Kathryn Simpson was murdered in 1988, the defendant Jakob was in her house on the night in question, and history is unchangeable, which means his presence didn't modify anything. I don't see how one could come to any other conclusion but that he was the cause of her unfortunate death. I do, of course, speak with some degree of hyperbole; truly, I haven't made up my mind. I know rationally that we've been privy to but a fraction of the trial." A knowing smile crept onto Ime's face. "Perhaps that is all inconsequential, though. Jakob's saving grace may prove to be the ineptitude of the prosecuting attorney. For instance, I'm quite certain that her opening remarks were largely plagiarized from a Broadway musical which came after your time. Plus a snippet from a blockbuster film too, I believe. She may have been counting on the jury's lack of familiarity with the works. Or perhaps she is merely lazy."

"Hmm. Well you gotta admire her for just going for it," I joked, before tacking a bit more sincerity to my voice. "I have to say I'm on the fence. Sitting right smack in the middle of it. But if I had to make the choice right now . . . well . . . I've been watching the guy just as much as I've been listening to the witnesses, and unless he's the world's greatest actor, my gut is telling me that he's innocent."

As Lisa nodded in appreciated solidarity, I thought about how ridiculous my sentiment was. Only cold, hard facts should shape my ultimate verdict, yet I couldn't shake the feeling that the early tides were erroneously turning against the defendant. Though I didn't dare utter it, I felt an uncanny kinship with him that surely shaped my premature viewpoint.

Still, as Ime said, there was plenty of trial left to make up my mind.

An hour later, we returned to the jury holding area and waited for official approval to reenter the courtroom. A much more relaxed Andrés greeted us individually with a reminder that going forward, we were to be sequestered in the WCO facilities. Aside from yesterday's metropolitan expedition, I truly couldn't see how this differed from our existing situation.

Four days in, the novelty of being in the twenty-first century was starting to fade, and I was left with a steadily expanding emptiness as each hour passed. Despite the growing bond I shared with my new friends on the jury, I felt isolated from my real life, the one back in 1985. My parents, my sister, my friends who I'd known since high school: all unreachable, and—though I did my best not to entertain the thought—probably long since passed. I never had the morbid curiosity or mental fortitude to ask Wally to confirm their status.

Amid the countless luxuries of the time, I knew I had little justification for which to complain, especially with the knowledge that I would soon be returning to the very life I coveted. After all, I wasn't a prisoner; if anything, this was more like a high-tech adult summer camp, though instead of boating in the lake, we deliberated over the pivotal details of a heartbreaking murder. Fun for all ages!

The ephemeral nature of the arrangement may have been a factor as well. Any new experiences and relationships forged here would be involuntarily wiped away at the conclusion, lost to a future we may never encounter again. Summer camp at least has the advantage that everyone departs under the hopeful pretense that they will remain best friends forever.

The trial abruptly resumed while I was processing these budding sentiments, snapping me back into the present moment.

"Doctor Ingles," the prosecutor began, "could you introduce yourself to the court?"

"Hello, yes, hi! Sorry, I'm a little nervous. I've never been in a courtroom before! Beautiful, isn't it?" Her delightfully disheveled appearance only served to augment the endearing rambling. "I'm, er, my name is Natalia Ingles, and I'm a historian at the Smithsonian World Organization with a specialization in the history of modern time travel." She let out a visible sigh of relief, as if she had finished reciting her big soliloquy in a middle school Shakespeare production.

"Thank you. Can you elaborate on your relationship with Kathryn Simpson?"

"Oh, well, yes, she's just incredible, isn't she? She gave us everything! Oh, and I've written three books about her. *The Mother of Time Travel, Our Inadvertent Utopia*, and uh, what was the most recent one? *Herstory*. That last one is markedly less academic though, extrapolating the rest of her life if she hadn't been . . . well, you know."

"Yes, yes, I do know," responded the prosecutor with exaggerated despondence. "Could you share with us a fragment of your knowledge, and take us through some of the key facts of Kathryn's life?"

"Objection, Your Honor," jumped in the opposing attorney. "I don't question this witness's expertise, but I do have trouble identifying the relevancy of such a broad question." Judge Kasem turned to the prosecuting attorney, prompting a response.

"Your Honor, the underlying biographical context is critical to understand the defendant's motivations for the actions he took and to establish the circumstances of the murder itself."

"I'll allow it," the judge condoned after a brief consideration. She turned to address the witness directly. "Please, do your best to keep it succinct and relevant."

Natalia froze, awestruck to be commanded by the all-powerful judge. She regained her composure and began.

"Ms. Simpson—Kathryn, I'm going to call her Kathryn— was born in St. Louis in 1939. She had one sibling: a significantly older brother who actually served in the later years of World War II. Kathryn idolized her brother, and when he used the G.I. Bill to earn a degree in physics, she wholeheartedly followed in his footsteps. Even as a child, she read everything she could get her hands on and quickly became a prodigy, especially as a female in the 1950s Midwest." She paused, briefly glancing at the judge for assent to continue, who, by lack of response, implicitly provided it.

"Right, so, skipping ahead a bit, she completed her PhD at twenty-three, though her dream of researching for a major university proved unattainable. If I may editorialize a bit," she said, turning to face the jury directly, "it really was dismal to be a smart, professional woman one hundred years ago. Anyway, she took a position as a local high school science teacher, all the while working nights and weekends on her true passion. About ten years later, she finally was accepted as an associate professor at Berkeley, based on the strength of her independent work.

"At Berkeley, she found a home, immediately becoming a favorite of students and mildly contributing to her burgeoning specialty of what we would now call chronophysics. In 1986, while working on a hypothesis related to predictive quantum behavior, Kathryn had her big breakthrough with a peerless formula that shockingly failed to make any waves in her field. Though she considered it her best work, she contentedly moved on to the next project, fully unaware of the formula's chronological implications. The following month—"

"Let's skip ahead to the murder," jumped in the prosecutor, startling Natalia out of her lecture. "What can you tell us about Kathryn's last day?"

"Oh, um, sure. There was some interesting stuff about her abbreviated sabbatical in Switzerland working for CERN, but that's okay. Let's see . . . last day. . . . Not too much is known; there certainly wasn't any evidence she knew her life was nearing an end. Kathryn followed her usual routine: coffee, a stroll around campus, a compelling lecture, some professorial administrative tasks. She returned to her North Berkeley home in the early evening, and from there we venture into the realm of uncertainty. I'm happy to share my theory—"

I glanced at the defense attorney, who was ready to pounce with an obvious objection.

"I'm sure your conjecture is extremely well-founded," the prosecutor commented, "but alas, that would be speculation, and thus isn't admissible. One last thing I would like to get your expert opinion on, though: What is Kathryn's legacy?"

"Her legacy? Well, like I said earlier, Kathryn gave us *everything*. Before her work was rediscovered and unlocked the crucial piece of the time-travel puzzle, the planet was heading down a dark path of seemingly inevitable doom, right? We can all agree on that, I think. And it's much easier to celebrate a person—especially one so universally generous and kind—rather than an arcane mathematical formula. She may not have intended it, but she is the face of time travel, and by extension a symbol of hope for all of humanity."

The prosecutor thanked Dr. Ingles and sat down. The defense attorney stood to address the professor.

"Just one question," said the defense attorney. "Why would anyone want to kill her?" That got her counterpart's attention. "Actually, let me rephrase before that question is stricken: Are you aware of anyone in Kathryn's history who would have the motive to kill her?"

"Oh dear, no, it's hard to imagine *anyone* wanting to kill her; she was such a sweet soul."

"Did Kathryn have any ex-partners, professional rivals, students who received a bad grade?"

"Yes, all of them, I suppose. She had one long-term boyfriend in her younger days, but he didn't join her in California. At the university, she was too focused on her work to sustain a relationship, at least as far as the historical record shows. I'm sure there were students with bad grades too, but that's no more than a motive to complain to friends, not kill! Er, what was the last one?"

"Professional rivals."

"Right, thank you," the historian said, taking a moment to scan through her mind for possible matches. "Honestly, she didn't live long enough to make enough of a mark in her field to have rivals, if such a thing even existed in the esoteric world of 1980s pre-chronophysics. And to reiterate, by all accounts she was a sweet and caring person personally and professionally, beloved by everyone she met. Similar to how all of us feel about her now, I suppose." She glanced over at Jakob with the slightest hint of disdain, so quickly that I nearly missed it.

The penultimate witness of the day was announced: a chronophysicist beamed in virtually from the Massachusetts Institute of Technology. The projection was so unnervingly convincing that I had to constantly remind myself he wasn't actually ten feet away. With my energy already fading, I was not looking forward to trying to follow what I assumed was going to be an avalanche of incomprehensible scientific terminology.

"Professor, could you introduce yourself to the court?" prompted the prosecuting attorney.

"Yes, hello all, I am Doctor Ravi Sharma, Professor and Department Chair of Chronophysics at MIT. You may know me as one of the researchers who conducted the first successful time displacement trials in 2033."

"Are you familiar with Kathryn Simpson's work?" the attorney asked with a hint of procedural monotony.

"Yes, of course. It formed the basis for much of my own."

"In layperson's terms, could you explain for the jury her contributions to the field?"

Dr. Sharma nodded pensively. "I'll do my best; some of it is quite complicated. As you all know, Kathryn's field of study was not time displacement; like most of the scientists of the twentieth century, she did not even begin to entertain that as a possibility, at least not outside of the realm of science fiction. I'll admit *I* barely believed it until I witnessed Gus appear in front of us nine years ago. Her—"

"Sorry . . . for the jury's benefit, who is Gus?" interrupted the prosecutor.

The scientist turned to face us. "Ah, yes, you don't know of Gustavo the time-traveling rat," he clarified, a laughably incongruous statement to be coming from the esteemed academic. "He was our loyal test subject, and the first sentient time traveler. Something about his brief test journey opened the floodgates; we welcomed the first visitors from upstream moments later. Anyway, to answer the question more directly: her primary contribution to chronophysics was an elegant formula, which she theorized could forecast quantum movement up to a picosecond in the future. That's *one trillionth* of a second, by the way. Kathryn's original hypothesis for the formula was later proven true in practice, but that was just a drop in the bucket. The full, world-changing implications of the work sadly were lost on her and the scientists of the time.

"Miraculously, the formula was rediscovered by a researcher on my team, all but hidden in a forgotten scientific journal that was recovered shortly after the infamous lab explosion in 2032. The complex physics underlying it completely unlocked our research, which, in turn, allowed us to establish the theory of temporal immutability. Temporal immutability is the foundation of the entire field of chronophysics and opened the door for temporal displacement. There is no question in my mind that

Kathryn's discovery moved our research forward by years, decades even, or maybe we *never* would have reached without it."

The prosecutor appeared to be genuinely fascinated hearing the first-person retelling. The level of reverence—celebrity even—I'd witnessed toward both Kathryn and science as a whole was refreshing coming from a home century rife with an unhealthy obsession on celebrity scandals and tabloid gossip. Though I'd only been exposed to a tiny fraction of the new world, I hoped maybe there was a chance that mankind had matured beyond that vacuous 1980s inclination that I tried my hardest to ignore.

"Thank you, Professor. For the court, could you take us through the two established laws of time travel?"

"Yes, of course, though 'laws' is perhaps not the right word; we usually label them as 'constraints.' Regardless, they are well-defined: first and most importantly, the timestream is immutable. In simple terms, the known future is sealed; time travelers cannot alter anything with their knowledge, and therefore paradoxes cannot arise.

"Secondly, downstream travel is limited to 2033; specifically the moment Gus made his maiden journey, like I mentioned earlier. This seemingly arbitrary barrier is the focus of my current research; all attempts beyond it simply fail." He shifted his commanding gaze to Jakob, who so far had been withdrawn and still throughout the proceedings. "I'm *very* curious to find out how *he* did it," the witness added with a delicate mix of admiration and contempt.

"No further comments, Your Honor," said the prosecutor before taking her seat.

"Professor," opened the defense attorney for cross-examination, "the bedrock of my client's defense rests on the fact that he traveled downstream with motive to *protect* Kathryn. Does this defense have scientific backing?"

"No, how could it? As a chronophysicist, Jakob is fully aware of the same temporal constraints that I just elucidated. If Ms. Simpson died in 1988, nothing about that eventuality can be altered."

"Allow me to present this evidence to the court," the attorney flicked her wrist performatively, bringing up an official-looking form. "It's the WCO record for the logs of Jakob's downstream journey. Professor, based on the data in front of you, did Jakob successfully jump to 1988?"

Dr. Sharma took off his glasses to study the projected document in detail. I was surprised that anyone was still near-sighted in 2042; perhaps the professor retained them merely for sartorial flavor.

"I'd love to study the logs in more detail, but yes, the registered displacement quantities are indicative of a downstream journey well beyond the barrier . . . somehow," he appended, shaking his head with barely concealed academic envy.

The lawyer paced a bit, allowing the previous answer to sink in. "Professor, earlier you described two fixed constraints of time travel. To recap: the timestream cannot be changed, and downstream journeys before 2033 are impossible. Yet in your previous answer, you testified that you do believe the defendant Jakob Olsen made a successful jump to 1988. Given that he invalidated the latter constraint, isn't it possible that the former is equally nullified?"

The defense attorney looked very pleased with herself, all but winking at the jury; her hammer had dropped.

"Well, er, yes . . . and also, no," Dr. Sharma stammered, a bit rattled by the question. "How can I say this? To start, it's a fallacy to say that these two constraints are inextricably linked, that by disproving one it disproves the other. That said, I am a scientist first and foremost, and I can't say that the new evidence doesn't cause me to rethink this particular chronophysics hypothesis. However, based on the information I have at this moment, I still fully believe in the theory of timestream immutability. Without that constraint, well . . ." He trailed off, staring into the virtual distance.

"Thank you, Professor," the lawyer responded professionally, trying to mask her obvious disappointment that her trap had been only partially successful. "No further questions," she concluded unenthusiastically as the holographic scientist faded from view.

After a brief, restorative break, the prosecution's final witness was called to the stand. A recently retired UN/WCO employee and former colleague of Jakob's, he carried a dignified air of importance, though I immediately recognized the trademark characteristics of a lifetime background player. It takes one to know one, I figured. His hands shook as the prosecutor began her questioning.

"Good afternoon, Mister Brown. I want to start by asking you about the defendant's time at the WCO. Specifically, what was his role and specialty?"

Mr. Brown nodded slowly. "His title was Chrono Research Engineer, Level II. He jumped around to various projects, but primarily was focused on microscale timestream fluctuations in upstream travel. A few years ago, he was on the team that figured out how to pluck objects and people from their orgtime and return them safely. *Pulling* upstream instead of *pushing* downstream, essentially. It's what allowed the jury to be here, as I understand it. Ironic, really."

"Yes, I suppose so. Did Mister Olsen have access to a time-travel device that he could have modified to travel downstream to 1988?"

"Yes, almost every department has at least one, though usage is heavily monitored and restricted. However, I have to say, even putting aside the impossible science, I don't understand how he could have had the time, resources, or tools to do so."

"Were you aware he was working on—" The prosecutor halted midsentence and turned to the back of the courtroom, a look of pure disorientation crossing her otherwise stern face. An increasingly alarming din was rising behind the doors of the small space; the disharmonious sound of dissatisfaction and disorder. Not sure if this was concerningly atypical, I looked around the room for clues. The tension was palpable—time traveler or not. Everyone I observed was somewhere between dismissive confusion and outright fear as the escalating roar neared.

The rabble pressed through the door and streamed into the room. I was relieved to see that while they seemed frenzied, it was the same band of protestors I had seen last night, who at least seemed to be peaceful by nature. More and more dissidents loudly pushed into the room, chanting, aggressive, but so far harmless. They quickly outnumbered the actual trial participants, overwhelming the bailiff, who was doing his best to shepherd them out with wholly ineffective cries of "Please disperse!"

One man stood out from the crowd—silent, austere, and wearing a contraption on his back that could only be described as an unholy mashup of a ray gun and a vacuum cleaner. He snaked through the massing protestors toward the front of the room, ignored amidst the chaos surrounding him. With great effort, he raised the barrel of the heavy device toward Judge Kasem, who took no notice of him as she desperately tried to reclaim her courtroom. Finger on the trigger, he took aim.

"Watch out!" I called out; too inaudible and late to really make a difference. Suddenly, the bailiff leapt out of the throng, tackling the man by the shoulders. The trigger was involuntarily pressed down by the force of the impact as the weapon wrenched to the right, directly toward me.

The room broke apart into a billion specks of colored light, each floating in place for a lingering, beautiful instant. Then, black.

9

_____

"Who the fuck is this guy?" I heard a mere moment later—or had it been an eternity? My body and senses thankfully seemed intact, aside from temporary blindness as my eyes struggled to adjust to sudden darkness.

"I thought we were pulling the *judge* upstream?"

"That was the plan; maybe our guy fucked up?"

"Well, obviously, this isn't the judge, so I'd say that's a safe fucking bet!"

"Maybe it was the machine?"

"No, the machine is good. It pulled *someone*, didn't it?"

If the inane bickering was intended as an elaborate form of torture, they would have broken me instantaneously. I decided to intervene before they devolved all the way into a vaudeville slapstick routine.

"Hey, guys, I guess I wasn't who you were targeting with your time gun or whatever, but my name is Aaron and I can answer your questions but I'd really just love to know where—or when—I am first?"

"Uh yeah, right. Hi Aaron. You're in Du—"

"Stop! We shouldn't tell him anything, I don't think."

"Why, what's the difference?"

As they continued their nonsensical squabbling, my vision returned enough to take in the surroundings, though there wasn't much to see. Beyond my two captors—if that was their intention—I spotted four blank walls and the outline of a disabled time machine, presumably the one that brought me here. Though I was sitting up and not restrained in any noticeable way, impromptu escape felt unlikely; this seemed more like an outwit than outfight situation, anyway.

They ultimately decided not to share any information with me, instead opting to defer until their third stooge later joined them. Despite the inauspicious circumstances—not to mention my tendency toward paranoia—I was surprised to notice a conspicuous absence of foreboding for my personal safety. Maybe it was the obvious ineptitude on display, or maybe Lisa's incautious nature had rubbed off on me.

After a few awkward minutes of silence, a petite yet sturdy woman joined us in the cramped room. She gathered briefly with her partners, all barely aware of me waiting patiently in the opposite corner. I probably could have joined in their huddle without any notice. Even without actively listening, I picked up a few choice words: "driver," "shithole," "joke," as they hurriedly debated my fate.

"Aaron, right? I'm sorry to meet you under these circumstances," the newcomer opened with a compassionate tone, though I had doubts about the authenticity of the sentiment.

"Bo, could you turn on a light? Why the horror movie setup?" she commanded one of the minions. The additional illumination only accentuated how barren the room was.

She returned her focus to me. "My name is Damitra, and you are in Dubai, 2087. I hope the journey wasn't too strenuous. We certainly don't mean you any harm, and you have my word that you will return to the courtroom in 2042. Am I right that that's where you upstreamed from?"

For the briefest of moments, I considered a path of duplicity.

"Yes, that's right," I replied, immediately abandoning the impulse.

"Were you a witness on the stand? How did you come to be here?"

"I was a juror, and some guy shot me with a sci-fi gun . . . but wait, did you say 2087? I thought time travel beyond 2080-whatever was impossible."

She raised an eyebrow, intrigued. Maybe I knew more than she anticipated . . . or maybe I knew less. "Aaron, I think we should take a walk so I can explain everything, if that's okay?"

Damitra outstretched her hand, close enough that I was unclear if she wanted me to actually grasp it. Before I had to commit to anything, she made a quick move to the door, sparing me an inevitable faux pas. I followed her through, the lackeys right behind us. The doorway opened to a long, concrete gray hallway. A dull stream of natural light passed through narrow slits close to the ceiling. If I had to guess, we were in a military bunker, though none of the activity I'd seen so far screamed armed forces. Maybe the world *had* ended in 2086, and what was left of humanity had no choice but to retreat to subterranean safety.

"Aaron, let's chat," Damitra said, maintaining an unexpectedly fast pace down the seemingly infinite walkway. "How about I ask you a question, then you can ask me a question, okay?" I nodded, inviting the first query. "You said you were a juror, yes? Are you from 2042 or another orgtime?"

Alright, starting with a softball. "I'm from 1985, actually, Chicago. I was pulled to 2042 to participate in the trial. I barely understood what I was doing *there*, and I have absolutely no idea what I'm doing here. Please, could you tell me where I am and why you brought me here?" As I spoke, she shared a quick, decisive nod over her shoulder to one of our escorts, who responded in kind.

"I'll answer only the first question, to honor the established rules." The glint in her eye clarified that she was being cheeky rather than pedantic. "As I said, you are in 2087, in Dubai. This is an abandoned base that was repurposed to protect—and hide—the last functional time machine."

It was quite a challenge not to follow up immediately on that revelation, but rules are rules.

"My turn," she continued, "what happened in the courtroom before you came here?"

"Um, well, a group of protestors broke into the room, completely overtaking the proceedings. A man with a weapon of some sort—I don't think he was a protestor—aimed at the judge. He was tackled as he fired, and his weapon hit me instead, it seems." She nodded, her suspicions of what transpired confirmed. "Don't you know all of this already, though?" I continued. "It happened forty-"— it took me an embarrassingly long time to do the math, especially for an accountant—"five years ago, right?"

"The historical record mentions that there was a disturbance in the courtroom toward the end of day one, but nothing specifically about any type of weapon or attack. I would suspect that information was redacted, which is exactly how we planned it. Why do you think you're here, Aaron?"

We finally reached the end of the hallway, only to pivot toward another of identical length and dismality.

"Didn't I just ask *you* that? Anyway, I think it's pretty obvious: you wanted to bring Judge Kasem here to influence the outcome of the trial, and I'm no more than an unlucky accident."

"It sounds harsh when you put it that way, but somewhat accurate nonetheless. I have to admit, it's not the most devious plan ever devised. But here's the great thing: you have influence too, don't you?"

I thought about this statement for a moment; I'd never considered myself consequential before. Plenty of other descriptors seemed more apt: insignificant, for one. Still, my integrity was unimpeachable.

"If you're trying to get me to change my position or sway the jury, it's not going to happen," I responded, resolute.

"We're not trying to get you to do anything, Aaron. Truly. But I'm confident you'll change your own mind once you hear what I have to say."

"I think it's my turn for a question, right? Why, or how, is there only one time machine left? What . . . happened?"

"Yes, that's the magic question, isn't it? How much do you know about basic time-travel theory, specifically the commonly accepted limitations it presents?"

Fortunately, I had just received a refresher on this very topic about thirty minutes prior in my personal timeline. "Enough, I think. The timeline is immutable, and you can't travel any earlier than the rat did."

"Very succinct, yes. As an aside, did you know that rat—Gus—would later go on to be the mayor of a medium-sized town in Iowa?"

"You're kidding! Mayor Gus, The Time-Traveling Rat?"

"I'm fucking with you, Aaron, c'mon."

"Right, yeah, of course. So, the time machines . . ." We took one more ninety-degree turn, following an ominous arrow that said *EXPLOSIVES*. This latest corridor at least had a few unmarked doors peppering the otherwise sterile walls.

"So, back to the two laws," Damitra continued. "Essentially, they are bullshit. You already know it's scientifically realizable to jump downstream beyond 2033; in fact, you've recently been in the presence of the first—and maybe only—person to do it. He was a true trailblazer. And we'll get to the other, even more spurious time-travel law in a moment. Basically, since the invention of time travel, there have been two groups fighting against widespread public use, especially for frivolous recreational purposes. The first group you've had the distinct pleasure of meeting already, stampeding through the courtroom with their uniquely useless form of nonviolent resistance. Most of them oppose time travel on religious grounds— 'only God should have this power' kind of stuff. Or they think it's harming their kid's developing brains, depleting the energy of the sun, having an affair with their wives, whatever. A lot of them are way out there, to put it nicely." She not-so-discreetly nodded over her shoulder toward the two men following distantly behind us.

"The other group is grounded in science, specifically around the flawed science of the law of immutability. We did our own, independently funded research, and though it's just as un*provable* as the counterargument, there is overwhelming theoretical evidence that the timeline is not locked, which implies that every single time someone has jumped downstream, they've forked a brand-new timeline. We all merely happen to be in the stream that is unchanged, which scientists and the wider public blindly latch onto as confirmation, blissfully ignoring the horrifying implications. Think about it: tens of thousands, maybe millions of jumps, each one branching a new timeline, exponentially multiplying the suffering in the universe.

"So we had no choice but to act, covertly and forcefully. The zealots and the intellectuals put our heads together and crafted a plan to end the scourge. You've heard of time as a closed loop, yes? Well, we prepared to break it wide open." Damitra smirked. "It helped a lot that public opinion was starting to organically sway our way, largely fueled by the greatest irony of all: the world already knew about the Cutoff, that one day in 2086 all time travel would cease, and they had long-since made their peace with it. A self-fulfilling prophecy, thanks to our tireless work.

"A few years back, we began to place our operatives in the highest ranks of the WCO, UN, and major world governments, lying in wait. On July 19 last year, we began a coordinated digital attack, completely taking down the network of time machines and the supply chain that feeds it. There was backlash, yes, but ultimately acceptance, or at least resignation. We capped off our success by building a wave of grassroots momentum that ultimately led to worldwide adoption of our sweeping anti-time-travel legislation, and the glorious disbandment of the WCO itself." By this point, she was noticeably out of breath, though it was unclear if it was due to the speedy walk, rigorous haranguing, or particular enthusiasm about the subject matter.

"Did that answer your question?" she appended with a grin.

"Er, yes, thank you, I appreciate the . . . verbosity." That was about the most supportive thing I could muster up; Stockholm Syndrome had not yet taken hold. "So that brings us back to the beginning, I suppose: Why am I here? I have to assume it's for more than a lecture on the political history of time travel."

As if in response, Damitra doubled her already-brisk pace. I couldn't determine if she was avoiding the question or had suddenly realized we were running late for our next activity. We passed by indistinguishable door after indistinguishable door, the constant déjà vu effect starting to make me feel dizzy. Without warning, she came to a jarring stop in front of one of them, unlabeled and unremarkable. Even on my newly rehabilitated legs, the hurried walk had started to wear me down, so the sudden pause was more than welcome.

"*This* is why," she gestured, grandiosely answering the question that I had somewhat forgotten remained outstanding after our closing sprint. The door popped open with a perfect sci-fi hiss. Despite her proclamation, the inside of the room only invited more questions. In the center sat another time machine, glowing brightly in the windowless room. The massive wall panel behind it showed a highly detailed world map with Dubai highlighted by a hypnotic, pulsing icon.

"Can you just give me a straight answer?" I said with simmering exasperation. It felt like we had walked for miles, only to end up in nearly the same room we had left. "This doesn't help. For one, didn't you say the *other* room had 'the last functional time machine'?" I added sufficiently sarcastic air quotes for good measure. "This one looks pretty darn functional to me."

"First of all, this isn't a time machine; it's a teleporter. Nearly identical technology, no universe-destroying side effects. Plus, time travel is illegal, remember?" she said with a wink that vastly overestimated our rapport. "Here's what it comes down to, Aaron: we need your help, and frankly, *you* need your help too. There is a task for you in London: a simple transaction to acquire more fuel for time travel. We need that increasingly scarce resource to send you home—or back to the trial, rather—as well as for our own use. Simply get the fuel, return here, and we'll merrily send you on your way."

"Got it. So I'm a time-jumping black market delivery guy now. And if I don't get the fuel?"

"You'll be stuck here with us for quite a while. But that won't happen. A simple transaction, remember?"

I sure wished she hadn't repeated the word *simple* so many times. "Is this what you had in mind for the esteemed judge too, if your original plan had worked?"

"Believe it or not, yes, among other activities. Given her easily accessible public records, she was the only individual in that room that we confidently knew had the exact skills we require. She may have needed a little more . . . *convincing* . . . but, like I said, this is the only way to ensure your timely return, as well as the continuation of this organization's critical mission to save humanity. Anyway, you'll do great; I have full faith in you. Bo here will join you and walk you through the details when you arrive. See you when you get back."

With a flick of her wrist and a dart of the eye, the wall screen came to life, dramatically zooming in from a global view down to a single London avenue. The effect was so photorealistic that I nearly lost my footing.

With our arrival location selected, I was inelegantly ushered into the narrow tube, once again unwillingly compelled through the vastness of spacetime.

10

————————

Though the jump itself was instantaneous, the aftereffects lingered throughout Bo the Henchman's prosaic explanation of our task at hand. For the first time, I had been mentally prepared to travel across a higher dimension; in the end, the knowledge probably only exacerbated the effect. The uniquely disorienting blend of speckled light, abrupt change in brightness and air pressure, and general fear of my atoms spreading across the galaxy hung around like a nauseating migraine crossed with an existential panic attack.

We had teleported directly into a bedroom; quaint and welcoming, it could easily have passed as a rustic bed-and-breakfast. Discussing illicit underground dealings felt dirty here, like the room was too wholesome to be exposed to such things.

" . . . so you won't show up in any of the facial recognition databases," Bo concluded, barely aware that I hadn't been paying the slightest bit of attention. "And you know how to drive, right?"

"Huh?" I mustered.

"You know how to drive classic?" he clarified, though my continued look of befuddlement prompted him to elucidate further. "We have a classic 2029 car model—steering wheel and everything—for our, you know, getaway. You can drive it, right?"

"I have a driver's license from 1982, if that's what you mean. But, you know, it expired fifty-something years ago."

"Great, that's what we thought. You should be fine, then."

"Wait, *that's* why you wanted me for this job?" I asked. "Because I can drive a freakin' car?"

"Well, yeah. It's very hard to find anyone these days who knows how. It'd be kinda like asking you if you knew how to ride a horse, I think. Nobody even manufactures human-driveable cars; way too dangerous and illegal in most places anyway. We thought we'd be getting a 'two birds with one stone' deal by upstreaming the judge, but hey, at least you can do this part. You're still one bird. Plus, like I said earlier," he added, "your best asset is that your old-ass face won't trigger any recognition alerts." Glad to be of service.

"So it's just in and out, right? We give someone some money, they give us some time-machine fuel?" I asked, hoping that Bo hadn't already gone over this.

"Money? Nah, there's no money anymore. Didn't they tell you that in the forties? We have something he wants; he has something we want."

"So, um . . ."

"Drugs, yeah, obviously."

"Right, great," I replied, opting to avoid any follow-up questions that would inevitably invite further derision.

Debriefed and ready, we headed out the door into the overcast London morning. Looking at the charming facades neighboring us, I was a bit depressed to realize that this unwelcome experience represented my first lifetime visit outside the US: a Dubai bunker and the seedier outskirts of London. Not quite the Parisian holiday that Jennifer and I had been fantasizing about as early as our first date.

Our "classic" vehicle sat idle for us, looking as futuristic to me as anything else I'd seen in the twenty-first century. The right-side door smoothly popped open as I approached, sparing me another embarrassing moment of selecting the wrong driver's side. Once comfortably inside, I instinctively fumbled for an ignition switch, finding nothing of the sort. Bo, caught between schadenfreude and impatience, blurted, "Just drive!" which ended up being great advice. The car accelerated effortlessly upon my command, following a path dynamically projected on the windshield.

Though most of the recognizable London landmarks were miles away, I did my best to take in the surroundings and enjoy the whisper-quiet ride. The silver linings of being a time-captive, I supposed. We approached a major intersection, vehicles weaving continuously through the center without any discernible pattern. I instinctively began to slow, though without the benefit of a stoplight, I couldn't fathom how we would ever navigate through the entropic traffic.

"Don't stop," Bo commanded unsympathetically, sensing my trepidation. "The other cars are all autonomous; they'll adjust, trust me."

Trust was a lot to ask from my literal kidnapper, but the logic made some sense. Against the wishes of every rational part of my being, I accelerated into the intersection, all but closing my eyes as other cars barely skirted past us.

After a few more intersections and some harrowing, unfamiliar right turns into oncoming traffic, we arrived at our destination. It is incredible how quickly you can traverse a city when you never need to stop. As charming as our starting point had been, this was the opposite: industrial, stark, and uninviting. To be fair, I hadn't expected the Ritz.

Bo donned a cloth mask covering most of his face, a marked improvement when compared to the alternative. "Alright, come with me," he ordered as he exited the vehicle, a satchel incongruously hanging by his side.

"Don't I get a mask?" I asked sheepishly.

"Why? You'll be back in another *decade* in a few minutes. What are they going to do, get their vengeance on your great-grandchild?" he mocked with a cruel grin.

If the comment was an attempt at reassurance, it failed spectacularly. I didn't know if I had any descendants, but I shuddered at the thought of inadvertently putting them in harm's way.

"Let's make this quick. And don't talk," he added.

I anxiously scanned the environment as we entered the creepiest of the properties; long-abandoned scaffolding dangled tenuously above the doorway.

A man stepped out from the shadows. "You got the stuff?" he queried with a near-indecipherable British accent. Bo held up the satchel in response, tossing it at the man's feet. He glanced inside, then jerked his head toward a couple of metal barrels along the far wall.

"Wait here," Bo commanded as he retrieved the contraband. What other alternatives he thought I might pursue, I couldn't fathom. Shadow Man and I stood in awkward silence as we awaited Bo's return, the quiet underscored by an eerie whistle of wind permeating through the cracked windows.

"So, who the hell are ya?" he questioned after about thirty strained seconds.

"Just some guy," I replied, the upper limit of precision I was comfortable with. Finding that answer satisfactory, he grunted and returned to the bag, investigating the contents with exaggerated interest.

"C'mon, Aaron, let's go," Bo ordered with a tinge of panicked urgency as he struggled to carry the two containers on his narrow shoulders. I was happy to oblige, though less so that he had needlessly used my name in front of someone whom I would bet my life had dispassionately killed a man or two in his time. Though Bo was still grappling to support the metal canisters, he rapidly accelerated the moment we cleared the building entrance, surging to barely short of a full run. I did my best to keep pace, hopping in the driver's seat just as he secured the loot in the trunk.

"Are we, you know, okay?" I asked.

"Shut up and drive. We'll be fine," he answered unconvincingly, his obvious apprehension barely concealed. He punched a destination into the vehicle's main console screen, and I smoothly navigated us back to the highway. The well-insulated car blocked out all road noise, leaving us with only Bo's sharp, anxious breathing. Finding it distracting and unnerving, I hoped maybe some light conversation would calm him down.

"So are we headed back to that same charming little—"

"Okay, you're going to need to drive faster," Bo interrupted. "Much, much faster. Like, your-life-depends-on-it fast."

The facade of calm broken, he theatrically stared behind us, and for the first time I saw a massive vehicle in the rearview mirror, cresting over a hill about a hundred yards behind and gaining.

"Are they chasing us? What the fuck is going on?" I screamed, suddenly on high alert, an unfamiliar and unsettling feeling. Survival instinct kicked in, and I punched the accelerator, launching us forward with a terrifying burst.

"They're trying to get the fuel back, dumbass!" Bo shouted back at me.

"But why? We gave them drugs, they gave us fuel. Fair deal, right?"

"Well, you'd think so, but we didn't actually have any drugs to give, and I think they figured that out."

"Fuck, are you kidding me?" I blurted as we barreled into an intersection at full speed. The vehicles traveling perpendicular paid no mind, calmly adjusting to avoid us.

"It's fine; I told you: just drive. We're faster than them; their car will be electronically limited to slightly above the speed limit. That's why we're in the classic. Don't be an idiot; follow the path and we'll be fine."

I dared a glance in the rearview. Bo was right; the pursuers were already nowhere to be seen.

"I think we lost them," I shared as I gradually slowed down to a more manageable speed. Bo stared backward for a minute before confirming. A few tense minutes passed, both of us waiting for something to go wrong. The surrounding buildings began to be increasingly residential and well-maintained; we were almost back.

Our vehicle passed through another major intersection; the same one I had panicked about on our outbound journey. Out of nowhere, the black behemoth peeled around the opposite corner, smoothly drifting with all four wheels turned into position immediately behind us. The truck lurched forward, crashing into our rear bumper with an ear-piercing screech of bending metal. We started to swerve against the weight of the pursuing juggernaut. I held on to the steering wheel with all my might.

"Go! Go!" screamed Bo. I smashed the accelerator to the floor, the powerful inertia compressing our bodies into the padded seats. We quickly regained enough separation for me to reestablish steering control, but the truck kept pace.

"Fuck, they obviously know where we're headed, that's how they were able to cut us off. We need to find another off-grid teleporter. Give me a minute." Bo's eyes lost focus, racing in all directions while he interfaced with his implant. His face was still covered by the cloth mask, creating the illusion of a man fully possessed. In lieu of any additional directions, I maintained our breakneck pace, opting to avoid any unnecessary turns in order to maximize our vehicle's speed advantage. The truck began to once again fade into the horizon when Bo snapped back to reality, immediately submitting a new destination into the car's center console.

"Okay, got it. A bit of a farther drive, but there's no way they'll figure out where we're going. Just keep driving like you are, and we'll be fine."

I allowed myself one deep breath and kept the pedal pinned to the floor, following the newly projected directions. Within minutes, we were out of the city proper and into the countryside, grazing cows unperturbed as we zipped by at a hundred miles per hour. Ten minutes passed without any sign of our pursuer.

"You've gotta be fuckin' kidding me!" Bo winced and craned his neck skyward, frantically scanning for something through our lightly tinted sunroof.

Against my better judgment, I risked a quick glance upward, spotting nothing beyond a soaring flock of migrating geese.

"I got pinged on my implant; we picked up a speed limit warning."

"Should I slow—"

"No! No time. We're already way behind schedule." His eyes locked on the target above us. "There," he said, pointing for my benefit, "a police drone on our trail."

I could see it now, dropping closer to road level. At roughly fifty feet, the drone halted its descent, effortlessly hovering precisely above us. The road immediately in front of the car suddenly transformed into a blue and red warning message, nearly identical to the one Lisa and I had seen on the sidewalk the day prior. All but the reflective lane lines were obscured by the flashing text, projected from above in four languages.

Every scrupulous bone in my body told me to heed the warning and stop. Police custody sounded much safer than the fuel-stealing, time-manipulating crowd with whom I currently ran. But they remained my best—and likely only—hope of getting back to 1985 by way of 2042. I suppressed the uneasy thought and maintained our velocity, the distracting message keeping pace in front of us.

"What do we do now?" I asked, knowing we wouldn't be able to rely on Bo's default strategy of outrunning any pursuit.

"Same answer as always: keep going and shut up. I've got a plan," he responded unconvincingly. We continued driving, the idyllic landscape belying the escalating panic coursing through me. Twenty stressful minutes elapsed without any change in our situation. On multiple occasions, passengers in vehicles traveling the other direction pointed and stared at us and our unwanted escort; we were, after all, the closest thing to a late twenty-first-century police chase.

"So, um, what else *were* you planning to do with the judge? I refuse to believe she was just going to be a glorified wheelman like me," I prompted, breaking the tense silence. I hoped our ongoing adventure together had built enough cachet that I could finally get an honest answer.

"Oh, you know, classic blackmail shit," he responded. "Threaten to release revealing information, photos, etcetera. All of it fake, of course, but the public wouldn't have known that."

"Uh-huh. Great. And, well, why? To dismiss the case?"

"Oh no, not dismiss it. I think Damitra wanted the judge to find Jakob innocent on grounds that multiple timelines exist. That would kickstart her whole crusade to end the 'great plague of time travel' forty years early. But since we ended up with *you*, she'll probably have to move on to her vaunted 'phase two' plan instead."

"Huh? Aren't you anti-time-travel too?" I asked, discerning Bo's unambiguous sarcasm. "Isn't that the whole point of your organization?"

"For some, yeah. But we did that already; we killed time travel! Mission accomplished! Woohoo, right? And now what's left is the crazies like Damitra who want time travel to have never existed. I don't give a shit about that part, though; I just stick around for the competitive benefits package."

"I'm going to assume that was a joke," I remarked. "Or is 2086 not as perfect as 2042? I thought there was no money, no work, widely available medbays, all of that."

"Yes, it was a joke, and as you know, there's nothing funnier than explaining it. The 2080s are fine. Idyllic, whatever you want to call it. Just like the '70s and '60s and '50s before it. And that's exactly the problem, yeah? Every decade is the same fucking thing. There's never anything new. Never anything exciting or unpredictable. I don't give a shit about Damitra's priorities nor agree with her extreme methods, but time travel had to end so we could actually feel alive again, you know? Living is shit, yes; it's going to abandoned factories and almost getting killed over a botched drug exchange, but what's the point otherwise? So a computer can do everything for you and tell you when and how you're going to die? No fucking thank you."

A few minutes later, we approached a short, tree-lined tunnel, golden sun cascading through the far end.

"Finally!" Bo began punching a new code into the car's display. "Do exactly what I say," he directed, snapping out of his introspective zeal to get back to business. "Stop in the middle of the tunnel, keep the car running, then get out immediately. Got it?"

"Got it," I confirmed; simple enough. As instructed, I came to a stop under the obscured protection of the tunnel and quickly hopped out, trying to conceptualize the remaining elements of this plan. The drone had not followed us in, but my expectation was that it would apathetically wait above for our eventual exit.

The moment our vehicle came to rest, Bo wordlessly burst into action, removing the precious cargo from the trunk, placing one canister on the curb next to me and plopping the other into the driver's seat. He secured the seat belt around the bulbous object, pressed a few buttons, and slammed the door shut. The car smoothly drove off into the bright light, presumably with the drone in tow.

"Huh?" I asked, flabbergasted. The entire transition had taken maybe ten seconds, like a pit crew that specialized in police evasion.

"It's an old car, but it has some limited autonomous features. It'll just keep going until it runs out of power or can't auto-navigate an obstacle, the dumbass drone following along the whole time. By that point, we'll be long gone."

"Yeah, but why the canister?"

"The car needs to think there's a driver available for emergencies, and that thing weighed ninety pounds easy. Damitra's not going to be happy that I had to sacrifice half our haul, but I didn't see an alternative."

"That . . . actually makes a lot of sense. One problem, though, do we have to walk the rest of the way, carrying this thing?" I tried picking it up and could barely nudge it off the ground.

"What? No, of course not," Bo replied with the same dismissive tone I'd heard countless times today. "I already summoned a car to pick us up. It should be here any . . . now." He nodded toward the entrance to the tunnel; a sleek, unmistakably modern car quietly stopped inches from our feet, the side door sliding open with a welcoming tone.

It was much easier to enjoy the tranquil English countryside when not being actively pursued. I zoned out amid a tapestry of green, rolling hills and brilliant midday sky.

———

Ding!

"C'mon, Aaron, hurry up," Bo enjoined while I struggled to regain my bearings in my groggy state. I certainly hadn't intended to fall asleep, though to be fair, I had already been awake for over twenty-four hours. I'd experienced jet lag before; this was a whole other level. Call it chrono lag, I suppose.

Bo laboriously carried the remaining fuel tank up the front stairs of an enchanting country cottage. Lush forest surrounded the modest building; if not for our transport now leaving on the dirt road, we easily could have been in 1850.

"Where are we?" I asked, catching up to Bo.

"Colleague's house. He has an unregistered teleporter we can use to get back to HQ."

I followed him inside and was immediately hit with a wave of subconscious, uncanny terror; something wasn't right here. It easily could have been the hundreds of vintage maps blanketing the walls or the juxtaposition of absurdly contemporary, minimalist furniture in a place of such antique sensibilities. No; the true source, I realized after a moment, was the conspicuous and absolute absence of sound. The spritely chirp of the birds, the gentle rustling of the leaves, even our footsteps on the hardwood floor, all muted; only our voices broke through the eerie silence.

"Yeah, it's weird," whispered Bo, sensing my obvious unease. "This guy's super freaky, but we'll be out of here soon enough."

Bo led me down the rest of the hallway, past a sparse kitchen and inviting meditation room. We reached the office at the end of the hall where a bearded older man was meticulously shuffling through some papers in a wooden filing cabinet. Though all non-vocal noise was suppressed, he immediately sensed our arrival and rose to his full height.

Our eyes locked as dawning recognition snapped into focus; this was a face I'd seen before. Quite recently, in fact. Though his hair was no longer blond, the broad chin and sad eyes were unmistakably the same. I spied a sly smile on his face as the realization became mutual.

"Welcome to my home, juror number four," Jakob announced with sinister, unbridled glee.

11

"Oh right, shit!" Bo exclaimed. "I forgot you two know each other."

"Not really . . ." I responded on autopilot, still dumbfounded as I stared at the man who had indirectly triggered my entire temporal adventure. Last I had seen him in court—a mere handful of hours ago—he was deflated yet youthful, a lifetime of wasted promise quite possibly in front of him. Though forty-something years had passed since then, he looked maybe late-fifties now, undoubtedly a beneficiary of the twenty-first-century medical advances.

"Can we go?" I mumbled to Bo. "Not to be rude, um, sir," I added, turning to our host, "this is all just way too weird for me."

"Wait."

With long strides, Jakob approached us, our height imbalance negated by the sunken office in which he stood.

"The teleportal is warming up; why don't we chat for a minute?" He made no attempt to sound any less menacing, though

I may have been projecting my own rising terror. This older version emitted none of the muted notes of decency that had lured me to his side throughout the trial.

"Joe, right?" he prompted my ersatz colleague. "Can you fetch us all some tea?"

Bo hesitated, glancing quickly at me, then back at Jakob. "I think I should—"

"The kitchen is just down the hall, friend," he added, halting the protest in its tracks. Clearly intimidated, Bo followed the instructions without further objection, tacking on a faint "back in a minute" as he exited.

"Come, have a seat," Jakob offered with a gesture meant to look inviting. I saw no recourse but to oblige. "Did you come here straight from the trial? The protester with the unidentified weapon upstreamed you?"

"Uh-huh," I answered passively as I sat down, annoyed at how snug the chair felt after my exhausting day.

"Quite intriguing, I must say. I didn't know such an advanced device existed—even now—though I admit I suspected it at the time. I have often considered the immense, untapped power of such a technology. What a shame that it was wasted on such frivolity; I would have suggested something much bolder had they asked. Alas. Speaking of which, when did you arrive in 2087?"

"Er, about nine hours ago, I think." I was already quite impatient for Bo's return as a necessary social buffer.

"Yes, yes, that is interesting. Your presence here is quite the outlier, I must say. Upstreamers were rare even before the Cutoff, and after—well, my friend, you may be the only one. I assume you were not the original target. . . ." Jakob trailed off, deep in thought. "Yes, interesting. Tell me, juror," he finally said, "have you talked to anyone outside the realm of your natural influence, or made any unpremeditated decisions that could have permeated the established timeline?"

Ignoring the question—which I barely understood anyway—I instead blurted out the lone thought that had been nagging at me since identifying our esteemed host. "Did . . . did you kill her? Kathryn Simpson?"

He looked taken aback, though more performatively than reflexively, as if that was the reaction he thought I would expect to see.

"Your accusatory undertone is unwarranted, friend. Why do you ask this question?"

"Because you are—were, rather—charged with murdering an innocent woman, and to be honest, the evidence doesn't leave much room for interpretation, even when trying to give you the benefit of the doubt."

"I do not care to relitigate. If I correctly recall the timing of the courtroom incident, you are yet to even hear my own testimony."

"Wait, your lawyer let you take the stand?" I questioned. Even with my limited legal knowledge, I knew this was usually a terrible idea.

"Quite reluctantly, yes, upon my resolute insistence. I hide nothing, you see; trivial perjury to protect the innocent aside, I could not pass on the opportunity to impart the exculpating truth to yourself and your fellow jurors."

"So if you don't hide anything, I'll ask again: did you—"

"No, sir, I did not," he interrupted. "And it is my greatest regret that I could not prevent her death in this nor all timelines. I take comfort to know at least that there is another in which I was successful. That is all I wish to speak on the matter."

"I thought you would try to convince me to sway the jury's decision," I shared.

"Ah, fascinating. You assume I was convicted?" Jakob said with a hint of anguish, pausing to deliberately consider his next words. "Regardless, nothing I say to you now will change the result in *your* temporal reality, plus I respect your right to act on your perception of free will."

While I processed this disconcerting statement, Bo returned with hot tea for each of us, precariously balanced on a serving plate, clearly not intended for the purpose. I took a polite sip to remind myself how much I loathed the stuff before placing the cup and saucer down beside me.

"Alas, my favorite variety of Camellia sinensis went extinct in 2039," Jakob shared, taking a less reluctant sip of his own. "We may have turned around climate change in time for human survival, but there were still some unfortunate victims. I have been trying to cultivate it on my estate using the recorded genome, but it's just not the same, is it?"

"I like it," I lied. Bo mumbled affirmatively as well.

"Every day," Jakob continued with escalating fervor, "I activate the home's noise suppression algorithm—my design—and ruminate over a cup of genetically engineered tea. And every day I come to the same realization: the world simply doesn't deserve me." My poker face held strong against the onslaught of remarkably unfeigned introspective wisdom. Out of the corner of my eye, I caught Bo studying the crown molding in great detail.

"I figure out how to jump downstream beyond 2033, they make it illegal. I protect Kathryn, I get put on trial for it. I've worked my whole life to better the world, and here I sit, unheralded and alone, in a timeline primarily shaped by my actions. Your people got it right," he added, turning to Bo, "time travel is simply too dangerous for the plebs to possess, blindly placated by the bald-faced lie of immutability." Bo nodded passionately, though it was difficult to distinguish if the action represented mutual agreement or an attempt to avoid further elaboration.

"Tell me, juror number four—"

"Aaron is fine, thanks," I interjected.

Jakob snorted and furrowed his brow in reaction, disconcertingly scrutinizing me anew before recollecting himself. For the briefest of moments, he looked like a different person, the one toward whom I had instinctively been sympathetic at the trial. As his demeanor returned to its menacing baseline, the contrast became all too stark. Forty years would change any man, but this felt like something more, something darker.

"Tell me, *Aaron*," he corrected, "what is the worst thing you've ever done?"

I hesitated, hoping the question was purely rhetorical. Jakob leaned forward in expectant anticipation. "I, um, cheated on my previous girlfriend, I guess," I contributed.

"Ah, you must have led a privileged life so far, my friend. If that is indeed the case, I truly envy you. Perhaps, young man, your answer will change someday soon." Now he was just being outright threatening. "I find your response difficult to believe, but it will suffice to make my point, nonetheless."

Good instinct, I thought, especially since it had never happened. Kerri had broken up with me because she couldn't come to terms with my predilection for wearing a baseball cap at all times. But the possible sociopath across from me didn't need to know that, nor anything else about my personal life.

I returned a half-hearted shrug, fully aware I was inviting his next bombastic monologue.

"Imagine for a moment that you could visit the timeline where that event never occurred," Jakob began. "This other prospective partner of yours took a wrong turn or had a teleporter malfunction, leaving you alone yet relieved that you narrowly avoided breaking your beloved girlfriend's trust. Perhaps your life is different at a micro level, but I think you'll agree that it would be fundamentally unaltered at the macro. Maybe you still have your affair the next day, or the original relationship fizzles in some other way." Like because of a throwback Cubs cap.

"For many, life is not so simple. The smallest individual event can generate massive personal ripples. The largest events, for all of humanity. War, terrorism, genocide, natural disaster, etcetera. The origin of my personal ripple occurred when I was eleven, my genius just beginning to blossom. I was skating on Maridalsvannet Lake with extended family when my younger sister darted off outside the safe zone. I followed, impotently watching the ice crack around her while executing an amateur layback spin in imitation of her hero, Sonja Henie. After a hard fall, she broke through the surface and into the freezing water below. We both had received precautionary lessons for precisely this situation, yet neither of us reacted accordingly. She did not survive, as you may have surmised from my prelude. Ten years later, that ripple met another—the invention of time travel—and my life's purpose came into view. Perhaps there was a way to save her, at least for some parallel version of myself."

Jakob delivered the story of this tragedy with forced monotone, dampening the first sign of true human emotion I had witnessed coming from him. It was impossible not to feel compassion, even for someone I recently called a sociopath.

"So, did you do it? Go back and change things?" Bo asked impatiently.

"If I had, friend, how would I be aware of her death? You know as well as anyone, changing the past branches off a new timeline. Yet I am stuck in this one, the darkest timeline, as they say: no Heide, no Kathryn, unheralded and alone.

Bo still looked confused. "Why didn't it work though, if you're so sure you can change the past? You were able to go to 1988, right? Why not, um, 2020ish, if I'm guessing your age correctly?"

"I tried, sir, oh I tried," Jakob responded with undisguised exasperation. "I spent years attempting to overcome the myriad theoretical and technical hurdles. In the end, it simply proved unfeasible. My working theory posits that there exists a chronophysical barrier that obstructed me from occupying that moment in time in both my adolescent and adult forms. A barrier that is unique to pre-2033 time travel. Alas, as I am the only known individual to attempt such a feat, this theory regrettably remains uncorroborated.

"As a desperate alternative, I leveraged my advancements to downstream to 1988 instead, in an attempt to save my idol, Ms. Simpson. This effort was not purely driven by devotion to her, nor selfless desire to better the world. Rather, I foolishly surmised that her survival would advance the field of research enough for me to save my sister, or at least jump laterally to a timeline in which she survived."

A subtle alert sound echoed throughout the home, accentuated in relation to the artificially established silence.

"Ah, perfect timing," shared Jakob, instantly breaking out of his state of unaffected monotonal delivery and back into vaguely theatrical hospitality, no less sinister but much less uncomfortable. "The teleportal is rebooted and calibrated. Please, friends, finish your tea and remain as long as you wish."

We both stood up without hesitation.

"We're in a hurry," Bo explained, securing the fuel canister onto his shoulder.

Jakob led us into the lone unviewed room across the hall. A crude, unmistakably homemade teleporter acted as centerpiece around miles of tangled cables and inscrutable screens. The contraption barely appeared to be qualified to microwave a bag of popcorn, never mind send a living being hurtling through spacetime.

As Bo confidently stepped into the clear tube, Jakob handed him an unlabeled package. The two shared a subtle, knowing nod; moments later, Bo disappeared in a quick flash of intense red light.

Any trepidation about following after my newfound partner in crime was sufficiently suppressed by an overwhelming desire not to be left alone with Jakob. I stepped into the precarious device and waited anxiously as he made an unhurried adjustment on one of the screens, finally turning to stare at me with his sorrowful eyes.

"See you soon, my friend." I caught a faint hint of a smile as the world melted away, somethingness giving way to peaceful nothingness and back again.

12

———

"Order! Order!"

I found myself back in the courtroom, embroiled in pure pandemonium. As prepared as I had been to return to the moment of my departure, it remained utterly overwhelming to be dropped in medias res among dozens of roaring protestors, scrambling jurors, and the remainder of the violent takedown of my attacker. Still, I was miraculously and safely back in 2042, and I embraced an all-encompassing wave of relief.

"Order! Order in the courtroom!" Judge Kasem continued to shout in a vain attempt to reassert control. Her pounding gavel was barely audible among the rumbling chaos. The bailiff had successfully pinned the attacker to the ground, though he was now powerless to assist elsewhere. Most of my peers on the jury were hiding behind their chairs or seeking alternative forms of refuge. I sat motionless, perhaps appearing unflappable, but, in fact, I was slowly regaining my bearings.

I directed my focus to Jakob, looking impossibly youthful

compared to the embittered old man I had just spent an uncomfortable hour with. He likewise seemed unfazed, taking in the commotion with the same unaffected leer I had witnessed throughout our previous interaction. I half expected him to turn and acknowledge me with his sinister and all-too-familiar grin, a mutual indication that he, too, had just returned from a formative trip to the future. Alas, nothing of the sort occurred, and he continued to sit, patient and unsettlingly observant.

Any lingering affinity for the man had been cleanly wiped away by his panic-inducing behavior in the deep future. It felt like the veneer had been washed away; I could finally see him for who he truly was. A megalomaniac at minimum and a perjurer by admission, with a dash of sociopathy: all of the ingredients in the murderer stew. I found myself aching to find him guilty, to punish someone so deeply detestable for the crime he must have committed.

After some amount of time—my chronological perception was still off-kilter—additional law enforcement officers hustled into the room, quickly redirecting the minimally resistant protestors back out the ornate main doors. The perpetrator was similarly removed, with unlinked, brightly lit cuffs secured around both wrists, seemingly no less effective without the metallic chain.

With her courtroom restored, the judge quickly reasserted her authority, asking for all participants to return to their seats.

"On behalf of the court, I sincerely apologize to all involved," she proclaimed with renewed gravitas. "This situation never should have occurred, and I can assure each and every one of you that we will take all necessary steps to ensure it never does again. Thank you, Bailiff, for your decisive action protecting us from harm. I am truly relieved to see that nobody was hurt. Despite the demonstrators' best intentions, the trial will continue. However,

I move that we adjourn for the day. I ask everybody to please collect themselves and return tomorrow with a fresh mind. Thank you, that is all."

———

Comfortably back in my room, I collapsed into the chair in a state of bleary-eyed enervation. I wanted to think about anything other than the overlong day's events, yet found that the distressing images were stuck on repeat.

"Hi, Aaron, welcome back! How was the first day of the trial?" Wally's attentive and congenial questions didn't help. "Remember, anything you share with me will remain between us. Robot-patient confidentiality, am I right?"

As much as I longed for interpersonal connection, I didn't have the energy for the AI's exuberant disposition right now. "It was fine, Wally, but I don't really want to talk about it. It's good to see you, though."

"Good to see you too, Aaron! Anything I can do to assist you for now?"

"Yeah, can you send a dinner to the room? The curated, healthy option is fine; I don't want to choose."

"Absolutely, Aaron! That should be here in twelve to thirteen minutes. I'll switch to standby mode now."

"Thanks," I mumbled.

A mere hour earlier, I had been no less exhausted but without any leverage to abstain from conversation. After the jump from Jakob's cottage back to Dubai, Damitra had requested a second-by-second debrief of the day's events, primarily seeking to rationalize why we had returned with half our expected haul. I spent the entire exchange terrified that retribution for our shortcoming would trap me in the deep future for an extended period. Damitra was clearly displeased but seemed placated by the unexpected package Jakob delivered via Bo. I didn't dare ask about the contents, but given the individuals involved, I assumed I didn't want to know, lest I add another item to my list of illicit activities for the day. Ultimately, she kept her word, fueling the machine and sending me downstream as soon as she had extracted every ounce of recollection.

For the first time in a while, I felt at home. I was sound asleep before the food ever arrived.

———

Morning softly filtered through the artificial window, gently stirring me from a reinvigorating slumber. I could already feel that today was going to be better; all I had to do was remain in the current decade, an admittedly low bar to clear.

"Good morning, Aaron," Wally softly chimed, the precise moment I returned to full consciousness. "Your sleep efficiency last night was 98 percent; excellent work. You have 109 minutes until you are required to report to the jury room." I had fallen asleep so early that I had some extra time to kill.

"Thanks, Wally. Can you order me breakfast, both the healthy one and the indulgent one? I'm very hungry. Oh, and can you check with Lisa's assistant if she's around for a call? It's been forever since I talked to her, and I want to make sure I have the chance before we're back in the courtroom."

"Absolutely, Aaron, your order is placed, and I will share Lisa's availability as soon as possible," the assistant responded. I was beginning to appreciate his omnipotence.

I took my sweet time getting ready, luxuriating in the shower with its hundreds of adaptive mini-nozzles, then exhaustively customizing my outfit from the provided wardrobe. The robot-delivered breakfast hit the spot, a feast of yogurt topped with fruits and various "superfoods"—whatever those are—plus a heap of banana pancakes that I unabashedly shoveled into my mouth.

Just as the sugar high peaked, Wally let me know that Lisa was on the line. Out of habit, I looked around for a wall-mounted telephone, until Wally gently reminded me to face the curved wall about a foot to my left. Lisa immediately appeared, as clearly as if I was standing in her room, though the background was partially blurred for privacy. We were scheduled to report in about twenty minutes, yet she wore only a plush pink robe in signature "Lisa doesn't give a fuck" fashion.

"Hey Aaron, what's up?" she said. "You know I'll see you in a few minutes, right?"

"Morning! Well, um, there's not too much opportunity to actually chat in the courtroom, and there actually is something more urgent I had on my mind." I had debated all morning whether or not to tell her about my harrowing adventure in the deep future, ultimately opting to embrace the Lisa paradigm and just go for it. She wouldn't remember in a few days anyway, though neither would I. With an eyebrow lift, she invited me to share. I took a deep breath and began.

"So remember when that one protestor with the backpack tried to attack the judge?" I asked, still questioning if she would even believe the tale. She nodded, wordlessly prompting me to get to the juicy part.

Right as I was about to dive in, an obfuscated figure appeared behind her, gradually coming into focus as he moved closer. The man moved cautiously, skulking behind my entirely unaware friend. As I prepared to blurt out a barely formed interjectory warning, Lisa caught my sidelong glance and peered over her shoulder at what I now saw in crystal clear detail: Paul, wearing an identical robe that *just barely* provided enough coverage on his extended frame. He stared at me with an exaggerated squint, finally sharing a half-hearted wave. Lisa shrugged in my direction with a devilish nonchalance that said it all.

"Paul, *darling*," she said to her paramour, stretching out the second word in an exaggerated mock-British accent, "can you give Aaron and me a few minutes? It's time for you to go get yourself dressed, anyway." He wordlessly obliged, leaving me fumbling to get back on track.

Once he was out of earshot, I resumed my rapid retelling in what felt like one unbroken, run-on sentence: the accidental up-streaming attack, the Dubai bunker, the time-travel laws, and, of course, the misadventures in and out of London. I withheld mention of any meeting or conversation with Jakob, not because of the obvious legal conflict of interest, but because it likely strained the already questionable credulity of the narrative beyond the breaking point. Plus, I simply didn't want to think about that man a moment longer than I had to.

Lisa listened without interruption—a truly astonishing feat for her—nor the animated reaction I was expecting. When I concluded the story with my return to the courtroom, she nodded to herself, processing.

"I did think it was incredibly odd that you sat there like a robot during the peak of the commotion," she teased after a moment, "but mostly I'm just glad you're okay. That sounds really scary, and I appreciate you telling me. So, what's the *future-*

future like? It's hard to imagine something more advanced than where we are now."

"For some reason—maybe the whole 'prisoner of time' thing—I didn't get many opportunities to ask questions like that, but honestly, based on what I saw, it seemed exactly the same as here. Technology advances, sure, but the problem is that people are still people. And there are still plenty of bad apples out there."

"All too true," Lisa concurred. "But still a little disappointing that we don't have big squid-headed aliens walking among us or robots doing our every bidding." She turned her head, listening to something offscreen. "Or, maybe we do; Arnie keeps sending me increasingly insistent notifications that I need to get ready for the courtroom. Let's talk more at lunch, yeah?"

"Sure, sounds good. And hey, if you run into Paul for any reason, say hi for me, okay?" We shared a knowing smile as the projection dissipated.

———

Back in the courtroom for day two, the mood was noticeably uneasy. Despite the bolstered security personnel on hand, everyone seemed to be looking around for the slightest sign of disturbance. Jakob shuffled in with a confident defiance that had been absent yesterday; perhaps he had been buoyed by the show of outside support. Without delay, the trial resumed precisely where it had left off: Jakob's former coworker on the stand, the prosecuting attorney pacing the room.

"Mister Brown," she opened, "apologies that we were unable to finish your testimony yesterday. I have just the same final question for you that was oh-so-dramatically interrupted: Were you aware the defendant was working on the ability to travel downstream beyond 2033?"

"No, absolutely not," he said, shaking his head vigorously to emphasize the point. "As far as I know, he worked on this project in complete secrecy; it certainly wasn't sanctioned by the WCO."

"Would it be considered a violation of the WCO working agreement to perform such research?"

"Hmm, good question. The theoretical research part would likely be acceptable; the WCO wouldn't ever stand in the way of pure scientific progress. But he nor anyone else would ever be authorized to use official equipment for this type of radical experimentation, never mind actual time jumps."

"Thank you, sir," she remarked, returning to her table. The defense attorney quickly rose in response.

"Mister Brown, how are you today?" she began.

"Fine, thanks. Excited to leave this room." He laughed to himself as a bead of sweat crested over his pronounced forehead wrinkle.

The lawyer smiled in a blatantly insincere show of empathy. "You implied that the defendant used WCO property to conduct his sub-2033 jump experiments. Did you ever personally observe any such tests, or any research that was not condoned by the organization?"

"No, ma'am, I did not personally see anything. I admit it's mere conjecture, but I cannot see how it would be possible for there to be any other, um . . . possibility."

"Theoretically, would it be feasible for an expert such as Jakob to build the necessary apparatuses himself, outside of the confines of the WCO?"

"Hmm, yes, I suppose so. As in, if all of the parts, plus fuel, were laid out in front of him, I think someone with Jakob's expertise could assemble a working machine."

"If the defendant did exactly this, would it be illegal, per international time-travel law?"

"Objection," the prosecutor intervened. "This witness is an expert in WCO policies and procedures, not legal precedent."

"Sustained," Judge Kasem concurred.

"Withdrawn." The defense attorney took a moment to refocus. "Let's go a different direction then, Mister Brown. How well would you say you knew the defendant personally?"

"Well enough, I suppose. We were never on the same functional team due to our different specialties, but we certainly interacted plenty, both in a professional capacity and occasional 'watercooler talk,' as it was once called."

"What is your opinion of him?"

Mr. Brown took a quick glance at Jakob. "Hard worker, a little intense, a great scientific mind—just like everyone else who works there—perhaps overly sensitive to polite critique. Everyone knew to stay out of his way because he delivered results." He paused, reconsidering his last sentence. "What I mean to say is, everyone knew that he worked best if given some space; I didn't mean to imply that he isn't a team player."

"Thank you, Mister Brown, that is all."

Once the witness had departed, the prosecutor rose, not bothering to venture beyond her table for redirect.

"Mister Brown, you testified that Jakob would be capable of building a functional time machine. If such a device existed, would its operating history appear on official WCO logs, like the one presented as evidence earlier?" With a hand motion, she projected the document, still completely unintelligible to my untrained eyes.

"No, madam, an unregistered time machine would not show up

on the logs. That is one reason why I did not consider a homemade machine as a possibility."

"Thank you, Mister Brown. The prosecution rests, Your Honor," she declared with presumptuous self-assuredness.

If the trial was already approximately halfway over, I could be back in 1985 sooner than originally expected. I had mentally prepared myself for untold days of monotonous legalese, but upon further reflection, a dearth of testimony for a crime that took place sixty years prior wasn't too surprising.

A series of character witnesses were called up to establish the defense: a childhood friend, a graduate school advisor, and an additional WCO colleague, among others. All vouched for Jakob's character and genius in lockstep, preaching of a man who cared only about the sanctity of pure science and the betterment of humankind. The burst of heartfelt adulation felt genuine, though in complete contradiction with the man whom I had recently spent that fateful hour. There was no mention of the family tragedy that I knew had set his path into motion, nor his unhinged quest for recognition. The prosecutor tried her darndest to poke holes and establish inconsistencies in their messaging, but could never find a gap to exploit. I could feel my fellow jurors being seduced by the uniformity and sheer volume of the puffery.

After the onslaught of extolment, an exceedingly welcome lunch break was announced. How could everyone be so gullible, I wondered, and not see straight through the defense's blatant play on their naivete? I was now surer than ever: this monster was guilty. Jakob himself was on deck to be called up to the stand, and then everyone else would see through the shameless charade with me.

13

Jakob confidently strode to the witness booth, his footsteps reverberating loudly in the otherwise noiseless room. Terrified silence—or hushed awe, it was hard to tell which—emanated from the jury. Jakob took his seat, flashing a strained smile in our direction.

"Mister Olsen," opened the defense attorney, "let's start at the beginning, chronologically. Did you travel downstream to 1988?"

"Yes."

"There has been some attention in this trial on *how* you accomplished that feat, but what I'm more interested in is: *Why*?"

"Yes, that is the more relevant question, isn't it? Quite straightforward, really: it was my intention, madam, to branch a new timeline in which Kathryn avoids or at least survives the attempt on her life on the twenty-fifth of January. In oversimplified parlance, I jumped back to save her."

"Thank you. We will return to the events of that night later, but I wanted to get the obvious out of the way first: your intention was to save her." The lawyer stood largely motionless, her hands behind her back, locked in focus. "Let's back up. Prior to the jump, what was your personal relationship with Ms. Simpson?"

"As with most of the commonalty, I was regretfully unaware of her existence until she became internationally recognized for her contributions to the then-nascent field of time travel. I was twenty-one, and immediately identified a kindred spirit: a brain that could cogitate like my own, a genius who changed the world with only her intellect. I enthusiastically absorbed the entirety of available knowledge on the topic, including the Natalia Ingles books mentioned yesterday, though I must say that I found them overly simplistic. I scrutinized the entirety of Ms. Simpson's published works, making sure I obtained absolute comprehension of every nuance. During my academic years, she was my solitary source of motivation, a measuring stick against which to compare myself. And when I followed in her hallowed steps as an elite researcher, every action I took was based on a framework of 'what would Kathryn do?' In a way, I picked up where she tragically left off."

The defense attorney nodded politely as Jakob went on. "Did you ever feel jealous of her tremendous accomplishments in such a short lifetime, or resentful of her worldwide fame?" she asked.

"Never, madam. I resent only that asinine question," he snapped. Jakob quickly caught himself, attempting to laugh off the brusque comment to his primary ally. She moved on with a well-practiced blind eye.

"When did you decide that you were going to jump back to save her?" she continued, unflustered.

"Roughly two years ago, in early 2040. My team's work had progressed to a point where such a possibility became viable, though unsurprisingly only I had the foresight to register that fact. Over the course of the last two years, I solved scientific hurdle after scientific hurdle, primarily in my limited free hours. Just last week, the alignment tests all showed green for the first time, and without hesitation, I initiated my solo downstream jump mere hours later."

"Please, Jakob, continue. In your words, what happened in 1988? Spare no detail." It felt like everyone in the courtroom leaned forward in shared anticipation.

"The jump felt like any other; I materialized inside an empty Berkeley campus classroom exactly as I planned, though I was dispirited to discover that my arrival occurred ninety-one seconds later than predicted. I obviously plan to analyze that miscalculation as soon as this farce is over. Knowing my implant would be disconnected from any public data streams, I had prudently preloaded it with detailed maps of the area, allowing me to navigate quickly to Kathryn's nearby neighborhood slightly north of the university proper. Per standard time-travel code, I minimized contact with any timelocked individuals; I may be a trailblazer, but I'm not reckless. They paid me no mind in my period-appropriate clothing.

"When I arrived at her seemingly modest home, I admit I was awestruck. This was a building I had visited in VR from every angle, and I even toured the physical home some years ago after it was converted into a museum. I fell for that tourist trap, you could say. But now the dwelling was right in front of me, and as I approached, I could see Kathryn's metaphorical fingerprints in even the smallest places: the meticulously centered welcome mat; the pleasing Fibonacci spacing pattern of the potted plants; the double-pane, soundproof windows. I felt home too.

"I knocked on the door—per the custom at the time—and waited patiently for her to open. I heard a distressingly loud metallic clatter and nearly burst in to intervene, but she opened the door before I committed to the act. And suddenly there she was: homely and unkempt, an unexplained pot lid in each hand, yet glowing magnificently with incandescent wisdom."

The man telling this story was barely reminiscent of the bitter, disconnected version with whom I had spent that treacherous hour. He was nearly floating on air during the enthusiastic retelling of his fateful meeting with his idol.

"Dampening my accent as much as possible, I explained I was a prospective graduate student and an admirer of her work, and she invited me inside without hesitation. Americans used to be much more trusting of each other, it appears. I perhaps will save my unabridged description of being in her presence for my memoirs, but trust me when I say that I was—pardon the old idiom—losing my shit.

"As we heard yesterday, the specifics of her murder are unknown, so I was on high alert for the slightest sign of disturbance. While she poured us drinks, I artfully procured a chef's knife from the kitchen, fully prepared for the worst. One friendly acquaintance stopped by for a short time, but presented no immediate threat. Beyond that, my time there proved to be curiously benign.

"Deep into the evening, we conversed about physics, technology, and the prospects of the future, plus some fabricated academic queries I raised to maintain my cover story. I suppressed the baser urge to speak on the matters of which I most truly cared for: her life, her future, her work, her impact.

"With my allocated downstream time dwindling, I bid Ms. Simpson a reluctant farewell, confident that the would-be murderer had been deterred by my mere presence. I returned to my laboratory in the present and was dismayed when my implant reported that Kathryn's untimely death was unchanged in my active timeline."

"What was your reaction to that realization?" the defense attorney said, snapping me out of a state of transfixion from Jakob's story. I still didn't believe him, but the man could deliver a compelling narrative.

"My reaction? Madam, I think I have made that quite clear: dismay, as I said, and acute disbelief. She had been alive and well moments earlier, the fateful night nearly over. I still cannot comprehend how my actions were unsuccessful."

"What happened after that?" she inquired.

"I analyzed the results, of course. My hypothesis was disproved, so as would any true scientist, I scoured my work looking for a mistake. There wasn't one; the science was flawless. After all, I *had* successfully traveled back to 1988; that much was unmistakable. If I had been allowed more time in the lab, I certainly would have solved it."

His lawyer began to ask a follow-up question, barely getting the chance to open her mouth before Jakob interrupted.

"To proactively answer what I expect is your subsequent question: no, I did not anticipate my arrest the following week, I must admit. I suspect that once my clandestine timejump was discovered in the logs, an all-purpose security scan was conducted, which matched my fingerprints to the old case. A bit of bad luck, perhaps, but this event only delays my inevitable findings. I have already made my mark on history, and will do so again."

"Thank you, Jakob," the attorney said. "I think that's a great stopping point." She brushed shoulders with the prosecuting attorney as they swapped places.

"Mister Olsen, I think we all would appreciate some clarifications regarding the downstream night in question. Firstly, why did you not remain in 1988 until Kathryn's welfare was confirmed?"

"Madam, this was the first time anyone had jumped before 2033. I hope you will forgive that I was unable to create a stable temporal field of indefinite length. My return time was fixed from the moment I arrived."

"Was Kathryn alive when you left?"

"Yes, madam, of course."

"What was the last thing she said to you?"

"'Best of luck on your application, Jakob.' I would have preferred something more profound, I admit."

"On your way out the door, did you see any suspicious activity?"

"No, madam. As I mentioned, I was on high alert at all times. Her street was well-lit and devoid of any activity, suspicious or otherwise."

"Did you carry a weapon on your person?"

"No, madam."

"Did you see a gun in Kathryn's home?"

"No, madam."

"Did you see any medication or pill bottles, specifically, diazepam?"

"I did not."

"How much alcohol was consumed?"

"I would describe the quantity as moderate. Kathryn had perhaps two glasses of wine."

"We heard yesterday that your fingerprints were found on the kitchen counter. When did this occur?"

"Anytime, I surmise. We spent the bulk of our time in her kitchen."

"Are you aware she was found dead *in* her kitchen?" the attorney probed.

Jakob was wholly unperturbed by the indelicate topic. "Of course, madam, I know all the public details of her death. It was impossible not to think of this fact during our extended discourse in that very room."

He had a convincing answer for everything, it seemed. I could only hope that the prosecutor was building up to a grand moment of elucidatory revelation.

"Let's change gears for a moment," she continued, immediately negating that wish. "The entire premise of your story is that the timeline is mutable. From where does that belief arise?"

"Forgive me for saying it, but from superior intelligence, I suppose. Timeline immutability is a delusion that is fed to the masses to ethically justify time travel and dismiss the implications of our downstream actions. You heard it yesterday; even the esteemed Doctor Ravi Sharma admitted his burgeoning doubt. I do not believe in conspiracy, only science, and the so-called experts are simply wrong. I even admit that I fell for it too, for a time.

"Imagine for a moment if the greater populace believed they could affect the future. In the early days, we all witnessed the boldest speculators attempting to make a quick buck with market manipulation or sports gambling. That was but a drop in the bucket. Everybody would have some motive—selfish or altruistic—to change the past. Save a loved one, prevent a catastrophe, become wealthy. I am but the first to act with full knowledge and conviction."

"Interesting," spoke the prosecutor, though her face said the opposite. "So you have the knowledge, and you have the technology. I ask, why Kathryn? An esteemed woman, yes, but still just one person. Why not try to prevent a more impactful tragedy? Countless natural disasters and wars, 9/11, the 2020 or 2031 pandemics? By your logic, you had the unique power to change these."

Jakob took a moment to answer, showing a rare gap in his consistent, studied composure. I had to imagine he was thinking of his fruitless effort to rescue his sister.

"Madam," he said, "I respect the spirit of the question, yet reject the premise. What could be more transformative than allowing our greatest scientist to continue her research? Perhaps we achieve time travel forty years early, prematurely shepherding us into the supposed utopia we enjoy now. Would that not benefit more people than any option you present? I never considered any alternative, and I have no regrets. I will try again the moment we are done here."

"Let's bring it all together. You testified that despite your early return, you were confident that her brush with death had been averted by your presence, and that a new timeline would be created as a result of her survival. If we accept these conditions as indeed true, then I must bluntly ask: Why, sir, is she dead?"

If it hadn't been so wildly inappropriate, I may have considered letting out an "ooooo" of destructive pleasure at the deliciously deep-cutting question.

"Yes, that is the very thing I have been asking myself since my return," Jakob responded, unfazed. "At this time, my leading theory is that a new timeline was indeed branched upon her survival. Yet this version of my consciousness, regrettably, returned to my original timestream."

"You're familiar with Occam's razor, yes? Have you considered the possibility that you simply . . . failed?"

He smiled. "Yes, madam, I am quite familiar with Occam's razor, and though it is commonly understood to mean 'the simplest explanation is the best one,' this is inaccurate. My working theory is in fact reinforced by the very law of parsimony to which you refer."

"Mm-hmm," the prosecutor mumbled. "In this new timeline you supposedly created, aren't you worried about the butterfly effect? What if you or your loved ones don't exist there?"

"Ah, quite the opposite," Jakob shared. "I have no concerns for my personal welfare, only the universal betterment of humankind. As I stated previously, if Kathryn lives, chronophysics inevitably matures that much earlier, and one can extrapolate the rest of the timestream from there. Certainly many of the disasters you mention would naturally be averted altogether."

"What is your ultimate ambition in your career, Mister Olsen?"

"The same answer, I suppose: the universal betterment of mankind, by way of my gifted mind."

"Would you like to be considered the preeminent researcher in your discipline?"

"Absolutely; I believe I already am."

"Do you currently have any recognition in your field? A Nobel prize, or something similarly prestigious within your field?"

"No, not yet. I suspect I will soon, though, yes? I already solved the most formidable challenge in perhaps all the sciences."

"Would you like to be famous?"

"For good reason, yes, certainly. Wouldn't everyone?"

"Would you be content if you successfully saved Kathryn, but nobody knew?"

"Yes," Jakob answered unconvincingly, another slight falter briefly visible in his bravado.

"What about the other way: Would you agree that the individual who did murder Kathryn Simpson would be among the most famous—or infamous—people in the world?"

Jakob looked offended by the implication. "I did not kill her because I wish to be famous, madam, if that's what you're implying." He immediately caught himself, though not before a few muted gasps could be heard.

"Ah, that was quite poorly phrased, I admit," he corrected. "Allow me to restate: I did not kill her, nor would I ever consider such an unspeakable act toward anyone, regardless of any personal gain. But yes, without a doubt, that person would be notorious worldwide."

"Indeed, they would. Thank you, Jakob, that is all." The prosecutor returned to her seat, forcing a look of profound and utterly unearned confidence. It was hard not to be disappointed by the lack of any overwhelming evidence connecting Jakob to Kathryn's death. I had been misled by decades of films to expect a dramatic bombshell, a moment when the tables are turned and the truth is explosively revealed. I suspected I had a daunting task in front of me to convince my fellow jurors of Jakob's furtive guilt.

Judge Kasem called for closing arguments; the end was in sight.

The prosecuting attorney returned to the center of the courtroom, her forced conviction turned up to eleven. A brilliant ray of sunshine shone down through the skylight overhead, highlighting her like a trained spotlight.

"Gentlepeople of the jury," she elocuted, "you now have the facts; a vast collection of evidence and testimony that incontrovertibly point directly to the defendant, Mister Jakob Olsen. The full picture of a man who—by his own admission—is borderline fanatical about the victim. Who has not just the resources and scientific knowledge to attempt to change history, but the grandiose vision of worldwide adulation to think that only he is qualified to do so. We *know* he downstreamed to the night of Kathryn's murder. We *know* he was in her home, spending the bulk of his time in the room where she was found dead. He claims she was alive when he returned, before the fateful night was over. Do you really believe that this man, Kathryn's number one fan, who spent his life's work finding a way to supposedly save her, would accept a partial protection plan?

"Ultimately, when the jury finds him guilty, Mister Olsen will have succeeded in his true mission. He will forever be a household name: the infamous killer of the great Kathryn Simpson. Thank you."

My thoughts exactly. The defense attorney was up next.

"Thank you for your mindful attention, members of the jury, on this groundbreaking case. As a reminder, my client is charged with *temporal murder*, an indictment which has only existed for a few short days. Despite the novelty, the burden of proof is no different now than with any other case. We know Mister Olsen was present in Kathryn's home on that fateful night in 1988, yes. The prosecution has needlessly hammered that point home even as Jakob admits the fact without reservation. Proximity, however, is not proof.

"The prosecution has tried to frame Jakob as a power-hungry mad scientist, a man who focuses his prodigious gifts solely on individual acclaim. Aptitude, also, is not proof. The prosecution has described Jakob as an overzealous, fanatical disciple of Kathryn Simpson, a borderline sociopath who has the maniacal tendencies of someone capable of murder. Passion, jury members, is similarly not proof. Their sensationalist descriptions of

Jakob—while manipulatively exaggerated—do highlight the essence of a man who has the uniquely perfect combination of intellect and verve to pursue something that the world thought was impossible. Why, I ask you jury members, would he risk his career, his relationships, and his unparalleled gifts on an undertaking like this, if *not* to change the past? He may have been unable to save her, regretfully for all of us, but failure . . ." She paused, solemnly nodding to herself. "Failure, too, is *not proof.* Thank you."

"Jurors," the judge said once the defense attorney had taken her seat, "the focus now shifts to you. You will have time and space to discuss and deliberate among yourselves on the lone charge of temporal murder. The decision must be unanimous. Once you have reached a verdict, please inform your jury coordinator and we will reconvene. Thank you. Court is adjourned for today."

I could sense a rustling in the seats around me, an anxiety stemming from the burden now placed upon us. As a whole, the jury of which I was a part felt ludicrously underqualified to decide such a monumental case. And I felt ludicrously underqualified to sway them.

14

Sam and I were alone in conversation on the meandering walk back from the briefing room, where Andrés had informed the jurors of what to expect over the next few days of deliberation. My unlikely friend and I hadn't spoken much since Lisa and I had spontaneously forsaken his tour group for our unguided adventure through eastern Manhattan. Luckily, he didn't seem to carry any lingering resentment, which only strengthened my fondness for him.

"So, how's the trial going?" Sam asked after we had dispensed with the requisite small talk. "I know you can't share any specifics, but you doing alright?"

"So far, so good, thanks. I had fortified myself under the assumption that it was going to take much longer, so it's great to see the light at the end of the tunnel. Now we just have to come to a decision, I guess."

"Yeah, maybe that's the hard part," he responded reassuringly. "Hey, I heard about the disruption at the end of day one. What was that all about?"

It took a lot of restraint not to tell him my full, time-hopping story, but unlike Lisa, Sam surely would be obligated to inform his superiors.

"It was scary, honestly; really scary. Dozens of protestors burst into the room and wouldn't leave," I replied with information he likely already knew. "There was this one guy who stood out among the rest, carrying on his back what looked to me like a high-tech weapon of some sort. Luckily, the bailiff took him down before he could, you know, hurt anyone."

"Yeah, sounds scary indeed! Just glad everyone's okay," Sam said, though his oddly disinterested tone was noticeably less consolatory than his words. "So the guy never got his weapon off, huh? You never saw it light up or anything?"

"No, I don't remember anything like that," I responded truthfully. "I don't want to know what would have happened if he *had* fired it," I added, much less so.

I could only hope the limited acting skills I'd picked up from my high school musical performances were enough to convince Sam of my uninvolvement. It didn't bode well that I had felt more comfortable depicting a going-on-eighteen-year-old Nazi than I was with my current performance, though.

Sam's mention of the protestors prompted a question that had been rattling around since my sojourn to 2087; one which he seemed uniquely qualified to answer.

"There's something I'm not clear on, Sam, and maybe you can help, given your field of interest. A big topic during the trial is whether the past can be changed. I think the term they used repeatedly is 'timeline immutability.' We were told during our orientation here that the timeline is fixed, that you can travel to the past but can't change anything. But Jakob—that's the defendant—

and, um, some other people I've talked to said that you *can* change the past, even hinting at some kind of global conspiracy. It seems like a major thing for everyone not to be sure about."

"Ah, well, you hit the nail on the head, didn't you?" Sam said, a twinkle in his eye. "Let me throw it back at you: Do *you* think you can change the past?"

"No," I responded, "otherwise every time traveler would be rich."

"Ah, that's a particularly concise way to put it, isn't it? Very similar to the sports conversation we had a few days ago."

We came to a wordless halt as we neared my destination, the third rung on the now-repetitive and claustrophobic loop of hotel room, courtroom, cafeteria, and back again.

"One follow-up before I gorge myself with more surprisingly palatable food—"

"You know a robot is cooking it, right?" Sam interjected lightheartedly.

"I . . . did not. So, wait, professional chefs are obsolete too?" I asked.

"Yeah, for the most part. As much as I liked my mom's special unseasoned microwaved green beans, the robots are just plain better."

"What jobs *are* left then?" I joked. "Um . . . accountants?"

Sam shook his head, eyes closed with exaggerated despondence. My mock-frown quickly morphed into a smile.

"So, anyway," I resumed, "you asked me my opinion, but how widespread is the contrarian view actually, regarding the timeline?"

"More widespread than most people believe, I think. And you have to admit, they have a point, right?"

"Do they?"

"Yeah, sure. Think about it: Might it be possible that if there are an infinite number of timestreams out there and we all just happen to be in the one that is somehow unchanged? And we choose to view that as proof of immutability, while meanwhile our actions in the past are branching timestreams with *all kinds* of unpredictable impact. Don't tell anyone at the WCO I said that, by the way. I'd probably be kicked out of my internship merely for acknowledging the idea."

I zipped my lips and bid him farewell, envious that he could leave this stifling building at the end of the day.

A bountiful spread of cheese, meats, fruit, and refreshments were laid out before us; somebody up there did not think we were going to come to a verdict quickly. Only the twelve of us were permitted in the jury room, and seeing the group assembled in such a way served as a disheartening reminder of my natural introversion. Over the course of five days, I'd somehow never spoken directly to at least seven of them—eight if you don't count Paul's near-nude virtual visit—and now I had the self-assigned duty of convincing these near-strangers of the defendant's not-so-obvious guilt.

Ime was selected as our foreperson without objection; unlike me, he was somehow best friends with everyone here. As his first action, he called for a preliminary vote to take the temperature of the room. Unsurprisingly, the vast majority submitted their verdict of not guilty. Only Feng and I—conveniently seated together at the wide head of the rectangular table—had our thumbs pointed downward.

"Let me explain," Feng said, likewise sensing the palpable disappointment from the others that this deliberation was not going to be an abbreviated affair. Lisa glared at me and only me, mildly unamused.

"I openly admit my biases: I'm fully aware I am one of only two here who even knew of Kathryn before this week. And that has shaped my verdict, without a doubt. You must understand, her life—and especially her death—is still a constant topic of discussion, even when I come from. There is a collective guilt that she didn't live to see her work not only validated, but heralded and world-changing. I know the evidence is a bit shaky, and Jakob definitely hired the better lawyer, but still! He was incontrovertibly there, with her, on the night of her death. He openly admits it, and he claims nobody else was there. No other fingerprints were found, no other leads. There is only one possible conclusion in my mind. Prior to Mister Olsen's admittedly convincing testimony, I have to imagine at least a few of you felt the same."

I caught a few reserved nods among the group.

"A fair point, Feng, and thank you for opening up the discussion," Ime responded. "If I may speak for many of my fellow acquiters—apologies if that non-word was untranslatable to your native language—I think it would be helpful to outline *my* position on the matter. As you indicated, there is a distinct lack of evidence directly linking Jakob to the crime. His lawyer put it well: proximity is not a crime, and it certainly isn't proof. Feng, you imply that Jakob deliberately lied on the stand, and while that is possible, I did not feel the same. Taking him at face value, I see a man who—while overzealous and wildly condescending—had good intentions at the core of his actions. Again, the absence of proof linking him to the actual homicidal act is too glaring to ignore. If she was indeed coerced into a drug-induced suicide under threat of violence, I ask: Where is the murder weapon? Where is the motive?"

His point made, Ime grabbed a plate and filled it with a tasteful mix of fruit and cheese. With the dam now broken, most of us followed suit, inviting a temporary lull in the escalating discussion. The tray of food hovered silently over the table surface, automatically gliding to each juror who requested it.

"I'd like to invite anyone else to share their reasoning now," Ime said once we were all sufficiently satiated.

"I'll go," Lisa volunteered through a mouthful of the same delicious smoked gouda that I was actively snacking on. She gave me a quick look before continuing.

"Jakob is the worst; I think we can all agree on that. Remember when he briefly went after his own lawyer? Jeez. I think he is conniving, manipulative, and weird. He's also kind of hot, but that's neither here nor there."

"Um, I thought you voted to acquit?" another juror asked sarcastically.

"Yes, I did, I sure did," she responded. "I'm getting there. While I wouldn't ever want to hang out with him, I have to admit I found his testimony convincing. I didn't see that coming at all, but the story checks out, right? I do think he simply reveres Kathryn Simpson and would go to extreme measures to try to save her, perhaps even inventing a scientific theory to justify it with that whole 'branching timeline' thing."

"Can we talk about that for a minute?" jumped in Feng. "When I come from at least, the whole idea is simply preposterous. I have a lot of trouble believing that anyone—especially a man of science like Jakob Olsen—would subscribe to a theory that so blatantly flies in the face of established thought. Even the MIT professor said that the breakthrough in time travel was only possible because of that discovery. I'm paraphrasing, but he said something like 'chronophysics is grounded by temporal immutability.' Room, can you confirm?"

"Of course, Feng." The walls were talking, something I doubted I would ever quite acclimate to. "The official transcript lists Doctor Sharma's statement as 'temporal immutability is the foundation of the entire field of chronophysics and opened the door for temporal displacement.'"

A new juror chimed in, the surprisingly jovial German woman from the 1970s. "True, but the professor also said he may consider revisiting that theory given Jakob's recent advancements, yes?"

Feng appeared annoyed. As someone wholly allergic to conflict of any kind, I appreciated that she was taking the brunt of the debate.

"How do I say this?" She stared at the empty wall as she took a moment, forming her thoughts. "Our foreperson here just said he didn't think Jakob had a motive. I wholeheartedly disagree, and if anything was disappointed the prosecuting attorney didn't hit this point harder. Like I said earlier, I cannot stress to you quite how renowned everything about Kathryn is. Imagine Einstein, Gandhi, and Superman all rolled into one. That's how most people of the time-travel era see her, and Jakob seemingly takes it even a step further.

"Did you catch his reaction when the lawyer asked if he had any professional awards? He was not pleased, to put it mildly, but tried to mask it as much as possible after his earlier outburst. I think *that* is his truest motivation; maybe not fame in a traditional sense, but some form of recognition, status, acclaim. And I think he saw an opening to achieve it once he had his breakthrough about how to travel to 1988.

"So, putting it all together, I submit that he *knew* he couldn't actually alter the past, and that he traveled back to end her life, not save it, and make sure he got the credit. That would also explain her method of death, right? Coerced into an overdose of sleeping pills? That sounds like the most humane way to go, something he would want for his hero. Maybe he even told himself he was helping her pass peacefully. And back to my original point: I propose that the malleable timeline junk is merely a cover Jakob invented, hoping that all of you time-travel newcomers would accept it at face value from an accomplished scientist like himself. And if you *do* believe this outlandish theory, despite any actual proof, and you're using it to justify his actions, I don't see how you can at the same time claim there's not enough evidence to convict. She's still dead, after all; so you can't have it both ways.

"If you accept that there's one immutable timestream, then it follows that you accept that Jakob knew perfectly well what the end result would be, and therefore, the *only* valid reason to go downstream was to kill her himself. That's what I'm saying, basically. The alternative is that he changed the future with his presence, but we can still refer to the rich tapestry of evidence that still points to Jakob and only Jakob. Not to mention, a decision of 'not guilty' would mean that this jury's decision negates a decade of established, foundational science!"

Probably without realizing it, Feng had risen from her seat and by the end was confidently pacing the room. She sat back down with a sigh of relief as the rest of us processed her persuasive speech. Nobody else spoke for a minute; given how articulate her message was, it was a tough act to follow.

"I admit I did not think of it that way, Feng," Ime commented. "I can't say I agree with some of the extrapolations on his character you made based on a few innocuous comments on the stand, but you make a good point."

"Hey, can I finish my thought?" Lisa asked, not bothering to wait for a response. "What I was going to say, coincidentally, is why does it matter if the multiple-timeline thing is real or not? It only matters what Jakob believes. Even if there is only one timeline, everything he said in court could still be truthful. If he can't save her because of the vaunted laws of time travel or whatever, it doesn't mean he killed her."

"I must say, I was on the fence, and I now plan to switch my vote," shared Paul. Lisa redirected her impatient glare from me to him. "I barely understand most of the science, but frankly, I do not believe this presents an obstacle in my ruling. I have seen too many men like Mister Olsen in my time, and I do now agree there is enough motive and intention. Along with his admission that he was present at the scene of the crime, I believe him guilty."

"Thank you for letting us know, Paul," Ime said authoritatively; leadership suited him well. "We'll conduct another informal vote after everyone who wishes to has had a chance to share their initial reasoning. For now, let's collect our thoughts on the board so we don't lose track throughout the discussion."

Upon Ime's command, the room assistant created a virtual blackboard on the far wall, featuring discrete columns labeled Incriminating and Exculpatory. A superfluous, borderline grating chalk sound accompanied as text was filled in based on the group's most cogent arguments so far.

"Aaron, would you mind taking us through your thought process for your opening decision?" Ime offered, catching me by surprise.

As every face turned toward my direction, I flashed back to this group's very first moments together, when I had invited their derision with an ill-timed utterance. Even after a few days together, the prospect of being able to express rational, compelling viewpoints out loud seemed far-fetched. I would accept somewhat intelligible and lightly dispassionate, honestly. I went into a career in accounting precisely to avoid this situation.

"Um, yeah, of course," I started, trying to organize my thoughts on the fly. It would have been oh so much simpler to instead relay that Jakob had all but admitted his guilt to me directly in the distant future. But alas, we would have to get there the hard way.

"Feng made some great points already, exactly what I was, er, thinking. Let's see. Oh! The murder weapon, right? There's a lack of clarity on that. I am convinced that Jakob lied on the stand, since he obviously wouldn't admit his guilt. But I still think most of what he said is true, especially about his journey to 1988 and other bits and pieces. He made a point to mention taking a knife out of the knife block. A 'chef's knife' specifically, in his pompous way. I'm assuming you can't time travel with a gun, right?" I glanced at Feng for confirmation.

"Right, Aaron, no metal of any kind," she confirmed.

"Okay, so, there's the weapon; he told us without telling us."

"Aaron, I'm not saying you're wrong," Ime stated, clearly about to tell me how I was wrong, "but he said he grabbed that knife for proactive defensive purposes. Even granting you your innate distrust, what leads you to make such a leap of logic?"

"Well, um, again, my premise is that he told us as much of the truth as possible short of actually incriminating himself. So if he did threaten her life with a weapon, I believe that was the one, considering we know he didn't have anything when he jumped."

I was having trouble focusing, locked in my anxious state, but I did catch the phrase "Chef's knife: murder weapon?" as it was digitally scribbled on the chalkboard. At least I had the room assistant's piddling approval, just enough of a confidence boost to embolden me to pursue the chain of thought.

"And yeah, I suppose it is a leap of logic," I continued, "but so is the situation he outlined. He grabs this knife soon after arrival and presumably has it on hand the entire time there. I can accept that Kathryn wouldn't notice it missing, but are we to believe that he either hid a kitchen knife somewhere on his person for hours, or rationalized it to Kathryn somehow? So, um, yeah, that's what I'm thinking, knife-wise."

"Wait, I think you might be onto something there . . . sir," declared the German woman supportively.

"Aaron," I provided. To be fair, I didn't recall her name either.

"Yes, Aaron, you made a good point, and there might be more to it. Room, can you pull up the image of the crime scene?"

A three-dimensional diorama of Kathryn's kitchen appeared above the table, the same one the original detective had used to pinpoint the fingerprint locations.

"There!" she said, pointing to a spot on the floor between the kitchen table and stove.

"Room, can you highlight where Martina is pointing, then zoom in and enhance?" Ime requested.

"Highlight, yes," the room assistant responded, "but I'm afraid I'm unable to zoom and enhance; the image fidelity is too low to extrapolate the missing pixels." Despite that limitation, there remained no doubt: a large knife was plainly visible in the spotlit area, resting unperturbed on the kitchen floor.

"It doesn't prove anything," said Martina, "but I do think this strengthens Aaron's point. It's hard for me to imagine a situation in which he departs her home in the prepared, cordial manner he described, yet leaves the knife on the floor. I acknowledge that this does not preclude the same knife being used as the murder threat weapon by *someone else*, but that does feel like a stretch, yes?"

"Yeah, and you know what else?" Another thought had occurred to me, building on the momentum from my surprisingly successful start. "I think he also lied about his arrival. I don't know about what it's like where—or when, really—you come from, but back in the '80s, we didn't simply open our door for anyone who popped by our home, especially not a woman on her own at night. For those that don't know California geography, Berkeley's neighboring city is Oakland, which in my time at least was one of the least safe cities in the country. So I don't think she happily welcomed with open arms some stranger with a flimsy excuse for being there, especially at that time of day."

"Ugh," Lisa groaned reluctantly. "Aaron's right. I truly hate to admit it, but he is. There's no way I'd let anyone in *my* apartment—I agree with that—but there's even more to it. Aaron, you forgot a key fact that the original investigator shared: there were signs of a forced entry, and Jakob's fingerprints were on the front doorknob. Jakob even testified that he *almost* broke in; maybe that was another case of truth-telling up to the limit of admission. God damnit Aaron, you and your incoherently persuasive points," she concluded. The rest of the room, unfamiliar with our unique rapport, looked confused.

Ime brought us back to center. "I acknowledge that the presence of his fingerprints on the doorknob is certainly noteworthy, but once again, it could be circumstantial, or further proof that the true murderer arrived after Jakob left."

"That's actually the thing that stands out to me the most," I said.

"What is?" Ime fired back.

"'After Jakob left.' I still don't understand that part. He said he jumped back to '88 nearly immediately after all the tests passed, knowing full well that he couldn't stay the entire night. Can you remind me his exact words on this, er, Room?"

"Absolutely, Aaron," Room responded with the familiar catchphrase. This particular assistant must have been talking to Wally, or were they one and the same? I planned to look into the question later. "Mister Olsen's statement was 'I was unable to create a stable temporal field of indefinite length. My return time was fixed from the moment I arrived.'"

"Right, and I have to admit my thought at the moment was 'that's fair,' considering he had just achieved something scientifically monumental. But I don't think it holds up under even minimal scrutiny. This is a man who dedicated a large chunk of his life to supposedly *saving* his hero. Yet he didn't have the determination to solve this one last hurdle, the one that would ensure that he could be present throughout the fateful night?"

"We can't fault him for being impatient," suggested Felipe, who had been enthusiastically nodding along with every speaker throughout our debate. "An abbreviated time is still much better than nothing."

"This isn't just impatience, it's imprudence," I retorted, hoping someone would appreciate the wordplay as much as I did. "If there's one thing I've learned about time travel, both real and fictional, it's that there's *always more time*. He could have taken a few more days, weeks, even years to figure out how to stay the full night, and *then* traveled back to the very same moment. So why didn't he, I ask? Because he never intended to save her, and thus didn't have any reason to delay his jump to iron out those last few hurdles." I was in such a zone that I even cogently employed the word 'thus' for the first time in my life!

"Now that, Aaron, is an excellent point."

Ime had said the words, but I could tell that he spoke for the majority. The automated blackboard notes behind him brimmed with unofficial endorsement.

"I'd like to call for another vote and see where we are."

15

Back in the courtroom for the last time, the jury members solemnly took our seats, fully aware our adventure in 2042 was coming to a close. For me, the realization was met with bittersweet relief. On one hand, I dreaded the prospect of saying goodbye to my small group of new friends; this unique experience had been brief, yet intensely unifying. On the other, I was emotionally exhausted and entirely homesick. Lisa had seen it early; there was a numbing banality to the utopian future that counteracted its paradisiacal intention. Maybe I was extrapolating too much from my individual experience, but it felt like the edges of human experience had eroded away, leaving just the sterile, gray middle. I couldn't wait to return home, if only to feel those extremes again, the highs and the lows.

It was little comfort in the moment knowing that none of my memories or sentiments would persist once my precious neurons were expunged. Still, I remained cautiously optimistic for the unaware, orthopedically enhanced Aaron, who would continue into 1985 and beyond. Ignorance is bliss, as they say.

If the jury box was lightly downhearted about the impending end, Jakob projected the sheer opposite. Here was a man fully convinced of his imminent acquittal, something his lawyer had surely reinforced as well. I felt like I could read his mind: visualizing the near future, seeing himself triumphantly cascade down the (non-existent) courthouse steps with a horde of press begging to hear of his miraculous journey to the twentieth century. He would write his long-awaited, best-selling memoir, telling the eager masses precisely what Kathryn was *really* like. And maybe get a creepy, isolated cottage in the English countryside to occasionally escape from the adoring public.

"All rise," the bailiff declared in now-familiar ritual. "Judge Kasem presiding."

"Thank you, Bailiff, and thank you, jurors, you may be seated," she began. "As this trial reaches its conclusion, I once again want to express my sincerest gratitude, jury members, for your service in this grand experiment. I truly hope we never need to conduct another temporal court, but if we do, your professionalism, integrity, and resilience have set the highest possible standard. That said; foreperson, has the jury made a unanimous decision?"

"We have, Your Honor," Ime replied assertively. He handed over the envelope, which contained our verdict, signed by each of us.

"This trial has been nothing but unusual, and now I need to ask for one more such occurrence. To ensure the final verdict remains confidential, I invite all non-essential personnel to depart the room. We cannot risk a leak into the timestream that would pollute the judicial process. That includes the bailiff and court reporter, please."

With a huff, a dozen people exited, leaving only the judge, jury members, lead attorneys, and, of course, Jakob himself. The judge inelegantly flicked her wrist at the ceiling, an unfamiliar gesture I initially struggled to understand. Gradually, the overhead skylights dimmed to near-opaque, casting the courtroom into an eerie yet perhaps appropriate gloom.

"Apologies for the high security, but the WCO has wisely advised that we maintain strict protocols for this portion of the trial. Similarly, I must remind all still present that under international law, it is a violation to discuss the verdict or sentencing you hear today with anyone. This is punishable—at minimum—by disconnection from all public networks and resources, including medical scanners and time machines."

The judge carefully opened the envelope and scanned its contents. If the decision surprised her, she hid it well, though I may have caught the slightest hint of a smile in the corner of her mouth.

"In the absence of the usual court staff, I will now state the jury's verdict." Jakob sat straight up, a ball of kinetic energy just waiting to detonate.

"Jakob Olsen, on the charge of temporal homicide, the jury finds you . . . *guilty*." An involuntary gasp escaped from his attorney as Jakob shot out of his seat.

"No, no, no. Friends, you are wrong." He took a belligerent step toward the bench. "This is an outrage!" he shouted to everyone and no one. He hesitated, instead falling back and collapsing into his chair; I suppose hyper-geniuses can process the stages of grief that much faster than the rest of us. The attorneys shared a quick look of mutual relief that they weren't going to have to hold back a fiercely indignant Scandinavian.

Upon the judge's request, Ime verbally confirmed our verdict, sinking Jakob deeper in his seat, head in hands.

"Mister Olsen, given the circumstances, your sentencing will take place forthwith." The judge turned to face us. "Jury, depending on where and when you're from, you may be expecting mandated incarceration; however, this is no longer accepted best practice, even for homicide cases. For the official record, I hereby order Jakob Olsen to be discharged from his position at the World Chronology Organization and barred from any future position in the field of chronophysics. Mister Olsen will bestow all of his private research to the WCO. Furthermore, he is to be blacklisted from any form of time travel, both recreational and academic. These rulings will be publicly evident and may be perceived as a sign of Mister Olsen's guilt, so let it be known that a similar decision would have occurred regardless of the final verdict, with the blessing of Mounira Calwi, WCO Director.

"The rest of the sentencing will remain unknown publicly. Mister Olsen's implant will be over-coded with monitoring software, which will enforce strict compliance with probationary directive. Mister Olsen is additionally required to conduct biweekly in-home therapy with a dedicated, secure bot. Mister Olsen is barred from publishing or otherwise sharing his experience from 1988.

"This decision is final and unappealable. The verdict and sentencing are to be sealed until January 1, 2086—the Cutoff—at which point concern about timestream contamination diminishes."

Throughout sentencing, Jakob never lifted his head off the table. His lawyer was subtly inching away from him, her well-funded support drawing to a close along with the trial.

"I just wanted to save her," he finally muttered; one last resigned, pleading gasp.

———

For the final time, Andrés welcomed us back to the jury room. Even Mounira graced us with her presence, an appropriate bookend to a singularly novel experience.

"Jurors, your service is now complete," she declared. "On behalf of Andrés, myself, and the entire WCO, I cannot express the great debt that we owe you. I wish you the best of luck in *your* future, and perhaps for a few of you, our paths may cross again in mine. If you opted to receive a medical scan, I hope you flourish with renewed vigor. My only regret is that you cannot retain the memories of your exemplary work. We truly could not have handpicked a more honorable, amicable group than the twelve of you. All that said, it is with endless gratitude that I now bid you a fond farewell."

"Thank you, Mounira," Andrés shared as she departed. "Our time here is nearly over, and we will soon be taking you in small groups to the time-travel facility for immediate return to your orgtime. I welcome you to say your parting words to each other at this time."

Before anyone had a chance, Lisa politely raised her hand.

"Will we be returning to our rooms first?" she asked.

"Lisa, no; per WCO regulations, we need to return you to your orgtime as soon as possible to minimize timestream impact. Take comfort that the raw materials of your provided belongings and wardrobe will be rapid-recycled for the next occupant."

"Yeah, I don't care about that; I just want to say goodbye to Arnie."

"Sorry, who?" Andrés asked, thoroughly confused. "Ah, right, your virtual assistant, yes." I caught a few others nodding in support. I wouldn't mind saying goodbye to Wally myself; he'd been my most consistent companion over the last week.

"I can set that up for you, yes. Give me a moment . . ." He

trailed off as he interfaced with his implant, eyes darting around unpredictably. "Okay, anyone who wishes to speak with their personal assistant may do so now. You are each set up with an isolated, narrow-band audio interface."

"Wally?" I cued; I couldn't help but feel self-conscious speaking aloud in the otherwise silent room.

"Yes, Aaron, it's Wally, I'm here. I heard the trial is over; congratulations! You can return home now!" As always, I imagined an anthropomorphized version of the AI carrying a permanent, lopsided grin.

"Thanks Wally, I'll, um, miss you, I suppose. Thanks for all your . . . assistance." Around me, nearly all of my peers were deep in private conversation with no one, just like I was.

"Absolutely, Aaron, I'll miss you too."

"One minute," Andrés warned us.

"Hey Wally, can you do me one last favor?" I inquired, speaking quickly to make sure I squeezed the request in before the allotted time ran out.

"Absolutely, Aaron."

"This is a little awkward, but . . . if I'm still alive right now, in 2042, I mean, and I don't want to know if I am, but could you send old-me a message about what I did here? Spare no detail; I have a feeling I'll find it fascinating. How old would I be now, ninety-something?"

"Yes, you would be ninety-one, in fact! Regarding the message, I will verify with my ancillary compliance protocols. If such an action is permitted, then it would be my honor, Aaron, to contact you."

"Thank you so much. This way, I figure, I can forget the whole thing happened a whole other time! Get it? It's a dementia joke."

"Got it. Although most neurodegenerative diseases were cured in—"

"Goodbye, Wally, thanks again!" I intervened, preempting the meandering explanation.

"Absolutely, Aaron, and goodbye, my friend."

———

The first batch of jurors made their way out the door, one short walk away from their return home. I had little to no relationship with any of them, opting to go with generic platitudes such as "nice to meet you" and "great work" as they made their way around the table. I instinctively adopted the same rote, mumbled tone as at the end of my childhood Little League games. Two-four-six-eight; who do we appreciate? Pre-1980 jurors!

Lisa was included in the second departing group, and once she had released Paul with an affectionate tap on the rear, I sidled in next to her.

"You gonna miss me?" I teased.

"Yes, indeed I am, Aaron. C'mon, I'm not *always* sarcastic," she added in response to my exaggerated astonishment.

"Okay then, fine, I guess I have to say it also: I'm gonna miss you too. Hey, will you look me up in 1994? Or better yet, just catch me on NBC on Thursdays? I assume my comedy career will have taken off by then."

"Ha, yeah, you're a regular Jim Carrey." I hoped that was a compliment. "Seriously though, I know we won't remember this whole thing, or even this conversation, but I do want to say that your friendship meant a lot, and maybe if there is a higher power up there, then we'll get to have some kind of serendipitous meetup and do it all again."

"I sure hope so," I replied affectionately. "You made this

experience fun—other than the whole murder trial thing, I suppose—and opened my eyes to another way of living with your whole *carpe diem* vibe. Maybe I'll even break a rule one day and think of you."

"I truly hope you do. Well, thanks for everything, 'thank you guy.' Take care." She smiled sweetly and gave me an unexpected peck on the cheek, then strolled over to say her farewells to a few others before departing in style with an embellished curtsy.

Once her trio was led out the door, only four of us remained. Among the twenty-first century trio of Ime, Feng, and the elusive cloud engineer, I was a conspicuous outlier. I wished my best to each of them and waited patiently for the WCO staffer to fetch us. Though by now I was a certified time-travel pro, I still felt the customary apprehensive jitters build until my whole body was shaking uncontrollably. I took in deep, peaceful breaths to try to combat it, to limited effect.

Finally, it was time. As I stood up, I looked around the featureless boardroom and wordlessly broadcast my final thoughts on my time here: pride that we put a guilty man behind proverbial bars, fulfillment that I was one of the lucky few who was chosen to participate, and hope that humanity had maybe figured things out for good.

At the door, the staffer politely stopped me. "Sorry, Mister Barnett, just a few more minutes for you. Please wait here for the next team member."

"Can I ask why?" I questioned, shell shocked.

"I'm not sure," he responded, "only following orders. I don't think you'll need to wait very long."

"Oh . . . kay," I mumbled, trying to rationalize the oddity of the circumstances. "Well, bye Ime, bye Feng, good luck with everything." They seemed equally confused about my predicament as they waved back, leaving me completely on my own.

Apprehension building, I thought about all the reasons I may have been singled out. Did they know I had been upstreamed and were merely waiting until after the trial concluded to fully interrogate me? After all, I had quite blatantly broken the law in future London. I hadn't really processed the full implication before, but I was technically an international fuel smuggler now, on top of being a run-of-the-mill police drone evader. But no, there would be no way for that information to be sent back; it occurred after the Cutoff.

Worse yet, what if there was a problem with the return process? Maybe there was a lunar eclipse in 1985 that briefly scrambled the fourth dimension, and I would be stuck here forever? *No*, I told myself, *you're just freaking out. Get a grip, take another deep breath.*

The doorknob rattled, snapping me out of my tailspin. Even in the depths of raw panic, my brain still took a moment to be surprised that the humble doorknob persisted; I would have expected everything would be whoosh-doors by now.

"Aaron!" a familiar voice said before popping into view in the doorframe. "Hey man, so sorry to keep you waiting." It was Sam! A friend, a confidante, and most importantly: an intern. I may be insignificant, but even *my* measly arrest would warrant more than an intern. The pent-up anxiety rapidly melted away as he emerged into the room.

"What . . . what are you doing here?" I asked, completely unable to hide the unadulterated relief in my voice.

"I'm going to take you back. Back to 1985, I mean. By special request!"

"Oh—that's great! Maybe a little warning next time though, so I'm not sitting here alone in a pool of my own panic-induced sweat?"

"Oh, my colleague didn't tell you I was coming? It definitely wasn't supposed to be some big secret. Anyway, I'm here: ta-da! You ready to go home?"

"I am. I really, really am." I stood up, took one last look around, and headed out the door, tapping the doorknob on my way out. The walk was short, though even with Sam by my side, I still was compelled to stare at the floor for directions; the habit was fully ingrained. I realized if I had ever had to navigate the repetitive hallways of this monolithic building on my own, I would have been disoriented in seconds. Like many of the modern novelties, the projection provided massive convenience in exchange for near total dependence.

"You know, I've never actually sent anyone back in time before," Sam shared. "I thought, who better to start with than a friend?"

As amiable as the thought was, it was not exactly comforting to hear. Sam seemed wholly unfazed by the possibility of potentially vaporizing me into atomic oblivion.

"You've, um, had training, right?" I confirmed.

"Don't worry," he said with a chuckle, "the computer does all the work; I only press a button."

"Okay, good. I wasn't worried," I lied. We had transitioned to a new building in the meantime; less luxury hotel, more futuristic laboratory. "Sam, I gotta say, it's been really nice getting to know you a bit. I never thought I'd form a friendship with someone seventy years younger than me. Best of luck to you with the rest of your program here and college and beyond. I'm sure you'll do great things."

"Thanks, Aaron, I really appreciate that. I'm sure you will as well. And we are here!"

He opened a door to a spartan yet high-tech room. The all-too-familiar transparent tube lay at the center, surrounded by an array of brightly lit screens, nary a physical button or wire in sight. The juxtaposition between this and Jakob's patchwork setup in his remote cottage renewed my copious relief that I had made it back here in one piece.

"Sam," I remarked, "before we go in there, can you answer one quick thing: Why me?"

"What do you mean?" he queried, gesturing for elaboration.

I tried to summon up all the earnestness I could. "Why was *I* chosen for this? Am I actually special in some way like they kept telling us, or am I just a name drawn out of a hat?"

"Which answer would you prefer?" Sam asked rhetorically. I wouldn't have been able to choose, anyway. "If you want to reduce a complex supercomputer's algorithm to a hat, then it's that one. Sounds weird to say this to a friend, but no, you're not special. At least, not in that way. Anything they told you was just puffery to get you to stay in '42 and fulfill the obligation. They didn't even look at personal history, ostensibly to remove any possible biases, so you really were no more than a name, coordinates, and timestamp in a massive database. But hey, that doesn't mean you're not significant and memorable to me." Sam winced. "Poor choice of words, I admit."

"That's okay, you're memorable to me too, at least for another minute or two." I let out a deep sigh. "Well, take care, Sam. I'm ready; ready to go home."

We shared a heartfelt handshake before he beckoned me into the booth and took a seat at the computer station, punching in some commands on a touchscreen. The banks of displays surrounding the time machine sprang to life with indecipherable techno-gibberish.

"Alright, let's do this. Gotta start with some boilerplate stuff first. You are Aaron Barnett, of sound mind and body, and you consent to this displacement through time?"

"I do."

"And do you have any metal objects on your person?"

"Nope."

Sam looked up at me with a smirk. "Actually, there are about three more pages of this, plus all the safety briefings. Let me speed it up: Do you want to go home?"

"Very much so."

"Alright," he said after swiping the remainder of the travel authorizations away. "October 19, 1985. This one's actually worth double-checking. Is that correct?"

"It is."

"Nineteen. Eighty. Five," he slowly repeated to himself, eyes narrowed in concentration as he tried to conceal a quick glance in my direction. While I stood fixed in the cramped, claustrophobic tube, he moved over to another console and hurriedly entered some unseen commands. He locked eyes with me; a mix of dread, hope, and conviction evident on his youthful face, finger resting on the button that would finally send me home. Sensing his hesitation, I gave him a subtle nod of friendly encouragement.

With a tap, the totality of light in the universe dissolved into the void, leaving behind only Sam's final, haunting words.

"You can save her."

PART 3

16

___

Cold. That was my first thought; a chill on exposed toes, a frigid dryness in the air. I was lying in my bed, Jennifer asleep to my side, the morning birds outside the apartment chirping a familiar song to the nearing dawn.

I had been a twenty-first-century resident for over a week, and not once had the ambient temperature been even slightly outside my comfortable range, not even for a moment. This was my *second* thought, as full consciousness slowly reemerged.

Twenty-first century! I bolted upright, inadvertently smacking Jennifer, who grumbled and slid me some excess blanket. The memories came flooding back in such force that I didn't even have time to convince myself it was just an intensely vivid dream. I remembered everything: Wally, the medbay, Central Park, the trial. And Lisa, who admittedly did have a certain dreamlike quality to her.

I quietly climbed out of bed, waking an excited Rex who now expected an immediate walk outside. First, I needed to confirm it was all real. So I squatted; a simple bend of the knees. First once, then a few more for good measure. No clicks, no pain, much confusion.

How was this possible? The first fact I had learned in the future was that the entire experience would soon be unlearned. No, *how* was the wrong question; Sam had done something, that much was obvious. The better question was *why*, and I was not nearly lucid enough to start going down that path quite yet.

I snuck out of the room and prepared myself a cup of coffee, still feeling unusually groggy. I couldn't tell if that was because I had been asleep for eight days (from a certain point of view), or if I was overly habituated to the pampered wake-up routine Wally had provided. I sat down with the morning paper in a vain attempt to reconnect to the present. *My* present, I had to remind myself. I never truly belonged in the future, yet reacclimation was so far much more challenging than I had expected. Another reason for the standard memory wipe, I figured.

After some time, Jennifer joined me, helping herself to a cup as well. She looked sluggish too; I must have woken her prematurely. To her, this was merely another day; we would each soon depart for our respective jobs with a detached peck on the cheek, reconvene for dinner and some rote conversation recapping said mundane jobs, cuddle for an hour or two on the couch, and then do it all again the next day.

For me, though, she was a true sight for sore eyes, a steady beacon of light after a week on unknown seas. I suddenly had an urge to immediately tell her everything; we could both call in sick and I could regale her with every unbelievable event I'd just experienced. Unbelievable was perhaps too apt a word; I still had minimal faith that she—or anyone—would accept the story. A few pain-free squats likely wouldn't be convincing enough as corroboration.

I stood up and lovingly wrapped my arms around Jennifer from behind, startling her out of her early morning haze.

"Aaron, c'mon, what are you doing?" she asked as she pivoted within my tight embrace. "Let me at least get some coffee down first." Face to face, she did a double take, as if she was seeing me for the first time. I released her from my affectionate hold, alarmed by her unexpected reaction.

"Did you . . . put on makeup or something?" she asked, taking a step back.

"Nope. What are you talking about?"

"You look, well, great, honestly. Must have just woken up on the right side of the bed. And maybe you could share some of whatever your magic skin care product is."

I had entirely forgotten that the medbay had performed some minor facial work. I now wore the unblemished face I had always pictured in my mind's eye, the airbrushed version of what nature provided. And thanks to the future tech, today they were one and the same, perhaps decoding why it felt so unremarkable to me.

"Oh, yeah. Thanks, Jen! I, um, actually have something quasi-related that I want to talk to you about. It's not quite on the topic of skin care, though, sorry."

"Not to be rude, love, but can it wait? You know quite well I have that big presentation to Phil and Andrew, so I want to get ready early to get in some extra prep."

"Yeah, okay, no problem. Raincheck, tonight? I'll pick something up from Jimmy's and we can have a special dinner and catch up on everything. Or better yet, I'll cook."

"Jimmy's sounds good, sure." That was the correct decision; I was no Jimmy in the kitchen, nor did I employ any robo-chefs to pick up the slack. "I could use something unhealthy and delicious after what I'm sure is about to be a very stressful day," she added.

If she had previously informed me of this particular presentation, the memory was long gone. It felt like the eight days in the future had pushed everything else out of my brain. And now I was expected to suddenly return to tedious normalcy, the knowledge of humanity's future weighing on me like an anchor behind my back. During the abundant downtime, I had occasionally asked Wally to catch me up on world history, show an interesting documentary, or expound on twenty-first-century scientific progress. Many times, I regretted the request, feeling like I was buried under a growing mountain of human suffering and strife—wars, pandemics, natural disaster, politics. Yet it always turned around in 2033, the future bringing salvation to the past.

I knew exactly what I had to look forward to—video games and the Web seemed like upcoming standouts—but I also knew what I had to dread. Adding a few existential sprinkles on top of my existing anxiety was not a great recipe for success.

Admittedly, there was some comfort knowing that there was nothing I could do. Immutable timeline and all of that might imply an absence of free will, as Ime had once astutely observed, but at least that freed me from any burden to attempt to change things.

After an unsatisfying shower (one measly nozzle!), I put on some worn-down workout clothes and stepped outside with Rex for a jog in the brisk October air, wishing Jennifer good luck on my way out the door. This simple act had been my north star throughout my stay in the twenty-first century, keeping me centered through the ups and many downs. By minute ten, I was cold, drenched in sweat, and uncomfortable, yet for the first time in a long time, I was truly home.

I called in sick to work—*cough, cough*—and started planning out the rest of my life. By conscious request, Wally had never divulged an iota of knowledge covering my personal future, so my destiny was unsealed.

First step: financial security. I hadn't bothered to research anything that would be particularly useful with an eye toward speculation, so I worked with the limited information I did have. I called up a stockbroker friend and bought ten thousand dollars' worth of shares balanced among a handful of tanking companies I knew to be omnipresent sixty years later. His increasingly pleading counsel to consider other options fell on deaf ears. I could only hope I would start to profit off these investments while I still had plenty of time to enjoy it.

With that done, I grabbed a sheet of paper and scribbled down every relevant date and fact I could remember. I was gifted with my memory for a reason, and I refused to squander the opportunity with insufficient preparation. Most of the general-purpose knowledge would prove to be entirely useless, I knew, but at least I wouldn't find myself in New York in sixteen years, nor take frequent vacations to certain parts of the Middle East. For good measure, I included every detail that applied to Kathryn: where she worked, lived, and the unfortunate circumstances of her death. I delicately folded the invaluable page and tucked it deep into my already overstuffed wallet for safekeeping.

"You can save her." The words still reverberated through my head on a loop, a permanent echo sent from the distant future. I tried my best to repress them. I couldn't remotely understand why Sam made the choice he did. I just hoped he was okay and hadn't sacrificed his budding career for nothing. Because, in fact, I could not save her; her death, regrettably, was set in stone. Jakob's guilt demonstrated this; the whole concept of the fixed timeline proved to be the principal argument for conviction, after all.

Further validation of this came in my endeavors to contact a younger Lisa. I knew she lived in Los Angeles at this point of her life, though she'd yet to settle into her lucrative career managing television ad placement. I started with a call to my only contact in the area, a college roommate who was quite surprised to hear from me after nine quiet years. The oddity of my request didn't help: the phone number of every Lisa Barnes he could find in his local white pages.

I sat down in my favorite chair—Rex on one side, push-button telephone on the other—and proceeded down the list, twenty-two in all. Of the handful that answered, none were the right Lisa. I knew from the beginning this was a futile effort; the time-hopping 1994 version was fully unaware of me, a foolproof indicator that we had never met prior. Not to mention, *my* Lisa would never deign to speak to a strange, uninteresting man calling from Chicago. Fate would conspire to keep us apart, I acknowledged with resignation, though I didn't regret the attempt. Until I had to pay my long-distance phone bill, at least.

More than once throughout the day, I called out to Wally for assistance, cruelly reminded of his absence during the embarrassed silence that followed. By the end of my time in 2042, I had somehow begun to take for granted having the entirety of human knowledge available at my fingertips. I consciously knew I could no longer order the perfect meal, nor enjoy whichever incredible sci-fi movie had been curated for me; instead, it was the little things that were most frustrating, such as when I hoped to find out which region a particular area code corresponded to during my Lisa search. I imagined such informational convenience would have also gone a long way toward mitigating the unnecessary arguments Jennifer and I often got into about frivolous subjects like the age of various celebrities.

She returned home as the last bit of sunlight began to recede. The phone calls had taken up a good chunk of the day—Lisas were a loquacious bunch, it seemed—but true to my word, I had picked up our favorite lasagna and eggplant parmesan. I tried my best to amp up the romance factor: candles, flowers, even our folded cloth napkins, which had never before seen the light of day. The environment had to be just right for Jen to meet the new me: stronger-willed, somewhat in touch with my emotions, perhaps even borderline gregarious.

"How was your presentation?" I asked as she sat down and helped herself to some delicious, overpriced Italian food.

"You know, it went pretty well; thanks for asking. Andrew said the investors were impressed by our value-add opportunity, and the synergy between . . ."

I nodded along as she continued, doing my best to be supportive while absorbing absolutely nothing. I was busy mentally preparing a presentation of my own, a lightly substantiated story straight out of a rejected script for a low-budget sci-fi miniseries. Should I tell her about Lisa, which might trigger an unwarranted jealousy reflex? Or about my unsolicited side-adventure in the deep future, involuntarily supporting chrono-extremists? No, simple is better; superfluous detail will only serve to diminish the already strained credibility.

"Jen," I began, taking a deep breath, "there's something I need to tell you, and it would probably be best if you let me finish before you ask the many inevitable questions you will have."

"Aaron, there's something I need to tell you too, and I think it would probably be best if I went first."

"Um, okay."

"I think we should break up."

"Wait, what?" I was flabbergasted, to say the least; struggling to rationalize why she would declare this now of all days, when I was on the verge of boldly stepping forward as a new, slightly changed man.

"It's not you, Aaron, it's me. Really, I mean it. I think I need to be with someone more . . . exciting. It's not your fault, but you're *you*, you know? Mister Suburban Accountant, nine-to-five, gray suit. The most spontaneous thing you've ever done is what, stay up past ten?"

"But . . . why? Why now? Why today? Maybe if you let me tell you my thing, you'll change your mind." I still was reeling from the blindside, and it showed.

"I don't think so, Aaron. I know you're having an off day today, and I'm genuinely sorry to make it weirder, but I have what, three years of evidence? Nothing you say now can override that, so for both of our sakes, don't bother. I only regret not doing it earlier. The success of that presentation really gave me the adrenaline boost I needed to finally rip off the bandage."

I couldn't go down without trying. "Jen," I said, laying the sincerity on thick, "last night I traveled sixty years into the future—"

"Okay, nope, not doing this," she interrupted, preempting any further elucidation with a deadly look I had seen too many times before. "I truly hope we can stay friends, but I need you and Rex out of here by the end of the week, okay? Let's just keep things clean, simple, and minimize the acrimony, okay?"

The war was lost, that much was clear. I felt dismayed, yet oddly unsurprised. We had shared many reasonably good years together, though Jennifer had somehow never felt like "the one." Regardless, I had always envisioned us getting married in the near future, honeymooning in Paris like we always dreamed about, following the fixed course that societal norms had mapped for us the moment we said "I love you."

As the shock slowly receded, a feeling of unfettered volition superseded it. Me, boring? This century-hopping, fuel-smuggling time juror? No, my dear Jen, I had learned a thing or two from Lisa in the art of spontaneity. I had plenty of money saved up, a partial map of the future, and nothing in Chicago tying me down anymore. There was another path out there for me, forged by the unlikeliest of circumstances. Perhaps timelines could change after all.

"You can save her."

Sam's words returned in full force, shaking me from my short-lived funk and into clear-eyed certainty. I now knew my destiny after all, and who cares if the laws of chrono-whatever allowed it? I needed to at least try. I needed to save Kathryn.

17

_____

By the start of the weekend, my life was thoroughly uprooted. Rex and I were on our way to California, leaving behind a stable job and an utterly confused group of extended family. And Jen, of course, though she may have been the least surprised of them all when I declared my westward plans.

"You're kidding!" she responded as I sealed up my last remaining box of books. "Is this just because I called you a bland automaton?"

"No, it was not that at all, and I'm pretty sure you chose different words at the time. And to be honest, you were spot on anyway. I keep trying to tell you though: I've changed."

"Yeah, okay. I'll believe it when I see it. What are you going to do when you're out there? For work, I mean?" she asked.

A fair question. I had been at my company for eleven years, a stalwart of consistency and professionalism. When I strutted into my boss's office and turned in my notice, he politely refused to accept it as anything more than a cruel prank for at least ten minutes. My similarly staid colleagues wished me well on my last day, though there was an undertone of bewildered apprehension when I informed them that I had nothing else lined up.

I wasn't being purely impulsive; my natural instinct to over-plan was still intact. And I had plenty of time to do so on the multi-day trek along the nearly complete I-80. I'd never driven west of Omaha before, and my mind naturally began to wander while passing by the endless brown fields. At least Rex didn't seem to mind, his floppy ears waving through the crisp autumn air of the open passenger window. The monotony of the journey triggered a longing for the picturesque green hills of England, not to mention a luxurious car that could take care of the driving.

By the end of the trek, I was exhausted, unkempt, and aching for a real cup of coffee, but I had made it. The calm water of the San Francisco Bay glistened brilliantly when viewed from my East Bay destination, forcing me to squint to see the famous Golden Gate Bridge and city skyline near it. Basking in the temperate setting sun, I wondered why anyone would ever choose to live anywhere else.

Within days, I had secured a cheap rental on the outskirts of Berkeley, close enough that I could visit campus when needed, but far enough that I wouldn't be surrounded by obnoxiously naïve students at all times. Rex appreciated the abundance of new smells, never once questioning why we were suddenly living in an entirely different city. He was a loyal companion through and through.

I filed paperwork for my new private practice: Futureproof Accounting, LLC. Corny, yes, but I was proud of the name. I planned to take on a limited group of clients, just enough to sustain a modest livelihood while funneling a small portion into the stock market, still blindly relying on the future of the same few struggling corporations. I calculated that I could work roughly twenty hours a week following this pattern; nine-to-five Aaron was officially dead. Except during tax season, of course. As the old accountant saying goes: there is no escaping that.

I tried my best to embrace the California lifestyle. For the first time in my life, I went more than a day without shaving and soon enough sported a healthy beard to go along with an increasingly untamed haircut. I hiked every mountain I could; first alone, then later with some like-minded friends I made in local accountant circles. I have a type; what can I say? I jogged along the Berkeley marina waterfront daily, continually stretching my range as the autumn season began to wane. Eventually, Rex bowed out as my loyal running partner once I started to regularly break the five-mile mark.

The choice to relocate had been assertive and abrupt, but there remained plenty that I missed from home. Real winter, for one; the northern California version was just a few pockets of rain and slightly less optimal temperatures. And while I thoroughly enjoyed the far superior ethnic food, I deeply yearned for the deep-dish pizza that had been an indulgent staple since childhood. And of course I missed my hometown family, friends, and sporting events.

Fortunately, I didn't have to wait too long to be reunited with any of it. I never intended to decisively renounce my old life, though many reacted to my news as if that were the case. So I returned for Thanksgiving, and Christmas a few weeks after that. I was overjoyed to see my sister at both events, my best friend and staunchest supporter. She eagerly inquired about my new life in California without any of the veiled condescension that almost everyone else exuded. For the most part, they seemed to be projecting their own envy onto me; most people don't get an opportunity to start over.

I never saw Jennifer again, though some mutual friends informed me that she was happily going steady with a new colleague from her company's merger. She had been right about the synergy after all.

I gave myself three months to settle into my new life, and as 1986 rolled around, it was time to increase my attention toward Kathryn. Her murder was still over two years away, so I knew there was little I could accomplish now, but I didn't want lack of preparation to be a potential reason for failure.

I began with deliberate circumspection, passively observing her movements from an obscured vantage point on a lovely bench outside the physics building. Even from afar, she carried an aura of innate brilliance. Her cogitative strolls across the courtyard gave the impression that she was perpetually engrossed in solving complex equations in her head. Maybe I was glimpsing the unassuming genesis of time travel. Until a student approached, at least, when she would snap into unbridled, genuine affability.

Among the hordes of undergraduates, staff, and faculty that swarmed the campus, Kathryn was as nondescript as could be. She was a bit older than the manipulative photograph that had been shown in court: her short, bushy hair had gone fully gray, and a pair of unflattering glasses permanently decorated her lived-in face. Yet she carried herself with a verve and energy that matched or even exceeded the passionate descriptions her disciples had espoused in the courtroom.

As I finished reading countless novels over many weeks of remote observation, I began to work up the courage to advance to a slightly more active form of reconnaissance. I imagined the envy of the twenty-first-century population, many of whom would have killed for a chance to meet their hero and indirect savior. Even if the future hadn't already indoctrinated me into the cult of Kathryn, I likely would have felt the same draw. She had a unique gravity to her, a magnetism that was genuinely striking even from my removed position.

I didn't want to squander the opportunity, yet at the same time I needed to ensure Kathryn didn't regard me as a creepy stalker, which, up to that point, wasn't too far from the truth. I concluded the optimal path was via the classroom, a rare chance to observe Kathryn in her natural element. With twenty-three months remaining, I moved on to phase two.

———

"Pardon me. Where is Professor Simpson's classroom?" I asked the secretary in the entryway of the Physics building. I was blindly guessing the location and timing based on the usual pattern of student movement.

"Who?" she replied, barely paying me any attention.

"Um, Doctor Simpson? One of the physics professors."

"Uh-huh. Let me see if we have anyone by that name." She started to page through a massive binder.

"Kathryn Simpson?" I tried.

"Oh, Kathryn!" she exclaimed, immediately brightening. It appeared the secretary had been pulled into her orbit as well. "Yes, of course. Her class—Physics 140, right?—started ten minutes ago, in room 385 upstairs."

I thanked her, turned a corner, then immediately exited the building. I didn't want to draw any unnecessary attention to myself by joining the lecture late. Most importantly, I had the information I needed, and confidently returned two days later with plenty of time to spare.

The classroom was smaller than I would have liked, a threat to my intended anonymity. As students trickled in, I buried myself in my notebook, fully aware that I looked positively ancient next to the sprightly cohort. I knew I had no hope of keeping up with the advanced material, but I planned to take notes regardless, partly as cover and partly in a vain attempt to connect with Kathryn. I had minored in math, so at least we shared the unwavering language of numbers.

Kathryn walked into the room with a beaming smile, instantly quieting the thirty or so seated facing her. I suddenly regretted being there; I stuck out like a sore thumb that she would see right through immediately. Not only was I twice the age of the other students, I was not registered and thus had no right to be there. Showing up a month into the semester was a poor choice that only served to highlight my intrusion.

Luckily, Kathryn either didn't notice or didn't care. She launched into her lecture on quantum something-or-other with electrifying gusto. I gave up on note-taking almost immediately; I didn't know a quark from a lepton anyway. Instead, I focused entirely on her: her effortless control of the room, her mastery of the curriculum, the perfect analogies that allowed even a dunce like me to grasp a handful of the advanced concepts. My college classes had been something to suffer through on the way to the glorious weekend. This was entirely different: engaging, intelligible, perhaps even entertaining. And I returned with wholehearted enthusiasm for more class the following week.

———

"Young man? Would you mind staying for a moment?" Kathryn surprisingly said to me as I was packing up after my third lecture. "I apologize; I don't recall your name."

"Of . . . course, um, Professor Simpson," I stammered. "It's Aaron, by the way."

"Nice to meet you, Aaron. Unless, of course, we've met before, in which case I should say 'nice to see you again,' though I have a good memory and suspect that's not the case. And don't be silly, call me Kathryn. That out of the way, I'm afraid I'm bound to ask: Are you an enrolled student?"

Well, that was it; my cover was already blown. This had always been a needlessly bad plan; I was fully aware of that fact and had been drawn in nonetheless. On the other hand, the creator of time travel was speaking to me!

"No, I'm not, I'm really sorry." There was no benefit lying to her; it was too easily disprovable.

"Rules are rules, Aaron, and I'm afraid I need to ask you not to attend this class anymore."

"Yes, of course, I understand."

It felt like I had disappointed my own mother.

"But perhaps instead, we could get coffee?" she offered. "I'm genuinely fascinated by someone who would choose to audit *this* particular class."

Well, this certainly was not part of the plan. We had jumped from phase two to phase twenty-two.

"I—I would love to, yes!" I responded, poorly masking my genuine excitement. "Like, er, right now?"

"Yeah, if that works for you. There's a nice place on Hearst, as close to campus as you can get." North campus, she meant, a location that I knew to be near her home. I had followed her there during my second week of clandestine observation, the apex of creepy behavior. An uncomfortable yet worthy sacrifice for a vital bit of information.

I was still in a state of shock as we strolled past the carefree students throwing frisbees on Memorial Glade and up the hill to the border of campus. In those five minutes, she somehow extracted detailed information about my hometown, the breakup, and the resulting move to California. I obviously left out the impactful eight days that preceded it.

I opted to curtail any return questions. As limited as my usual small talk capabilities were, the fact that I already knew the highlights of Kathryn's life added another complicating layer. It was a tricky balancing act to recall what I actually knew and what I should know as part of my undercover persona. Duplicity was not my forte.

We sat down at a small table over two steaming cups of needlessly sumptuous coffee. How a college student could hope to afford this was beyond me.

"So, Aaron, my adventurous auditor, back to the question that piqued my original curiosity: Why the interest in my class?"

I had taken advantage of the last few minutes to formulate at least a mildly coherent response.

"Call me an admirer . . . of the topic, I mean. I feel like quantum mechanics is the future, no pun intended."

"I don't think there is a pun there, Aaron, intended or not," she teased. "Do you have a science background?"

"No, I'm an accountant, actually."

"I see. So you haven't understood a single thing I've said in class then."

Her beaming smile completely disarmed me; already my defenses were weakened, and I battled the instinct to share everything, future and all.

"Very little," I responded instead. "But that's okay. Because, well, what do you think of time travel? I'm, uh, writing a movie script. A time-travel one. And I want it to sound scientifically plausible. I thought your class would help fill the gaps."

"Oh well, in that case, let me tell you all about the nuances of quantum entanglement." She chuckled to herself. "Aaron, c'mon, people don't want to hear about that, trust me. Do you know how many dinner parties I've been kicked out of?" Chuckle. "Why do you think it caught my eye that you attended *my* class, and more than once, to boot? A lot of the content goes right over the students' heads, and they're all physics majors!"

"Yeah, I suppose that's true," I conceded.

"So you're a time-travel fan? I simply adore time travel fiction. Have you read that new one by Ken Grimwood? It came out just last month."

"Not yet; what's it about?"

"Well, the main character dies in his forties—close to my age, actually. Hmm, hadn't thought about that. Anyway, he dies, and he wakes up as a kid, imbued with the complete memories of his original life. It's all about what he does with that knowledge. Fascinating, huh?"

"That sounds like a nightmare, actually. An adult brain trapped in the body of a child, unable to make connections with peers, burdened by knowledge of the future . . ." I trailed off, suddenly conscious that I was edging closer to describing my own unique situation.

Kathryn chuckled again, closer to a whistle than a belly laugh. "Well, first, the fact that you jumped straight into the fascinating

197

implications of the premise tells me that your screenplay is surely excellent. Though maybe I should have clarified that he goes back to when he was eighteen."

"Oh, well, that's better I guess." I added the novel to a mental checklist; ever since my upstream journey, I had been devouring any fiction that involved time travel or twenty-first-century prognostication. I found it very satisfying to appraise the authors' often-wild predictions.

"What about real time travel?" I asked, taking another sip of the delicious brew. "Do you think it's possible?"

"Ah, this is one of the triggering questions that often gets me in trouble at the aforementioned dinner parties. So I'll keep it brief and simple. Short answer: scientifically possible, yes. Will humans ever harness it? No way. The science is centuries away, and we'll probably all kill each other first, I hate to say."

"What about, um, predictive quantum behavior? Couldn't that lead to a breakthrough?" I asked, trying to make it sound off the cuff. I immediately regretted the query—a dead giveaway that I knew more than I let on—but curiosity had gotten the better of me.

"Fascinating! That is precisely my current area of focus. I hope to publish my findings by the end of the year. Nothing groundbreaking, of course, and time travel will still be impossible—sorry—but hey, me and maybe four other people in the world might find the paper exciting."

"Can't wait to read it," I joked, drawing another laugh.

"Aaron, I do have to run, but this has been lovely." Kathryn took a big, final gulp and stood up. "I feel that we've each found a kindred spirit. What do you say we meet here every couple weeks and talk science fiction? Call it a book club. And I'd be more than happy to consult on your script."

"Wow, um, sure, that sounds great!" I responded, unable to believe my luck. I was not remotely charming, handsome, or suave; and yet somehow, someway, this titan of intellect wanted to meet *me* again. I doubted that any additional interaction with Kathryn would actually aid in my ultimate mission; I truly just wanted to spend more time in her charismatic orbit.

Though our respective homes were actually the same direction, I parted ways with her to maintain my already threadbare cover story.

"Oh, wait, Aaron, one more thing!" Kathryn shouted after a few steps of separation. "I also could use an accountant."

18

Nineteen eighty-six was a blur. I tried my best to experience something new every day, and the Bay Area provided no shortage of opportunities: a leisurely hike among the majestic redwoods of Muir Woods, a sampling of delicacies in China-town, a ferry ride across the calm water. I all but lived outdoors, perhaps trying to make up for the time lost to the brutal winters and insipid office life of my younger years.

Kathryn served as my chief companion. We made quite an unlikely pair: the intellect and the ignorant, the affable and the laughable, the oft-humble with the oft-humiliated. We had quickly graduated beyond mere book club acquaintances into something more profound and earnest, underpinned by our shared love of the bountiful nature surrounding us. After years of being a homebody, Kathryn's kindly insistence had sparked that gradual awakening. She opened my eyes to the richness of our environment, a blind spot that had lingered for far too long.

Over the course of the year, the friendship blossomed from that most serendipitous of beginnings—at least as she saw it. I often felt a pang of guilt for the manufactured nature of our initial interactions: our true bond that was regretfully built on a lie. I recognized deep down that developing this relationship with her was unnecessary for my mission, and if anything could be a *threat* to its success, yet I persisted nonetheless. Perhaps it was merely self-serving, a greedy attempt to inflate my ego; after all, this world-changing genius wanted to be friends with *me*.

"Hurry up, old man!" she shouted over her shoulder on one of our early bike rides. My body hadn't quite figured out how to pump enough blood to the necessary muscles yet, and I could barely move after a roundabout two hours in the steep hills above Berkeley. Kathryn was patient but unforgiving. "We're almost there; I promise it'll be worth it."

She disappeared over a crest on the hilly terrain, and I mustered everything I could to keep pace. Over the pulsing sound ringing in my ears, I could hear a metallic clatter coupled with distant cheering, and I wondered what she was getting us into.

"Hey, you made it!" she welcomed me when I caught up. I huffed and gave a half-hearted thumbs-up as I limped off my bike, leaning it against a tree. "If only you had that teleporter from your screenplay, right?" she teased.

I had quickly come to regret my original cover story, the sci-fi screenwriter in need of guidance. For our first planned meetup, I had hastily thrown together a hacky piece of garbage, a typo-ridden screenplay that even my mom wouldn't produce. For lack of any actual inspiration, I loosely based the main character on Sam: a college student who works for the International Time Travel Institute and welcomes travelers to the present day of

2050. As one would expect, shenanigans ensue and pseudo-Sam miraculously saves the day, using (what else?) science! Even though only one person would ever read it, I didn't dare use any of my real knowledge of the twenty-first century to bolster the plausibility.

Kathryn had showered me with undue praise and provided some genuinely interesting bits of science that overshadowed the stilted dialogue and shoddy structure. She was incapable of harsh criticism, especially toward those like myself whom she justifiably considered to be a lower tier of brainpower. I thanked her for the feedback and never brought up the screenplay again, though she was apt to reference it from time to time.

We found ourselves on a small bluff, packed tight with an eclectic group of roughly fifty. I immediately felt self-conscious in my sweaty biking clothes, but followed Kathryn's lead and took a seat on the dusty ground. Like most west-facing lookouts in the area, it granted a view of the distant Bay, though today clouds occluded most of the usual spectacle. Below us, the massive football stadium sat unused, a shame given our prime fifty-yard-line view.

"Why—"

Kathryn shushed me, somehow layering a smile on top of the command. "Listen," she said.

As if on cue, a smooth drum beat started up, followed by a few other syncopated instruments and a roaring saxophone. We couldn't see the source, but the music sounded amplified in a way that was reminiscent of the individualized speaker systems of the twenty-first century.

"Jazz?" I exclaimed. I couldn't disguise my distaste of the genre.

"Yes, it's the Berkeley Jazz Festival!" Kathryn responded enthusiastically. "They're at the Greek Theatre, right down the hill from where we are."

"But we can't even see them!" I noted.

"There's a good reason they call this Tightwad Hill. You can't get everything for free. But jazz doesn't need to be seen, it needs to be felt. Just trust me. Listen."

Out of respect, I waited until the conclusion of the first meandering song before starting up again.

"I don't think this is for me, sorry."

"Well, you like *me*, right?" Kathryn asked.

"What? Yes, of course."

"Well, I like jazz," she stated.

"I don't think that's how the transitive property works, Kathryn," I teased.

"Oh, don't get me started on the transitive property!" She chuckled. "But I think you misheard . . . I said *I'm* like jazz. Jazz is chaotic and grounded, improvisational yet bound by set principles. That's exactly how I tick. Or at least how I rationalize my way of thinking. Jazz is also very much like quantum physics, so perhaps my chosen profession was foretold. And I think that if you can stand *my* idiosyncrasies, it's only a matter of time until you feel the same way about jazz. What type of music are you, Aaron?"

"Something . . . boring," I responded.

"Oh, don't sell yourself short. I think you're classical music! Everyone likes you, you can tell a riveting story, and there's a certain depth to you the more someone listens."

I opted to take the compliment, as well as the advice. Maybe out on this beautiful day with a new friend, jazz wasn't so bad after all.

———

Later in the year, I met Kathryn's brother Edward on a touristy walk along Fisherman's Wharf. He was sixteen years her senior, which made him almost twice my age. He was instinctively protective of his little sister, and thus eyed me and my newfound grooming choices with a fair amount of seasoned skepticism. While I was off playing an antique game in the penny arcade, Kathryn emphasized to him the complete and utter absence of any romantic connection between us. Afterward, he was the kindest man one ever could meet, the archetypal lifelong role model Kathryn had so often described to me.

I was less enthused to accompany her to a gathering of Berkeley colleagues: thirty or so pompous college professors sporting sixty or so elbow patches. I felt patronized the moment I stepped in.

"Oh, an accountant you say?" one particularly elderly academic said after Kathryn introduced me. "How charming!"

"Einstein once said 'the hardest thing to understand in the world is income tax,'" Kathryn quoted, the endorsement falling on literally deaf ears. She gave me an empathetic shrug as we moved on to the next circle of pontification.

After a languid dinner, we snuck out the front door of the gorgeous Walnut Creek home for a stroll through the neighborhood, a refreshing autumn breeze on our backs.

"Having fun?" she asked rhetorically, the ever-present twinkle in her eye shining brightly. "You know, Aaron, honestly, I don't like these events either, as much as I am bound to go for career sustainability."

"Oh, trust me, I get it. Do you know how many CPA conferences I've gone to? You may be surprised to know that tax code changes are not exactly the most riveting material. Although as a group, accountants sure can throw a mean party. Sometimes we even lightly interact with each other!"

That unsurprisingly drew her trademark chuckle; she had a weak spot for self-deprecating humor.

"At least you belong there," she continued. "This isn't really my world, especially since I didn't follow the usual path. Researching and teaching, I love. The politics, not so much. And that's a perfect lead-in, I suppose, for something I have to share with you," she continued, lowering her voice. "Don't worry, it's good news, I think. I've decided to take a one-year sabbatical abroad. It was a tough decision—leaving my students, leaving you—but I think it'll be a once-in-a-lifetime experience."

"Wow, no, that's fantastic, congratulations!" I exclaimed, quickly pushing aside a fleeting blip of disappointment over the temporary loss of my closest friend. "When, where, what—tell me everything!"

"Well, as you know, I'm finishing up my current research project here, the predictive quantum formula that I know you just *love* to hear about. And once that's published, I'll be moving to Switzerland and working for CERN. It's always been a dream of mine to go to Europe, and to be paid to do it is even better, right? I'll be only a couple hours from where Einstein developed his theory of relativity!"

"Wow, it sounds amazing! We'll certainly miss you here though."

"I know you will, Aaron. But don't worry, I'll be back before the ball drops for 1988. And hey, you can always visit me, you know? I'm not moving to Antarctica. Anyway, we better get back to the party; it's quite obvious when the lone female faculty member is missing."

Without Kathryn's buoyant presence, 1987 was a bit of a come-down, a reminder that this was not the life path on which I was originally set. For the first time, I began to question if this prolonged mission was even the right decision. After all, I was playing God, shaping the future in my own image, even if it was the righteous one. Plus, the undertaking was not dissimilar from what my nemesis Jakob had done before me, or rather, was yet to do.

I tried to fill my newfound time as best I could, branching out with some heretofore unexplored activities. In May, I reluctantly joined a friend to celebrate the fiftieth anniversary of the Golden Gate Bridge, a landmark for which I admittedly did share ample affection. To our dismay, nearly everyone else in the city joined in on the festivities. The simple walk across the bridge became a multi-hour slog, trapped shoulder-to-shoulder with 300,000 locals who, like me, all feared imminent bridge collapse. The most desperate threw bicycles and strollers over the edge in a feeble attempt to lighten the structural load. After that experience, I decided I needed to get away for a while.

So with nearly a year to go and little preparation remaining, I gave myself a new mission; or rather, a renewed one. I rented a house in Los Angeles for a month, and in between enjoying the plethora of new biking trails and beaches, I hunted for Lisa. I knew her name, birth year, eventual job, and not much else—for such a gregarious person, she had been quite reserved about large portions of her past—but that was enough to get started.

For lack of anything better to do, I fully threw myself at the problem, even buying a personal computer so I could install the latest computerized spreadsheet program. I digitally tracked the status of every Lisa Barnes in the greater LA area: whom I had spoken to, whom I had made visual contact with, and even the few who had justifiably called the police on me.

As a last-ditch effort, I cold-called every television ad placement agency I could find, knowing that by now she may have established her career in that field. None employed Lisa, though I did get an excellent rate for a prime-time slot on the brand-new Fox network.

As expected, the search was occasionally thrilling yet ultimately fruitless, and I began planning my overdue return trip home. A deep-seated part of me was convinced I would be triumphant this time, probably the same predisposition that had uprooted me in the first place to try to protect Kathryn. I thought if I could have connected with Lisa now, that was a strong indicator that I could change the future. Alas, it was not to be.

The picturesque June weather conditions on my last day in town were what travel brochures were made of, and I embraced it with a leisurely, scenic bike ride in Griffith Park, defeated yet at peace.

As I was coming around a bend, a fluttering tuft of distinctive dirty-blond hair caught my eye at a distance. It was her; somehow, I was sure of it. I couldn't believe my luck; here, on a sparsely populated trail, on my last day in LA, I had found Lisa.

With a rapid surge of adrenaline, I raced to catch up to her group, desperate to confirm the sighting and catch her attention. Careening downhill with reckless abandon, I narrowly avoided an adorable elderly couple holding hands, shouting a sympathetic "sorry!" as I zipped past. The dirt path narrowed as the downgrade increased, lurching me headlong toward my target with vicious speed.

I lost sight of Lisa around a sharp bend, forcing me to lean perilously in a manic attempt to reacquire the visual. Out of nowhere, I felt the bike start to slip out from underfoot, my usually steady balance betraying me. I fought to regain control with all my might. And I failed, spectacularly.

19

The overhead fluorescents overwhelmed my dazed senses, recasting the environment into blurred fragments distressingly reminiscent of that last moment before a time jump. For a brief moment, I wondered which decade I was in.

"Ah, good, you're awake. How are you feeling?" a distant voice asked. Based on the tone, I suspected a medical professional was speaking, though I couldn't focus on the source.

"Es . . . esellent," I slurred. My mouth somehow felt detached from my face, resulting in strained speech that would best be described as Sylvester Stallone-esque.

"What is your name?" I heard as the room slowly came into view.

"Aaro . . . Aaro. Ugh," I replied, trying to force the enunciation through.

"Good. And just vocalize whatever's comfortable. Can you tell me what year it is, and who is president? These are standard questions in the case of possible head trauma."

"Nineteen eighty-seven. And, um, Reagan."

"Great. So, Mister Barnett, you are here at the San Gabriel Valley Medical Center after a bike accident. Do you recall what happened?"

"Somewhat, I think . . . I remember the bike slipping out from under me, and then just . . . vague fragments."

With my vision mostly restored, I was able to distinguish the features of my doctor, whose patience with my labored speech was admirable. He looked all of twenty-five, and could easily have passed for Sam's darker-haired brother.

I let out a painful sigh of relief upon seeing my wiggling toes at the foot of the bed, but the rest of my status lay hidden beneath the veil of the meager hospital blanket. Too exhausted to verify more and undoubtedly numbed by numerous medications, I felt oddly disconnected from my body. Who knew what personal havoc I had wreaked in my impetuousness to catch up to Lisa? And what I wouldn't give for a quick pass through the medbays of the future to move past it quickly!

Well, only one way to find out.

"What's the, er, damage, Doctor?" I reluctantly invited, fearing the answer.

"Well, Mister Barnett, you were quite lucky. You sustained what I now believe is a mild concussion, which very well could have been fatal if you weren't wearing your helmet. On top of that, you have a cracked rib, a sprained ankle, and a lacerated lip. And now that I hear your hampered speech, likely acute TMJ as well. As I said, it could have been so much worse; you're quite fortunate that you fell the way you did, and that someone was there to summon immediate medical assistance."

"Wait—was it a woman my age, blondish hair?"

"Blond, yes, but I believe it was a man of advanced age. He said he was a stranger and didn't stay once you were safely situated. If you would like to contact him, he did leave his card." The doctor motioned to a side table, where I also spotted my few belongings.

"Oh. And when can I go home?"

"We'd like to keep you here for one to two days of observation and treatment for your injuries. And keep in mind that even a mild concussion may take a few months for a full recovery."

A bump in the road, perhaps, but this setback wouldn't derail me. I drifted back into unconsciousness shortly after, an agonizing dreamworld where Lisa *still* couldn't hear my desperate, pleading calls.

———

A ripple of indistinct panic coursed through my still-muddled mind as I awoke the following day.

"Are you okay, sir?" a passing nurse asked. "Can I get you anything?"

"No," I huffed, "thank you, I'm fine."

As soon as she was out of sight, I grasped for my wallet, the unlikely source of my distress. Frantically verifying the contents, I quickly accounted for the usual cash, driver's license, credit card, and a few family photos, but not the only item that actually had true, irreplaceable value: my handwritten timeline of the future and the key to saving Kathryn. I desperately scanned the folds again, my hopes dwindling with each unsuccessful attempt.

The business card on the side table caught my eye as I scanned the room again. It was time to make a call.

"Carrier Productions, this is John speaking." The gentle voice on the other end reminded me of my father.

"Hi, John? My name is Aaron. Aaron Barnett. I was—"

"Aaron, yes! Oh my gosh, how are you feeling? Are you still in the hospital?"

"Yes, I'm actually calling from there now. But I'm going to be just fine, and I understand a lot of that is thanks to you. That's why I'm calling, obviously, to thank you."

"Oh, yes, merely the right place at the right time. Anyone would have done the same. I'm very glad you're recovering well; if I'm being honest, between the bleeding and contorted limbs, I feared much worse."

"Me too, me too. I was wondering," I said, trying to sound as casual as possible, "did you go through my wallet at any point? Maybe to check the name on my license?"

"Yes, but I didn't take any cash, I swear."

"Oh well, if you had, I wouldn't have minded; I would have happily considered it a well-deserved tip for services rendered. But I'm actually talking about a sheet of folded paper, lots of tiny writing on it. Ring a bell?"

"Oh yes, the one with all the dates and times on it? I have to admit, it caught my eye."

"Do you know, er, where it is?"

John hesitated on the other end of the line. "It's gone; I think the wind took it while we were waiting for the ambulance. Sorry, was it important?"

"No," I lied, to myself more than my companion, "just some notes for a screenplay I'm writing." It was incredible how universally applicable that fabrication had proven to be over the years.

"Oh, sorry about that. You're a screenwriter? I'm in the industry, mostly production design for children's television, though we dabble—"

"One more question," I interrupted, rudely reflecting my disappointment back toward my benevolent savior. "Did you see a woman there? Midthirties, blonde-ish, irrationally self-assured?"

"Hmm . . . no, I can't say that I did."

"Alright." I sighed. I had been hoping my gnarly injury would have at least baited Lisa into an inquisitive visit to the scene of the accident. Even that pathetic version of a meetup would have gone a long way toward justifying my ultimately calamitous sojourn to LA.

"Well, thanks for everything, John. Keep an eye out for a gift basket I'll definitely be sending your way. Gotta rest now."

I abruptly ended the call, angry at myself for treating him so rudely over something seemingly so insignificant. Yet, this borderline illegible document had always felt like a lifeline, a puzzle simply waiting to be unlocked. By filling in the gaps, I could know exactly where to be, exactly what to do. Now, I was left to my own devices, with only my diminished wits to rely on.

———

"Hey, sleepyhead." A soft, familiar voice stirred me from my restful state the next day. A voice that couldn't possibly be by my side at the moment.

"I really love what you've done with the place," Kathryn added, gesturing to the laughably bland hospital room.

"Thanks," I mumbled. "Why, how—what are you doing here?"

"Why? I'm here to support my injured friend. How? I flew in

on an airplane. A truly magical machine. And what? Sitting by your side."

"C'mon, I'm concussed; give me a break." I tried my best to force my bruised face into a smile.

"Apparently, in your incapacitated state, you called for me specifically. That was enough for them to track me down, and I flew in as soon as I could."

"From Switzerland? I wouldn't ask you to do that."

"Well, some part of you would, it seems. They said you kept repeating my name. But it's okay, I'm here and I'm happy to be here and I'll take you back home soon."

"But your sabbatical? Ugh, I'm so sorry, I feel terrible."

"Aaron, I make my own choices, and I choose to be with my good friend. Plus, it's tough to be a quantum physicist in a world of particle physicists. We're just like two strongly opinionated electrons, repelling each other away."

I'd heard Kathryn deliver this very joke before, but it nonetheless proved sufficient in abating my crushing guilt. Truthfully, I was thrilled to have her with me, a bit of calming stability amid the disorienting fog of the accident.

"Well, it means a lot that you're here. How do I look?" I asked, mostly rhetorically.

"My advice is to avoid all mirrors for a while," she joked, prompting another painful, involuntary smile from me. "Hey, what were you doing in LA, anyway?"

"Oh, searching for a long-lost friend, you could say. And arguably taking one too many bike rides."

———

A few days later, Kathryn chaperoned Rex and me home. We had no shortage of conversation topics over the course of the seven-hour drive through the dull stretches of middle California. By request, she regaled me with stories of her travels around Europe: the wonders of Geneva, the Swiss Alps, and most envious of all, Paris. I greatly regretted that she had returned before I had a chance to visit; a holiday there would have been much more productive—and awe-inspiring—than Los Angeles had proven to be.

Now that I could call Kathryn a true friend—a fact that still staggered me—the intensifying reality of her imminent death completely scrambled my motivations. No longer could I tell myself that this was a mission to better the world with Kathryn's persevering genius; no, it was purely personal. I had originally envisioned myself as a silent protector waiting in the wings, a guardian angel sent from the future to intervene. Now, I just wanted my good friend not to die; it was as simple as that. Six months remained on the countdown, and it was time to kick my preparation into high gear. I committed myself to be ready to counter anything that might threaten Kathryn.

First step: mental preparation. Without my copious notes to fall back on, I attempted to summon forth every detail I could from the depths of my mind. I knew the bulk of what Jakob had told the courtroom—or me directly—was overtly false, but even a sprinkling of truth would bolster my chances of obstructing his actions. The focused meditation sessions weren't as directly productive for this purpose as I had hoped, but they did at least effectively allay my ever-escalating anxiety for a short time.

Within a few weeks, I had recovered from the accident enough to progress to the next stage: the physical preparation. Jakob would most accurately be described as a nerdy scientist, yes, but considering the medbays and supposed "superfoods" of the future, he would easily have won "most athletic" in any contemporary high school yearbook. I was no slouch myself, especially since moving to California, but I had focused on aerobics, not strength. Outrunning him wouldn't be particularly helpful in this situation.

I began making regular trips to the gym, pathetically pumping iron in a dubious attempt to bulk up. More pragmatically, I joined a self-defense class, not realizing I was going to be the only man in the group. The instructor—pleasantly surprised to have me in attendance—continually staged me as the attacker, resulting in a few light bruises and one unfortunate midsection injury. I hadn't understood how much of self-defense was groin-based.

With my dogged focus to intervene on the night of Kathryn's murder, it took me an embarrassingly long time to come to the realization that I had overlooked a significantly simpler path: all-out prevention. There was no reason to put her in the line of fire; we could simply stand to the side and let a bewildered Jakob flounder without his target.

While watching my beloved Cubs get crushed by the Giants at Candlestick, I gave it my best shot.

"Kathryn, I was thinking, what if we took a vacation together?" That got her attention; she had been engrossed in the game. "We could invite Stevie or Carol or Aaron Two, of course," I added, listing off a few of her other friends who I could feasibly tolerate.

"That could be fun, sure. What did you have in mind?" she replied, her eyes tracking another high-flying pop out from an overmatched Cubs batter.

"How about Lake Tahoe? We could go skiing or just sit around a fire and drink lots of hot beverages? I know a guy who has a place there and he could rent it to us in the last week of January." I didn't even remotely know a guy, but I could figure that part out later.

"Aaron, that sounds truly lovely. But is there any other time we could go? You well know that travel opportunities are more restricted for us instructors. I certainly couldn't do that to my students, especially so early in the semester."

"Okay, you're right, maybe that was a bad idea then. How about we go to a show at the playhouse instead? I'll have to check what they're putting on at the time. Or, better yet, the symphony! You like classical music, right? Or an NBA game; they're almost as fun as baseball, even if our local team is borderline unwatchable. What do you think?"

She dismissed my pestering with a playful shush, effectively adjourning the topic for the time being. I'd already pushed my luck enough.

———

As the momentous day neared, my desperation increased. Kathryn continually rebuffed my most reasonable suggestions to relocate her for the night. Often, I contemplated coming clean about her future, laying everything out on the table. Raw fear got in the way every time; I was simply too afraid of losing her cherished friendship. Plus, why would she possibly believe me? The risk wasn't worth the reward.

I decided to give it one more go during a particularly arduous biking excursion through the Berkeley Hills. The route was colloquially known as the Death Ride; I purposefully overlooked the ominous coincidence.

Out of breath yet exhilarated, we stopped for a picnic at the peak, taking in the sweeping vista of the Bay.

"Kathryn, I have to ask, why did you really leave Europe?" I prompted, a direction in mind for how to shape the conversation toward my desired result. "Say what you want, but I know it wasn't *actually* for me, nor because of some scientific discord."

"Oh wow, no small talk today, huh?" she joked while relishing a well-earned bite of turkey sandwich. "But I've got good news: you're completely wrong; it was for you! I got the call, and it was an easy decision. Or mostly for you, at least. I missed so much else about California: my brother, the Pacific Ocean." She gestured across the bay to illustrate the point, and given the spectacular view, it was hard to argue. "And my students! The sabbatical really reinforced to me that I'm a teacher who also researches, and not the other way around."

She sighed, her body language and tone noticeably shifting after an introspective pause.

"I would only tell you this, but, if I'm being honest with myself, I suppose I may have been looking for a reason to leave. Geneva is incredible, but I just . . . well, I never felt like I belonged there. It brought back some old memories, some painful memories. Even now, it's hard—really hard—often being the only woman in a world of men. But it was much worse when I was younger. I was bullied purely for being smart. Or more specifically, for being smarter than the boys. They *really* did not like being embarrassed by the nerdy, quiet girl.

"To make matters worse, I later had a long-term relationship with the worst of them. He had made my life miserable as a teenager, and then continued the trend in young adulthood with my diffident blessing. I had enough going on as I worked through my PhD program, and I think I compartmentalized my depression, even from myself. Thankfully, before it could devolve any further, my brother returned home, immediately identified the spiraling situation, and liberated me."

"You never told me that," I contributed softly after a sympathetic beat.

"What an odd thing to say!" Kathryn exclaimed with a chuckle, snapping back into her default joyous state. "I'm well aware I haven't told you that; that's exactly why I shared it now! Anyway, though I was always treated with utmost respect, I nevertheless always felt like an outsider at CERN, between my field of study, my gender, and my age. And it brought back a lot of those same emotions. So, in conclusion, I suppose it was *somewhat* about you, but perhaps more about me. Does that answer your out-of-nowhere question?"

It did, though with much more rumination than I had been prepared for. I awkwardly fumbled to get us back on track, though my plan to steer the conversation had already been derailed.

"Well, um, would you have any interest in going back soon, to Europe?" I followed up. "No physics, just three friends biking their way through France. Me, you, and Mona Lisa."

She sighed. "This again? Let me guess, you have plane tickets for the last week of January?"

I should have known I couldn't sneak anything by her, but at least I had an excuse ready to go.

"I do," I confirmed. "I can't go any later; tax season, you know."

"Aaron, I don't understand your fixation with that week. Why do you keep trying to get me away from campus at such an oddly specific time?"

"Well, do you trust me?" I questioned. It was time to deploy my most desperate, far-fetched plea.

"Of course."

"Then I'll tell you what I can. I have it on good authority that, well, there's going to be a major earthquake that week. I don't want either of us anywhere near it."

Kathryn chuckled, though I detected a distinct note of disappointment.

"That's a joke, right? You can't actually expect me to believe what you just said, for oh so many reasons. For one, no 'good authority' could anticipate the date of a major earthquake, especially not down to a week! Also, many of your previously suggested activities are still very much within the destructive range of this hypothetical disaster. You're lying, and I don't understand why."

"I'm only trying to protect you," I shared truthfully.

"I can protect myself just fine, thank you very much."

"No, you can't. I know that's hard to hear, but it's true. Please . . . please let me help you," I pleaded. "All you have to do is leave town with me for one day."

She sighed again and looked into the distance. The conversation had not progressed as expected. With no other cards to play, I once again revisited the option of releasing the floodgates of future knowledge, but again stopped short.

Kathryn wordlessly packed up her remaining food and hopped back on her bike. Our rides were always quiet, but this downhill trek was positively frosty. She barely acknowledged me upon reaching her house, a promising day coming to a disastrous close. I stewed the entire ride home, furious at myself for needlessly sacrificing our friendship in an impetuous effort to safeguard it.

I barely saw Kathryn over the last few weeks of the year and into early 1988. I desperately and repeatedly tried to patch things up, but each effort only seemed to exacerbate the situation. As the historic day approached, she stopped returning calls and rebuffed attempts at reconciliation, including one not-so-accidental meetup at her favorite spot on campus under the towering redwoods. I couldn't blame her; I could feel myself becoming increasingly unhinged by the weight of my impending task. Without her, I felt truly alone, a reminder of why I had no choice but to succeed.

With time rapidly dwindling, I contemplated anything and everything to get her out of her house that night, no matter how ridiculous: mailing anonymous threats, temporary kidnapping, even blatant arson. Alas, I could never bring myself to so boldly break the law, even with the purest of intentions.

Ultimately, I opted to trust myself and the years of preparation I had poured in. With complete conviction, I now truly believed: *I can save her*. For myself, for Sam, for the future, and most of all, for Kathryn.

20

January 25 arrived, temperate and serene, no different from any other California winter day. The newspaper was flung onto my porch with the same incautious energy; the usual trio of neon-clad women listening to their portable cassette players marched by on their daily route; the bells of the Berkeley campanile chimed with their customary timbre. Only Rex and I seemed to be aware of the portentous occasion.

I went out into the fading early morning darkness for a jog, a knowingly futile attempt to clear my head. I had barely slept the night before, suspended in a coiled nightmare of feasible failure. To my right, the sun steadily dawned above the Berkeley Hills, seeming to hover directly above Kathryn's house in a cruel taunt of inescapability.

Upon return, I grabbed a premade supply pack and set out according to my established plan. From the moment Kathryn left her house, I tracked her from a distance; I needed to be absolutely sure nobody else was doing the same. It did not escape me that my long-term mission had begun much the same way, all those years ago. I certainly never thought I'd be the type to reminisce about covert surveillance past.

As expected, Kathryn proceeded on her standard weekday morning routine, starting with the very coffee shop at which we had first conversed. Overpriced drink in hand, she took a leisurely, meandering stroll through campus, proceeding along a spiraling path which culminated at her academic building. Knowing her, the unpredictable, snaking route corresponded to some arcane mathematical equation; why bother being a genius if you couldn't apply it directly to the more monotonous moments of your own life?

I tried to keep my head on a swivel, scanning for any and all threats who might be tracking her with a more malicious intent. On such high alert, I encountered a few false positives along the way: innocuous students who happened to share Jakob's hair color or build, visitors snapping a poorly timed photo. Kathryn just kept walking, peacefully oblivious to the majority of her surroundings.

The rest of the day proceeded much the same: anticlimactic and uneventful. By the time Kathryn started her walk home, I was exhausted. Full-time stalking was hard work, at least for an amateur.

Once she was securely inside her home, I switched to sentinel mode, concealed behind a conveniently placed bush. I had scouted the location on numerous occasions, even once positioning a crude doll to confirm that the overgrown shrub could properly cloak me from all angles. The early winter darkness did a lot of the work bolstering the rudimentary camouflage as well. I slid on my gloves, ravenously dug into the food and water I had prudently cached there in the morning, and waited for my moment to act.

226

I knew Jakob would be materializing inside a Berkeley classroom at any moment. Shit was about to get real.

———

My backlit digital watch had just ticked past eight o'clock when I saw a shadowy figure cross under a distant streetlamp. Without even being able to discern any features, I had no doubt that it was him: the man I had thought about every day for the last two and a half years. It was the very same sense of uncanny recognition that the faintest glimpse of Lisa had triggered on that fateful Los Angeles afternoon.

As he neared Kathryn's home, I patiently observed the young, cocksure Jakob I knew all too well from the courtroom, composed and self-confident as ever. Contrary to his testimony, his wardrobe was plainly not of this century; the half-collared shirt and tapered fit screamed 2042 to me. It had been two and a half years since I had encountered him in the courtroom, and while my appearance had changed considerably—longer hair, a scruffy beard, a physique that didn't require constant concealment—Jakob looked like not a day had passed. Because, in fact, it hadn't: he was a few days younger, and noticeably sprier without the weight of the trial on his shoulders.

He paused in front of Kathryn's house, taking in the tastefully lit facade with sincere admiration. For the briefest of moments, he allowed his inner emotional state to peek through: a glistening in the eyes, a puckering of the chin. I had never distrusted his expressed fanaticism toward Kathryn, and therefore was not even remotely surprised to see him beset with emotion at the imminent prospect of coming face to face with his luminary. I knew the feeling all too well. He stiffened back to his default lack of affect and smoothly paced up the porch steps.

As he knocked on her door, I was painfully aware that I was likely waiting too long to intervene. Curiosity had gotten the better of me; I wanted to see how this was going to play out just a bit longer, and especially to validate the veracity of his testimony.

While Jakob waited, a forced smile unnaturally appeared on his face; he was getting into character as the hopeful grad student.

A deafening metallic clatter from Kathryn's kitchen window startled me out of my practiced stillness, briefly threatening my concealment. Luckily, Jakob was distracted by the sound as well, pausing for a moment before frantically rattling her doorknob in a hurried attempt to break into the house. I took a deep breath, prepared to burst into action, when suddenly Kathryn calmly appeared at the door. She looked splendid in the blue science-themed apron I had gifted her last Christmas, and as Jakob had once described, inexplicably held two pot lids.

Jakob froze, awestricken, before launching into his well-practiced introduction. I was unable to overhear the content, but I knew the idea, and I especially knew that Kathryn would never hesitate to support a prospective student, even a fraudulent one. Within fifteen seconds, an invitation had been extended. As Jakob went through the doorway, I caught a malevolent glimmer in his eye, a feature I knew all too well would eventually become a permanent fixture.

Now was the time to act. Distantly observing their interaction on her porch was one thing, but I certainly couldn't leave the two of them fully unmonitored. Standing up, I noticed a woman sauntering on the opposite sidewalk. She looked vaguely familiar, likely a neighbor I had once been cheerfully introduced to and immediately forgot about. Fearing identification, I quickly crouched down again and impatiently waited while she proceeded at an interminable pace down the opposite sidewalk.

Finally clear, I took one last gulp of water and sprinted toward the door. My sleeve immediately snagged on the bush that had been concealing me, and once freed, I fell face first onto a neighbor's well-manicured lawn as my feet moved faster than the rest of my body. So far, my stint as an action hero wasn't going great.

Recovered from my briefly humiliating setbacks, I bounded the porch stairs in one leap and redirected that momentum straight into the front door, shoulder-first. Nothing happened; I barely made a proverbial dent. Through the open window, I heard only silence, a worrying sign that I may be too late already. I vigorously gripped the door handle and threw my weight at the door again. To my great chagrin, I realized that it was already unlocked. I hurled the door open with agitated contempt and raced straight into the kitchen where I knew them to be.

At full speed, I launched myself at Jakob's midsection from behind, taking him to the ground and sending the telltale knife scattering across the room. I geared up for a haymaker, but he quickly flipped over and threw me off his body. He lunged toward me, opening himself up for me to seize his arm just like I had learned in class. For a moment, he was immobilized, and I summoned the strength to take him down again. Before I could, Jakob smoothly swung his weight around, barely missing a direct hit to my exposed face. He followed through, tearing his arm out of my grasp and taking a freeing step backward.

He was more primed for combat than I was expecting, and now that the element of surprise was long gone, I was thoroughly overmatched. We circled each other, neither of us committing to a move.

"Where is she?" I demanded, trying my best to sound imposing.

Getting no response, I feinted toward him in vain hope that he would make an exploitable mistake. Instead, he landed a forceful kick to my stomach, sending me sprawling backward into Kathryn's small kitchen table. I gasped for breath, temporarily incapacitated.

"You will not hurt her!" he shouted as I struggled to right myself. He took one long sidestep and reacquired the knife, never taking his piercing eyes off mine.

Kathryn bounded into the room holding two full glasses of wine.

"What in God's name is going on here!" She scanned the room, her face transforming into abject shock upon seeing me panting in the corner. "Aaron, what—what are you doing here? Explain, now!"

"Madam," Jakob interjected, somehow showing no signs of exertion. "If I may, this man—"

"No, young man; you'll get your turn. I must insist that I hear from my friend first," Kathryn said, her naturally authoritative presence taking full command of the situation. "And put that knife down at once."

"He's not going to do it," I asserted moments before Jakob obediently placed the weapon at his feet. Kathryn looked at me, eyebrows raised, demanding explanation. I had visualized this very situation hundreds of times in my head, and still had no idea quite what to say.

"Kathryn, please, you have to believe me; he's here to kill you."

"Madam—" She held up a hand, stopping Jakob in his tracks and prompting me to continue.

"Okay, well, here I go. This is going to sound crazy, so please stay with me. It's all true." The words were delivered in quick bursts as I struggled to regain control of my breathing. "He is a time traveler from the mid-twenty-first century, where you are a world-renowned figure. He spent his professional life figuring out a way to jump back to this year, to this very night rather, specifically to get to you. And I'm here to protect you, although I freely admit I may not be doing the best job of that so far. And you must see now, this is exactly why I've been so awkwardly and ardently trying to get you out of the house—or better yet, the city—tonight. I knew he was coming for you. And all I want to do is keep you safe."

She turned to Jakob. "And what do you have to say to this assertion, young man?"

"He's right, madam. I am from the future, and yes, tonight is the night you will die."

21

"See!" I declared. "He's here to kill you! Kathryn, just run away right now. I will do my best to delay him. You should—"

Kathryn calmly raised her hand once again, then turned back to Jakob.

"Ah, yes, that was quite poorly phrased. Apologies," Jakob continued, glaring at me all the while. "Allow me to restate: tonight is the night you die in the *original* timestream, but this will change as a result of my presence. I freely admit that I have been duplicitous with you, and for that, I truly apologize. I am here for only an abbreviated, imprecise window of time and did not anticipate that I would have the luxury to fully explain at the door."

"So, why *are* you here, future man, if not for some friendly grad school advice?" Kathryn inquired.

"To safeguard you, of course. From him." He pointed at me, eyes searing with deadly intensity.

Kathryn emitted her trademark high-pitched chuckle, a wildly incongruous response in the moment.

"Jakob, yes? May I introduce you to Aaron, my dear friend. He is no more likely to kill me than that toaster on the counter. Actually, much less likely; that thing is quite temperamental."

"Ma'am," Jakob pleaded, "I gather that he has ingratiated himself to you, but you must now see that it is under false pretenses. How else could he have known to be here this evening? How else could he have knowledge of future events? How—"

"Kathryn," I cut in, "he's right, there's so much I haven't told you. And I truly, deeply regret it. But you know the real me; our bond is genuine. And I would never hurt you, you know that."

"Both of you just shut up for a minute," she said, attenuating her typical Midwest cordiality. She closed her eyes in deep thought, though I could still see the wheels spinning in her head. Jakob and I stood facing each other, neither daring to make a move.

"Let's make this simple," she finally said. "Raise your hand if you are here to 'save' me." The air quotes did little to soften the derision in her tone. Jakob and I raised our hands together.

"Yes, that's what I thought." Kathryn sighed. "You're both idiots." She turned to face me.

"Aaron, if Jakob here wanted me dead, he's had a hundred opportunities by now. And yet, I am quite noticeably unmurdered after an ample amount of time together. If he is a time-hopping assassin, he's very, very bad at it. For God's sake, Aaron, what kind of murderer wears a bright white linen shirt? They're very hard to get bloodstains out of, trust me." That flippant joke extracted another situationally dissonant chuckle.

"And Jakob—wait, is that your real name?" He confirmed with a polite nod. "Right, so Jakob, like I said, Aaron is a true friend and confidant, even if he did withhold information to an infuriating degree. I am a good judge of character, and at the core, he is as gentle as they come. And again, the distinct lack of being eliminated over the last few years is a pretty decisive sign. He could have simply pushed me off the side of a cliff on any number of hikes over the years."

I was quite impressed how quickly Kathryn had moved on from the chaotic melee in her kitchen as well as the outright threat to her wellbeing. The woman was nothing if not matter-of-fact.

And the uncomfortable fact was: she was right, as always. Jakob was not here to kill her, I now recognized with great humiliation. Key evidence that had formed the basis of conviction—the knife, the forced entry, the shoe print—had just as likely been my doing, not his. I felt a crushing, momentary onslaught of guilt that I had played a decisive role in sentencing an innocent—albeit insufferable—man to a fate he did not deserve.

Fortunately, I was already in the process of making amends by saving Kathryn and thus preventing his trial altogether in the corrected timeline. I knew the man Jakob would become if we did not succeed tonight, and considering the part I had played to create that nightmare, this was the perfect opportunity to nullify past mistakes and clear my conscience. The mission was not over; cosmic justice demanded it.

Kathryn beamed. "So, let's move beyond the unpleasantness, and get to the juicy stuff. The future, you say?"

She downed a glass of wine in eager anticipation.

"Yes, madam," Jakob responded, slowly letting his guard down, "the very future that *you* forged."

"But in your future, I die tonight! So how can I forge anything?"

"Hang on," I interjected, turning to my friend in disbelief. "Kathryn, I'm sorry, you're just accepting all of this? I told you that he's a time traveler, and that I kind of am too, and you're ready to move on from that bombshell already? It's all true, but still, I honestly don't understand how you have so little skepticism."

"What was the point of reading all that science fiction—including that wonderful movie script of yours—if not to prepare me for this very moment?" she replied with a cheeky grin. "Plus, once you know, it's clear as day, isn't it? I wish I could claim some Sherlockian-level deductive reasoning, but honestly, there are clues everywhere. Look at Jakob's left wrist, for one, the tasteful tattoo portraying two conjoined hearts. When he stood at my door, that very same wrist showed an ice skate; I'm sure of it. A fascinating technology, I must say. Similarly, the rest of his skin is unrealistically flawless, as if it's been covered in a layer of concealer. Rather like yours, Aaron, I now realize, which makes a lot of sense. I imagine dermatology will advance quite a bit in the next century. Too late for me, regrettably," she added, gesturing to her own face.

"And most obviously, Aaron, your otherwise inexplicable actions over the previous six-plus months. As Jakob said, how could you know the future if you didn't, well, know the future? If I may imperfectly paraphrase the aforementioned Sherlock: when all the clues point to the same thing, however improbable, it must be the truth. So with that out of the way, back to you, young man," she said, returning her intense focus to Jakob. "I'll ask again: How do I make a mark in your future if I'm dead?"

"It would be my greatest honor to tell you," Jakob replied with unbridled glee, perhaps the most cheerful I had ever seen him. I reset the kitchen chair and took a seat, enervated, regretful, and bruised. Plus, I knew how exhaustively loquacious Jakob could be on topics he deemed worthy.

"In my original timeline, you are deceased, yes. But you have already published your seminal treatise on predictive quantum theory."

"Seminal? Hardly. Even the four people who read it probably gave it middling reviews."

"Millions—perhaps billions—of people have read it in my time, madam. I speak sincerely when I say that it is perhaps the most impactful single work in the history of humankind. Few have come to understand it as I have, though, madam."

"Please, young man, call me Kathryn. This 'madam' stuff is far too formal. And c'mon, why would anyone care?"

Over the course of the next two hours, Jakob enthusiastically expounded on the origin of chronophysics and the massive impact Kathryn's research had made. Even though the trial had familiarized me with much of it—and I was wildly underqualified to keep up with the meticulous science—Jakob's passionate delivery of the content was positively electrifying. Kathryn largely stayed quiet, serenely nursing her second glass of wine, though the intensity of her gaze left no doubt that she fully comprehended the gravity of the inordinately detailed information.

"And to bring this back to the beginning," Jakob concluded, "that's how, madam—Kathryn, sorry—that's how you became the 'Mother of Time Travel' and why you *must* live to see your legacy fulfilled."

"I see," Kathryn responded anticlimactically. She sat in stunned silence for a good minute, absorbing and processing the way only her unique brain could.

"Well, the whole 'Mother of Time Travel' thing is a bit hackneyed," she eventually stated, "but the science checks out. Every single bit of it. The implications are significant. . . ." She trailed off midsentence and peered into the distance, lost again in the deepest recesses of her mind.

"I just can't believe I never considered the impact of intersecting my work with the relativistic principles it unintentionally eschews," she resumed, as if there hadn't just been a minute of silence. "The 'Mother of Time Travel'! Ha! Who would have imagined? Aaron, did you know all—"

Jakob suddenly jumped in his chair, as if tapped on the shoulder by an invisible hand. His eyes darted side to side in a pattern that I knew was unremarkable in the twenty-first century yet looked absurd to me again after a few years' distance.

"Are you okay, young man? Jakob?" Kathryn pleaded with genuine concern. I had the same reaction the first time I'd seen the unnatural motion, I recalled with a nostalgic smile.

"Kathryn, he's fine, I promise. He has a chip in his head that he's interacting with right now."

"Ah, yes, of course. Could it order us some coffee then?" she responded, her quick wit unaffected by the unusual circumstances.

Jakob's focus returned to the small kitchen after a few more seconds, though his buoyant demeanor did not.

"I regret to inform you, Madam Kathryn, that my window in 1988 is coming to an imminent close. Alas, I do not have time to voice all that I wish to say to you. I implore you to stay safe tonight. Lock the doors, keep a weapon by your side. Your acquaintance here may be trusted, but a killer could still be afoot."

He walked over to the center of the room and faced Kathryn, his eyes noticeably teary.

"By being here and divulging your future, I have blatantly disregarded all standard international time-travel codes, yet I regret nothing. I am fully prepared to face the consequences of my actions, and I take great solace in knowing it will occur in a world in which you survive. I have no doubt your mere continued existence will dramatically further science and shape a better planet for all. I will continue to work on the chronophysical transmission application that you inspired and apply your teachings wherever I can. Goodbye, Kathryn, my muse. May you live to see the beauty of your creation."

Just as he reached for the invisible trigger to return upstream, an urgent thought struck me.

"Jakob, wait! You can't tell anyone in the future about me." He shared a quizzical look while I tried to pull together something coherent and authoritative without mentioning the trial. "I, um, am a traveler from beyond. Beyond the Cutoff. For obvious reasons, I can't share any more detail, but it is critical for the security of the spacetime continuum that nobody in your new timestream knows of my existence."

Jakob nodded. "I do not understand, Aaron, but you are a friend and protector of Kathryn, and I will honor your request, regardless. So, once again, Kathryn, Mother of Time Travel, I bid you farewell."

"Goodbye, young man, and thank you," she replied, matching his solemn delivery. "You have done well; I will be safe, I promise. And best of luck on your application, Jakob."

With a lone tear beginning its descent, he triggered his upstream return, noiselessly vanishing from the room in an instant. A raging current of air rushed to fill the void, tousling my overgrown hair and throwing loose paper all over the room.

"Well," Kathryn mused, "that sure was something, wasn't it?"

22

———

Kathryn sat motionless across from me with a distant stare, perhaps looking straight through spacetime itself. Without the need to mask her true state of mind for Jakob's benefit, waves of raw emotion were vividly cresting through a crumbling facade. As someone who naturally balks at even the simplest forms of human interaction, I felt wholly underqualified for the gravity of the moment. For lack of anything better, I reached out across the table and gently grasped her quivering hands in mine.

She looked up at me, her guise of modestly vindicated pride transforming into a full-bore sob.

"Kathryn, are you okay? Can I get you something?" She peered at me through tearful eyes and smiled.

"I'm more than okay, Aaron," she blubbered unconvincingly. "Did you hear what our new friend said? I . . . I changed the world. Or I will, at least. With science, with knowledge, with hard work, by following my core values. I, well, you know me, Aaron. I don't care about fame, or validation, or money. All I ever wanted was to pursue my passion, and maybe make a lasting contribution in my chosen field. Well, I suppose I've done that, haven't I?"

"You sure did, Kathryn. And I've seen the result, and it's incredible." I shared the most reassuring smile I could. "I know it's a lot to take in, so please, please let me know how I can help."

"You can help by staying right here for a few minutes," she replied, standing up. "This feels like it's going to be a long night, and I, um, need to get more wine from the basement. Want any?"

I politely declined as she exited the kitchen in a hurry. Wanting to be mildly helpful in the meantime, I committed myself to collecting the loose paper strewn about the room. Among scattered phone bills, I found a few handwritten reminders to buy milk or eggs, an amusing and reassuring indicator that even the most intellectual among us sometimes need a little cognitive assistance.

The undemanding activity was perfect to free *my* cognition to reflect on this unpredictable, illogical night. Over the course of the last few years, my energy had been purely focused on stopping Jakob and only Jakob. I never once considered that we would be allied in our intentions; I had been blinded by his young man's ego and old man's bitterness.

I attempted to comprehend the branching consequences of my actions. If I hadn't interceded, would Jakob's megalomaniacal tendencies have taken over, redirecting him toward a more violent end? And now that he had departed, was Kathryn's life still at risk? Regardless, I planned to spend the night here, diligently watching over her to ensure that was not the case.

Kathryn returned with a bottle of wine, already a bit unstable on her feet. She wasn't generally a big drinker, but given the stressors of the night, it was more than understandable.

"Aaron!" she said, taking a seat. She seemed to have progressed beyond tearful fulfillment and into woozy elation. "Now it's your turn, my good friend. I want to hear everything! You've been to the future? How? What's it like? Tell me all of it."

"I would be honored to, madam," I stated, feebly attempting a Jakob impersonation. Despite the second-rate accent work, it produced the boisterous trademark chuckle I was going for. "There's really so much to tell you, but I guess I'll start with what I *know* is your first question: no, there are no flying cars. But good news: the ground-bound ones do at least drive themselves. And you can talk to them to tell them where to go, and there are these omnipresent digital assistants that can answer pretty much any question. My room had one I named Wally, and he was the best."

"Your room?" she clarified.

"Oh, right, yeah, I was there for about a week, in 2042 specifically. They took us around New York and even rewarded us with a session in the medbays. The only reason I can bike with you for more than a few painful minutes is thanks to the futuristic ligament regeneration. I think it was nanobots, if that means anything to you."

"That's amazing, Aaron! I'm still a little confused, though. How did you get there?"

"Funny story, actually: I don't know. I went to sleep one night in October 1985 and woke up in 2042." I could not share the real reason I had been yanked upstream; that was a non-starter. Nobody should have to hear about their own murder trial, even if the event was soon to be lost to a discontinued timestream.

"God, I can't tell you how good it feels to be able to finally tell you all of this!" I gushed before continuing my retelling. "So they brought in a group of us—twelve in all—and toured us around New York as we lived in the lap of high-tech luxury. I met amazing people from all over the twentieth and early twenty-first centuries! Actually, one of them lives in LA. That's why I was really there over the summer. I was trying to track her down."

"Ah, you met someone in the future? How cute! A love across time . . ."

"Well, not quite. We were just friends . . . I think."

"Sure, if you say so. I saw those cheeks flush when you mentioned her." Had they, I wondered, or was she goading me?

"Aaron," Kathryn continued, coughing for a moment between words, "I don't know how to ask this without sounding rude, but: Why *you*?"

"Um, yeah, that's a great question. One that I've considered many times. Unless there's some chronophysical reason why it had to be certain people or certain orgtimes or certain locations, I honestly think it was merely luck of the draw."

"It just seems so risky," Kathryn added, "distributing this knowledge of time travel across the twentieth century. I believe that you would keep it confidential, but how can they entrust so many others? I'm truly surprised it's not public knowledge that this is even feasible."

"Well, yeah, that's the thing. As a rule, they erase everyone's memory of their experience upon return. I'm the only one who kept mine, and I think it's because of my proximity to your, you know, death. I had formed a friendship with my technician; he implored me to save you, then empowered me to do so by sending me back with memories fully intact."

"I see. So that's how you knew about me, because I'm famous in the future? And, oh, Aaron . . . *that's* why you're friends with me? Was it all manufactured to prepare for this one night?" As the thought struck her, the tears returned in full force.

"No, Kathryn, that's not true. Well, yes, it is, I suppose, to a degree. But I said it earlier: our bond is genuine. I did move to Berkeley for you, and I did follow you around a bit to learn anything that might help me protect you. But from that first moment you spoke to me in your classroom, that was me, the real me. I'm someone who has enough trouble with normal relationships; I definitely don't have the social aptitude to fake my way through one. I'm truly sorry I didn't tell you about all of this. You deserved to know, but I couldn't risk anything. I hope you can forgive me."

"Aaron," she said softly, "it's okay. I do forgive you. I'm just sad because this feels like the end, doesn't it? How can things ever be the same?"

I briefly broke eye contact in a vain attempt to hide the tears welling in my eyes.

"I love you, Kathryn. I really do. You are and always will be my best friend, and I'm sorry if I ruined it."

"You didn't. And I love you too, you know that. Thank you for being there for me the last few years, and especially tonight." She closed her eyes, wiped her tears, took a few choppy breaths, and gazed at me with a forced smile that did little to mask the lingering pain behind the veil.

"Please, Aaron, keep telling me about the future. I want to know every magnificent detail."

Compartmentalizing my crushing guilt, I enthusiastically fulfilled her request over the course of the next hour, regaling Kathryn with tales of every wondrous advancement I could recall. Upon her bidding, I also recounted the plot to every heretofore unreleased sci-fi movie sequel that Wally had selected for me. By the end, the genuine twinkle in her eye had returned, though she looked increasingly wobbly from the atypical alcohol intake and advancing hour.

"Wow!" she said sarcastically when I concluded the rundown, "so *that's* why you're always insisting that I buy those penny stocks, huh? After all these years, you finally make sense!" It wasn't particularly funny, yet we both broke into a period of mutual extended laughter, a needed release after a tense evening (to put it mildly). For a moment at least, everything was back to normal.

"You must know, Aaron," Kathryn murmured, snapping us out of our nonsensical revelry, "Jakob is wrong about one thing." She was noticeably battling to keep her eyes open as her distinctive homemade grandfather clock struck midnight.

"A man of his intelligence, I just . . . I just don't understand how he can't see it . . . but *I* see it; I understand it. It's plain as day. And you must too, Aaron, right? The science is foolproof, there's just no room for interpretation. The timestream is fixed, my good friend, and that can only mean one thing. Look at me, Aaron," she commanded softly yet forcefully, catching the confused look on my face through her semi-coherent rambling. I complied and was caught off guard by the intensity in her gaze. "Please, Aaron, I need to be sure you hear me say this: whatever happens tonight, whatever your goal was, *you succeeded*. Got it?"

"I, um, am not sure I'm following—"

"Aaron," she interrupted, barely audible, "one last question: Do the people in the future seem . . . happy?"

"Oh, um, yeah, definitely," I replied, relieved to return to a conversation topic more in my comfort zone. "They take for granted all the luxuries that offload a lot of their mental energy, but the people I met and society as a whole seem to be doing well. A few people maybe reject—"

Out of nowhere, something was gravely wrong. Time itself seemed to come to a screeching halt, my brain intuitively switching to fight-or-flight mode. I watched helplessly as Kathryn's eyes lost all focus. As her next words went unvoiced. As she inertly slumped out of her chair and onto the floor with a violent, shuddering thud. I was powerless, frozen, an unwilling observer of the very nightmare I was trying to prevent.

After a torturous few seconds, I heard her murmur as limited consciousness returned, her fluttering eyelids still struggling to reopen.

"Kathryn!" I shouted, leaping out of my seat and supportively wrapping my hand around her sweltering head. "Stay with me; I'll get some help, I promise!" The abruptness of her deteriorating condition locked me in place, incapacitated with fear.

"Aaron," she mumbled weakly, "it's okay. I'm ready to go."

"What? No! No one is coming anymore; you're safe."

"It's too late for me . . . I took . . . sleeping pills . . ." Her breathing was becoming increasingly inconsistent, her skin pallid.

"I'm going to call for help!" I reached for a nearby kitchen towel and placed it gently under her head, then stood up and bounded toward her telephone.

"Wait." She reached out for me, barely able to lift her hand an inch. With great effort, she willed herself to speak.

"Aaron, thank you for making my last few years the most fulfilling of my life and the last few hours a magical journey through the future."

"No, Kathryn, please, stop. Don't give up!" I pushed out through streaming tears.

"You need to leave, Aaron. For your own good. I couldn't let you take the blame for my unavoidable death tonight, but that only works if you leave. Right now." Her voice was noticeably weakening as the last bit of color left her face.

I hesitated, but there was little doubt that she was correct. This was about to become a homicide case, and if I was found on scene, even a regular old time-locked jury wouldn't have any trouble convicting me.

"Good bye, my friend," she whispered with faded vigor. "I hope . . . your . . . future is . . ."

I waited for her to deliver her final, strained syllable, clinging to every last moment together. I shut my eyes and exhaled in an ineffective attempt to reassert control over my turbulent emotions, then sprinted around the kitchen corner toward the front door and out into the incompatibly calm evening. In a state of borderline panic, I barely noticed my surroundings as I raced to the nearest payphone around the corner. I at least had the limited cognizance to confirm no one else was observing my incriminating action before grabbing the headset and frantically punching in 9-1-1.

———

Back in my previous hiding spot, my heart racing uncontrollably, I watched from afar as the ambulance blared down the street, stopping on the curb only a few feet away from me. There was still hope! A few neighbors briefly emerged to investigate the commotion, including the unidentified woman who had inadvertently delayed me earlier. The two EMTs jumped into action, rushing emphatically to precisely the wrong house, directly across the street from Kathryn. After a minute of back and forth, the confused paramedics were politely turned away, along with any surviving possibility for resuscitation.

The universe was mocking me; that was the only explanation. Mocking me for thinking I could alter even the slightest detail, that my measly existence meant a darn thing in the grand scheme. In the end, the entire endeavor served as nothing more than a cruel reminder of my impotency, forever drowning in the unwavering sands of time.

I crouched behind the all-too-familiar protective shrub, dejected and frozen in place by pure aimlessness. Now absent the all-encompassing, driving objective of the mission, I felt devoid of purpose, existentially aware of my uselessness to affect, well, anything.

Kathryn was gone; she always had been and always would be. She was so resolute in her steadfast interpretation of the science that she had been willing to die for it. How could she be so egotistical as to think that there wasn't a sliver of a chance that she was wrong, that the timestream could be tilted toward her survival? How selfish to not even give us the chance to try?

Or was it my fault? If I had just stayed away, maybe she wouldn't have believed Jakob's tale without my corroboration. Or maybe he never would have been compelled to share it at all, and stuck with his original cover story. Or maybe she wouldn't have felt the need to cover for my presence. Or maybe . . .

No, there was only one reasonable explanation, the one that I had blindly refused to acknowledge from the moment I set course to change history. I had let my hubris overwhelm rational thought, clinging to the theories espoused by the imprudent likes of Jakob and Damitra's post-Cutoff radicals. And Sam, of course, who I desperately wished I could contact, if only to show that I had tried. And I had, I really had, futile as the attempt turned out to be.

I thought back to Kathryn's last act, deliberately performed only to safeguard me from potential implication. The mission to save her may have been tragically unsuccessful, but at least I could make sure I honored her final sacrifice.

With the crowd fully dispersed, I crept back into Kathryn's house, intent on removing any evidence that may point toward homicide, of which I would surely be a top suspect. Though it was far-fetched to believe that the police would arrive before morning, I moved with cautious urgency as I revisited the scene. Forcing my eyes to avert their view away from Kathryn's lifeless body, I reset the chairs, wiped down the table, restored the knife, and rinsed the second, untouched glass of wine. A final scan of the room confirmed that everything that remained supported the tragic story of a planned suicide.

I started tiptoeing toward the front door when a soft creaking sound from the rear of the house froze me in place. On high alert, I softly curled back around the kitchen wall and hid behind the center island, listening for confirmation of the disturbance. It was easy enough to convince myself that the soft rustling of papers was a gentle breeze outside, but the nearing footsteps emanating from the hardwood floor were harder to overlook. Without taking my eyes off the doorway, I blindly stretched above for a weapon, grabbing the ineluctable knife.

A figure peered around the corner, surveying the room with a dispassionate, seasoned gaze. Their professional demeanor shattered almost immediately when they caught sight of Kathryn's crumpled body on the floor. As the shadowy individual walked over to investigate fully, the moonlight shining through the window spotlighted the very neighbor who had reappeared a few times over the course of the night. As she got closer, the brutal truth dawned on me: this was no vague acquaintance; it was someone entirely unforgettable. I stood up, chef's knife hidden behind my back.

"Hello, Damitra. Fancy seeing you here."

Startled by my sudden emergence, she leapt backward reactively before quickly recollecting herself into a combative crouch.

We each stood frozen in place, coiled in anticipation of the other's next move. She appeared to be weaponless, though who knew what futuristic shenanigans she had up her sleeve. Even with the power imbalance reversed from our last fateful encounter, I still felt like the unenlightened abductee, reliant on the good graces of my adversary.

"Who are you? Do I know you?" she replied, genuinely confused. I had anticipated a more dramatic opening line from my counterpart.

"Sure you do. We'll meet in about a hundred years." My sarcastic introduction belied the boiling rage I felt toward her. Fair or not, at that moment, I needed a target upon whom to direct my unprocessed grief. Damitra may not have been personally responsible for Kathryn's demise, but she felt tangentially so nonetheless. Her line of thinking, Jakob's line of thinking: that's what brought me here in the first place, the first link in the chain that guided us to this tragic outcome.

She studied my face in great detail, trying to place it. I was a bit older and much hairier, yes, but considering the danger into which she had once placed me, a little remembrance would have been nice. To be fair, it looked like significant time had passed for her as well.

"The juror? A-Adam?"

"Aaron."

"Wh-what are you doing here?"

"We don't need to trade off questions anymore," I seethed. "Kathryn's already dead; your task here is already complete, so why don't you just go?"

She eyed me with renewed skepticism. "*You* killed her?"

"No. I saved her. Or, I tried to."

"So, Jakob did it? Didn't think the old man had it in him."

"No, he didn't. He was trying to save her too."

Damitra glanced at the body between us. "So who—"

"Suicide." I sighed. "Or, death by inevitably, I suppose you could label it."

"Uh-huh. Odd. Well, as you said, my task must be done then. I'll see you around, Adam," she said with a presumptuous wink, already starting to exit the room.

"Hang on. That's not why you're here, is it? You already know that Kathryn's death tonight does nothing to prevent the 'scourge of time travel,' as you once put it."

She paused and turned back to face me with a self-satisfied grin.

"Ah, looks like you've learned a thing or two since we last met. I must admit, this phase—phase three—indeed has a different focus, though the objective remains the same. This one is a bit less subtle than phase one—back when we met—and a bit less . . . *explosive* than phase two. We continue to make progress along the way, each phase getting us closer to our ultimate goal of all-out preclusion. I should thank you, really. You're the one who enabled this, after all, by getting Jakob's design for pre-2032 travel to us. He had been obstinate and uncooperative prior to your visit."

"Whatever you're planning, it's not going to work. Haven't you figured it out by now? I'll say it nice and slow so you can understand: You. Can't. Change. The. Future. Jakob tried, I tried, and look where it got us. Absolutely fucking nowhere." I gestured in Kathryn's general direction to emphasize the point.

"You sound like the rest of them, stuck in your foolish assumptions. After everything you've heard, everything I've told you, you still think time is a closed loop? Ha! I'm going to splinter it apart until it's undeniable; you'll see. It gets tiring being the only one trying to save the universe, but alas, a true hero doesn't get to choose their mission. And with that said, Aaron, I'm afraid that I must be on my way. Duty calls."

She scurried out of the room at full speed, darting toward the front exit.

"Wait!" I shouted, too caught off guard by the unanticipated, mid-monologue departure to mount an effective pursuit. Still, I felt compelled to stop her; whatever she was planning, it couldn't be good. For all I knew, the known future depended on my success.

I hurriedly dropped the knife on the center island and sprinted after her. I heard the sharp object clatter to the ground behind me as I accelerated out of the room. I may not have been able to best Jakob hand-to-hand, but a foot chase I was well-equipped for. I didn't know what I would do once I caught up— the police *might* not believe I had averted a chrono-terrorist— but that was a problem for later.

As I hastily pursued Damitra through the door, a hint of bright white on the entryway table caught my periphery, abruptly halting me in my tracks. An overwhelming feeling of foreboding pervaded my entire being. There was little doubt over the purpose of the handwritten document before me, which I had somehow overlooked the last time I passed the table in my single-minded focus to summon emergency medical assistance.

Through the open door, I glimpsed Damitra disappearing around a residential corner. I had made my choice. Kathryn had been the mission, and while it had been a failure, I desperately craved any potential source of closure. Or, if I was being honest with myself, absolution. Plus, I could always thwart Damitra some other time; the words in front of me were now or never.

Suspended in benumbed inaction, I reluctantly forced myself to inch forward, simultaneously cherishing and dreading one last opportunity to indirectly commune with my late friend. Creeping silence permeated the space as I subconsciously held my breath, grasping the note for an elongated period before daring to bring it to eye level. My welling tears made Kathryn's hurried writing even less legible than it already was.

> *I truly wish I could have seen the wondrous future*
> *But this is the way it is . . . the only way it can be*
> *Predetermination is a real bitch, so I'm choosing the*
> *quick and easy way out*
> *I'm sorry to my friends, family, and students*
> *I love you all*

I desperately clung to the note for what felt like hours, frozen in renewed grief. The incongruence of such measured rationality in the face of such a horrific act—albeit a selfless one—staggered me. The touch of humor, the optimistic warmth, the acute sincerity; this was Kathryn on the page, and restoring the note felt like letting go for one final time.

After an eternal minute, I reluctantly replaced the document back to its original location and departed Kathryn's home for good, grabbing my gear from the nearby hiding spot on the way out. I staggered home on foot, feebly attempting to mask my muted sobbing from the dwindling passersby of the midnight hour.

The crushing disappointment of three wasted years of preparation, abortive from the moment I began, threatened to drag me deeper into the depths of despair. I found myself dwelling on the alternative version of my life that existed somewhere out there, the one where I remained a humble, boring Midwestern accountant. The path that could have been so simple, so passive, so unambiguous.

Absent Kathryn, it also would have been so . . . incomplete. She was unequivocally worth it, all of it: every misstep, every frustration, every defeat along the way. By her very nature, Kathryn had shown me—in life and in death—to plot my own destiny, to follow my instincts wherever they may lead. That genuine kindness and intelligence were not mutually exclusive, that joy and friendship could be found in the least likely of places.

If her premature demise was always a certainty, at least I had the distinct pleasure to enjoy the last few years by her side, a small man in the shadow of a future giant. For that, I felt only gratitude.

Amid the despair, I felt a crushing burden beginning to lift. The last few years of my life had been unknowingly set in stone from the moment I committed to this path; a car inconspicuously bolted onto a fixed track, the driver obliviously maneuvering a disconnected steering wheel.

Now, my destiny was once again in my control, with only the gleaming, unfettered road ahead.

Epilogue

1988

The next morning, I was brought in for questioning by the Berkeley police. As explained, they were covering their bases for the obvious suicide, though I knew from future experience that some fresh evidence would soon be discovered that challenged the assumption. All I wanted in the moment was to be alone, to process my overwhelming feelings in peace.

"Good morning, Mister Barnett," Detective James Mitchell opened. He was unaware that we had met before, sixty years into his future. Our time apart had done wonders for his health. "As you heard earlier, Kathryn Simpson was found deceased in her home this morning. I'm genuinely sorry for your loss. I know this is a tough time, but we called you in today to see if you had any additional information. To start, can you think of any reason Kathryn would want to harm herself?"

Though a simple lie about Kathryn's mental health would go a long way toward substantiating their prevailing suspicions, I refused to besmirch my departed friend's good name.

"Absolutely not," I replied. "She was genuinely happy last time I saw her, at peace even. She would have told me if something was wrong, I'm sure of it."

"And when was the last time you saw her?"

"Couple weeks ago, for a bike ride."

Another officer scampered into the room and whispered into the detective's ear. Over his shoulder, the bullpen was noticeably abuzz.

"Mister Barnett, my colleague here informs me that your fingerprints were found at the scene of the crime. You just claimed that you have not visited her home for at least two weeks. Care to explain?"

I let out an involuntary sigh of exasperated resignation. Emotionally empty, it was due time to embrace the protective barrier of predetermination. I knew no matter what I said—or perhaps because of what I said?—this was going to become a cold case soon enough.

"You found my fingerprints at my friend's house? Alert the media!" I mocked with rudely disinterested flippancy, a mild challenge given my typical deference to authority.

"Uh-huh. And where exactly were you on the night in question?"

"Home, sleeping, dreaming about being outside and not stuck in an interrogation room."

"Can anyone corroborate that?"

"Yeah, of course: my dog."

"Your disrespectful attitude, Mister Barnett, is not a great reflection on your character. We are investigating on your deceased friend's behalf; I would expect at least a modicum of support for the cause. You understand that you are now a person of interest, right?"

"I do, and you understand I didn't do anything, right? Kathryn is—was—my best friend. You have no evidence linking me to anything, because again, I didn't do anything. It's as simple as that. Can't you let me just grieve in peace?"

"To be frank, Mister Barnett, I do not believe you. My instincts are rarely wrong, and I know you're hiding something."

"I'm not," I retorted bluntly. The detective was visibly losing his patience, gritted teeth bearing at me from across the poorly lit table.

"Uh-huh. Well, since you obviously want us to solve the case so badly, can you tell me this: Can you think of anybody who would want to harm Kathryn?"

"I thought this was a suicide investigation?"

"We are obligated to consider all options, Mister Barnett," Detective Mitchell replied, nearly snarling. "And between you and me, it's looking less like a suicide by the minute. Last question, for now at least: Why weren't you surprised or even sad when we delivered the unfortunate news to you?"

"How I process my grief is none of your business, honestly. But since I can tell that you think you 'got me,' I'll still answer. Kathryn's brother called me before you did; that's why I wasn't surprised. Check my phone logs if you want. Like I said, Kathryn and I were close; close enough that her brother called *me* first. And I am sad, very sad—inconsolable even—which is why I would like to be done here."

"Fine. But as we continue to collect evidence, you can bet you'll be hearing from us again," the detective warned as I was finally dismissed.

I unsurprisingly never heard from him again, though I did obsessively track the progression of the case throughout the news

cycle. *PROFESSOR TRAGICALLY MURDERED IN HER HOME*
was just sensationalist enough to hold America's limited attention for about a week, during which time I declined numerous
interview requests from reputable and scandalous publications
alike. By the end, as interest waned and leads dried up, the updates barely cracked the local paper. Eventually, as I knew it
would, the case went cold and people moved on from the tragic
story of poor, innocent Dr. Kathryn Simpson.

1991

A small, nagging part of me will always believe I can change the
known future; it's perhaps the only thing about which I've ever
even slightly dissented with my late friend. Kathryn had the infuriating natural gift of always being right, so there was rarely
cause to do so.

Damitra did not share that gift: her vaunted phase three plan
turned out to be no more than a worldwide purge of Kathryn's
seminal work. In her oversimplified reasoning, if the foundational journal did not exist, time travel could never be invented.
As evil plans went, it was particularly unimaginative. Starting
mere days after Kathryn's death, Damitra began mailing me picturesque postcards from around the world, ominously listing
how many copies remained at universities and libraries, domestic
and abroad. And when the count eventually hit zero, she bid her
farewell to the twentieth century for good, assured that her mission was complete.

Occasionally, I considered chasing after her. It felt like the vir-
tuous thing to do. I may have been the only person even aware of
the steady depletion of the obscure scientific publication, so I knew

I was the only hope. On the other hand, I understood the very thing that Damitra refused to accept: the timestream could not be changed, and her mission—while ambitious—was ultimately futile. Whatever choice I made was the right one, since that's what I have done and always will do, and the one that leads to the future I knew. So, I chose the comfortable, effortless track and let her fail in peace, all the while floating down the smooth, lazy river of time.

Plus, while Damitra had been thorough on her deleterious path, she had overlooked the merit of indelible friendship, something which she assuredly lacked in her unhinged focus on timestream derailment. In a way, I pitied her for it, and for the resulting blind spot that made it all too easy to stymy her destructive agenda. With great pride, Kathryn had once gifted me an inscribed copy of her published journal, which had occupied the premiere spot on my coffee table ever since. Little did I know this cherished item would later become a tool with which to thwart her unknown antagonists. So every time I received a threatening postcard, I made another copy of the research for safekeeping, maintaining perfect equilibrium of Kathryn's beautiful legacy.

And once Damitra returned to her future, I began to redistribute them to their proper, original locations, one by one. I will happily extol my late friend's research to anyone who will humor me, an underqualified eulogist for her absurdly complex, groundbreaking work. Perhaps, if the future *can* change, a copy will reach the right physicist at the right time, and humanity can reap the rewards of her discovery a few years early. Or, more realistically, a secondhand copy of the journal will be discovered by an MIT researcher in 2033, just like it always has, and the wonderful loop can start anew.

_____

1995

Even all these years later, I often dream of those fateful hours in Kathryn's cozy kitchen. Usually, she falls into a spontaneously materializing rift in the middle of her kitchen floor. Her eyes widen as I desperately reach for her, her final plea swallowed by the oddly luminescent abyss. Sometimes Jakob is there, sometimes Lisa, Sam, or even my beloved Rex, who fell into his own proverbial abyss a few years ago. Chronological inevitability may have helped to cushion the psychological blow, but I still witnessed my best friend die that night in my arms, and I have paid the price since.

Over the course of the last few years, I became impulsively nomadic, traveling around the world at the slightest provocation or whim. Occasionally, I was joined by accounting circle friends, though I often preferred meandering solo journeys to the less explored corners of the globe. Money was tight—I continue to wait for my hopefully surefire investments to take off—but like Kathryn taught me, I will seek joy wherever I can.

Though my official residence and modest business remained, the East Bay couldn't hold the same allure absent my friend's enriching presence. I repeatedly heard her distinct laugh in the campus bells, saw her peculiar walking patterns in each passing flock of birds, and knew I couldn't stay forever.

This year, I finally completed an overdue move to Los Angeles with my new dog, Wally. (He's not as uniquely helpful as his namesake, though they do share a certain kindhearted overexuberance.) It was time to commence round three of my mission: locate Lisa. And while there were no guarantees, at least this time fate wasn't actively conspiring to keep us apart. My timing was deliberate; upstreamed-1994 Lisa did not and could never know me, but 1995 Lisa sure could. Plus, there was no longer a need for my armchair private investigator shenanigans; I knew exactly where to find her.

I strolled into her swanky Beverly Hills office building, the anxiety I'd successfully minimized—or perhaps repressed—for years brewing unwelcomed to the surface. I considered abandoning the plan for the day as the flop sweat threatened the integrity of my shirt. I hadn't seen Lisa for ten years—ten long, consequential years. A decade's worth of experiences that had shaped me into a different person than the one she had bonded with; a tad wiser, a bit more spontaneous, and, well, much older. Meanwhile, she had aged no more than a few months. What if we no longer shared the same undefinable, singular connection?

"Please come in, Aaron," her assistant prompted, removing the option for an unnoticed escape. "Ms. Barnes will see you now."

I thanked her as I proceeded into Lisa's office, tastefully adorned with artifacts of a life well lived. And there she was, exactly as I'd remembered: the knowing smirk, the probing eyes, the don't-give-a-fuck attitude.

"Aaron, right? We don't have any need for outside accounting services right now." She barely looked up at me as she spoke.

"Lisa . . . I mean, Ms. Barnes. I have to admit, I'm not quite who I said I am." That got her attention. "I mean, I am an accountant, but that's not why I'm here." Deep breath. "I want to, well, I want to take you out to dinner. Tonight."

She scoffed, a momentary dagger through my heart before reminding myself that for Lisa, derision is the surest sign of affection. As my bold-faced earnestness dawned on her, she gazed at me with renewed interest.

"Do I . . . know you?" she questioned.

"No, but you will." This wasn't intended as time-travel word-play; I just thought it sounded cool at the moment. Luckily, so did she.

Five weeks later, we were engaged; a high-speed rollercoaster of a relationship jammed into the briefest of time spans. Even that timeline felt unnecessarily plodding; we both knew within hours that we had found a sublime match. Whatever had kept us apart in 2042—our age gap, my timidity, the extraordinary circumstances—had been erased by the ensuing years. In many ways, I had become a bit more like Lisa in that time, an assimilation of the best parts of her and Kathryn alike.

Throughout that whirlwind first month, I pondered if Lisa, too, had retained her memories. Our rapport was so immediate, our chemistry so seamless, that it felt like we had known each other for years. On a few occasions, she would become suddenly pensive, pausing for dramatic effect before declaring she had something important to tell me. My heart raced with a mix of paranoia and excitement that I may not be the sole keeper of the future. And each time, to a tee, she would lovingly insult me, a tricky balance that somehow only she could make endearing.

Everything moves at breakneck speed with Lisa; we've already decided to adopt twin babies after our upcoming honeymoon in Paris. Luckily, and with great compromise, she consented to let me name them: Sam and Kathryn.

1996

"Uh-huh," Lisa remarked. I was hoping for a *bit* more, considering that I had just spilled my heart and soul in a multi-hour retelling of my time-hopping odyssey. She had hung on my every word, a supportive look in her eye that reassured me to continue as the story became progressively less plausible. It was a tale of friendship, of violence, of the wondrous future. But for the two of us, it was also the origin of our relationship, and I didn't know how she would respond to the imbalance that it introduced.

"Aaron, whatever led you to me—to us—is the way it was meant to be, no matter how insane. We'll have plenty of time for elaborations and questions—and trust me, I have many—but I do believe you, I promise. Who knows? Maybe my own memories are all buried deep in my brain somewhere, subconsciously validating all of it. And maybe that's why you and I are so natural together. Plus, I *did* wake up one day a couple years ago feeling freakin' awesome; that must have been the day I returned from 2042 with all the medbay magic, huh? Proof enough for me."

I was relieved, but I knew her well enough to know she couldn't maintain complete sincerity much longer. I took a calming sip of tea—I couldn't get enough of the stuff—and waited for the turn.

"I can see how hard it was for you to share, especially since you're really just awful at this kind of thing. And one day in forty or so years, on whatever day that time travel becomes a reality, you and I will walk out onto our majestic balcony overlooking the French Riviera and share a quiet toast to Kathryn. It's the least we can do.

"With that said . . . what the heck, man? You got poor Jakob convicted? He's a real piece of work, yes, but he doesn't deserve even the future's cushy version of prison. He did a better job protecting Kathryn than you did, really; at least she didn't die on his watch!"

There it was.

"Oof, harsh," I admitted. "What was I supposed to do? I went on the limited knowledge I had at the time, plus, did you forget the part where I met him in the future and he kind of indirectly admitted his own guilt for some reason? Anyway, what about me and you, how we *really* met? I think maybe you're focusing on the wrong part of the story!"

"Nope, I'm not, but don't worry: I know exactly what to do." Lisa ran off to the closet, creating a ruckus as her massive videotape collection was haphazardly strewn about the floor. She emerged with an oversized video camera on a tripod and began setting it up facing me.

"You're going to apologize!" she proclaimed.

"To you?"

"No, to Jakob. Duh. We'll vacuum seal the tape, put it in an envelope, postdate it, mention it in your will; whatever it takes to get this thing into his hands in fifty years."

Lisa was right: he deserved an apology; a token of recognition for his sacrifice, however futile. Old Jakob had once asked me about the worst thing I'd ever done. Well, persuading a roomful of jurors toward his oh-so-obvious guilt might just be my answer. I couldn't change the outcome—young Aaron had ensured as much, swayed by the hubristic rantings of old-man Jakob—but I owed at least this much to my longtime nemesis and short-time ally.

"Alright, let's do it," I prompted. I could feel the beads of anxiety sweat beginning to percolate, but it was best to rip the bandage off before I worried myself out of coherence.

Lisa finished the preparation and flashed an encouraging thumbs-up. I took a deep breath, and . . . action.

"Hi, um, Jakob, it's me Aaron, but you probably know that already, since in your timeline you just saw me like a week ago in Kathryn's house. I'm here in 1995, and, well, I know you don't use tapes anymore, so I hope this makes it to you after the trial and you can actually watch it. Sending you best wishes with the whole, you know, conviction thing. I know better than anyone that you don't deserve it, and if there was anything I could do to help, I would. I'm probably dead by now anyway, so it's gonna be especially tough."

Lisa rolled her eyes and gave me a "get to the point" gesture. I shifted to the most heartfelt tone I could muster.

"What I really wanted to say, Jakob, is that I'm sorry. I'm sorry Kathryn's dead, and I'm sorry you took the fall. It was suicide, by the way; I didn't kill her, but I think you know that. She was only protecting me and leaning in to inevitably. Selfless and noble to the end. I hope you can forgive me. And her, really, and yourself too. None of us can change history, that's the takeaway here. That's what Kathryn believed. I hope you can remember that as well.

"There's something you can do, one last act for Kathryn. There's a kid at the WCO, Sam, who is an ally of ours. He needs someone to help set him on the right path, especially since he probably got fired while trying to support you. He could use someone to watch over him. I'm hoping that can be you.

"Well, take care, Jakob. This is Aaron, signing off from the past . . . a blast from the past, really, and um, I think you can—"

"Alright, jeez, we got it," Lisa wisely interjected. "Not too shabby. I'll fix the rambling ending in post, and then I'll get my staff archivist to make sure this thing actually survives a half century. Feel any better?"

"Slightly," I answered. "But what if it backfires? I already know exactly what he's like as an old man. What if this tape is what drove him over the edge into a state of perpetual resentment? Or maybe it's proof that he doesn't get the tape and he descends into a cycle of self-pity?"

"That's a risk we'll just have to take, Aaron, you wonderful, stupid man. In the end, all we can do is the *right* thing, and let fate take it from there."

———

Perhaps there is an alternate timeline out there, one in which I never serve on that historic jury. That would mean no Kathryn, no Lisa; just my monotonous Midwest existence and a ticket to nowhere. Yes, ignorance may be bliss, but knowledge is revealing, and I wouldn't change a thing along the winding path that led me to where I am now.

I'm heartened that salvation via time travel is around the corner, if not for me, then at least for my incredible children and their collective generation. It's much easier to absorb the hits along the way knowing humanity is headed in the right direction. The upcoming century may not be perfect, but it sure is close enough. Call me an optimist, but as a policy I am anti-suffering, and in my humble opinion the fifty years of progress that time travel ushered in cancels out any technological dependence and "mediumness," as my now wife had once put it. Methods and rationale aside, maybe even Damitra had a point that time travel had an expiration date: it served its purpose, advanced society out of likely doom, and bowed out on top.

I sincerely hope that I make it another forty years to bask in the wonders of Kathryn's indirect creation. I'll just make sure to enjoy live sports while I still can.

The most prudent decision I made throughout my meandering odyssey was to not seek information about my own personal future. Nobody should be cursed with that knowledge; fixed or not, fate is too heavy a burden to bear. I know it better than most. Benign circumstance and the hope of serendipity gives us purpose, keeps us driven, and imbues life with meaning.

Surrounded by my wonderful new family, I already know exactly what my future holds, anyway. And I couldn't be any happier about it.

THE END

About the Author

JORDAN BERK is a software engineer by trade and a certified nerd by nature. He has loved time-travel stories for as long as he can remember, and *The Timestream Verdict* is his first contribution to the genre. In addition to writing, he enjoys basketball, tech-nology, and amateur songwriting (even though he can't sing to save his life). He lives with his wonderful wife and two kids near Los Angeles, California.

IngramElliott Publishing

IngramElliott is an award-winning independent publisher with a mission to bring great stories to light in print and on-screen. We publish stories with a unique voice that will translate well into film and television. Visit us at www.ingramelliott.com for more information.

Our *IngramElliott* imprint features full-length fiction and nonfiction titles designed with the book lover in mind.

Our *IE Snaps!* imprint features novella-length fiction in popular genres that are designed for a quick read on the go.

9 781952 961267